USA TODAY BEST SELLING AUTHOR
KRISTEN PAINTER

BOOK SEVEN

A SKY FULL OF STARS

For Melanie, who told me unequivocally that Edgar needed to live.

A SKY FULL OF STARS:
Shadowvale, Book Seven

Copyright © 2023 Kristen Painter

All rights reserved. No part of this book may be reproduced in any form or by any electronic or mechanical means, including information storage and retrieval systems—except in the case of brief quotations embodied in critical articles or reviews—without permission in writing from the author.

This book is a work of fiction. The characters, events, and places portrayed in this book are products of the author's imagination and are either fictitious or are used fictitiously. Any similarity to real person, living or dead, is purely coincidental and not intended by the author.
ISBN: 978-1-941695-87-6

Published in the United States of America

Shadowvale isn't your typical small town America. The sun never shines, the gates decide who enters, magic abounds, and every resident bears some kind of curse.

Lexi Gardner is a rare creature with a nearly unlimited supply of magic. Unfortunately, that magic has gotten a little low. That's all right. She's come to Shadowvale for a refill and thanks to an impending magical event, getting all the magic she requires shouldn't be a problem.

Until she crosses paths with someone who greatly needs her help. A man trapped in the forest. A man no one wanted anything to do with. A man considered by most to be a curse.

Lexi, however, sees beyond his past. She sees him for who he is now. And who he could become. The only problem is saving this handsome mountain of a man will take more magic than she has. In fact, it'll take all the magic she can get her hands on. Seems a small price to pay for his company, however.

She vows to help him if he'll help her in return, something he's glad to do. But he has his own issues to deal with. As do most people in town. Like Amelia Marchand, the witch who created Shadowvale. Will Lexi be able to help Amelia and her new friend while securing the magic she desperately wants?

Because a life without magic won't be any kind of life at all. Unless love turns out to be all the magic she needs...

CHAPTER ONE

Something of great import was coming. Amelia Marchand could feel it in her blood like an illness trying to take hold. The sensation had unsettled her for the last few days. She'd done everything she knew to suss out what it was, and nothing had worked. She had no more information now than when she'd started.

The tea leaves hadn't shown her a thing. Neither had her attempts at scrying, even in her finely tuned rock crystal bowl. She'd cast bones to no avail. Shuffled and dealt cards only to come up blank every time. Whatever this thing was, it wasn't ready to show itself yet.

There was no peace in that.

She tried to find some anyway. The cool evening breeze danced across her skin as she sat outside on the rear patio of her mansion, Indigo House, and watched the stars come to life in the deepening purple sky. She enjoyed the moment when the town's perpetual cloud cover scrolled back to let a glimpse of the heavens in.

More than a glimpse, really. The night sky over Shadowvale was a thing of beauty. A genuine wonder to behold. A vast velvet blanket covered in the diamonds of the cosmos.

"Age is causing me to wax poetic, Thoreau. And perhaps a bit melodramatic, too." She petted the tiger's neck and back, his fur indescribably soft under her fingers. She dug her fingers deeper to reach his skin and massaged the thick muscles under it.

He bent his head, pushing his neck into her hand, an easy rumble going through him that she'd come to recognize as a sign of his happiness.

He sat upright next to her, his head slightly higher than her own. She was not a tall woman, but he was no housecat, either. Despite his domesticity, he was still very much a wild animal. One she never grew tired of looking at.

"You are a gorgeous creature, aren't you?"

Thoreau had no response other than the twitching of his whiskers. Not that she'd expected one. Pasqual had been a gorgeous creature, too. Heartbreakingly beautiful in the way that only a vampire could be.

She missed Pasqual the most at night. She missed him all the time, of course, but the evenings were the hardest.

She let her hand rest in Thoreau's fur and tipped her head back to stare at the sky. The darker it became, the more stars appeared. The heavens were putting on a real show tonight. Nature joined in, providing the soundtrack. The muted sounds of insects turned into a melodious chorus. The breeze shifted and brought her the sweet perfume of the night-blooming flowers in her garden.

Pasqual would have loved an evening like this. He

would have poured them both a brandy and they would have sat together, just like she was with Thoreau, taking in the night and talking about everything and anything.

She'd created Shadowvale for him. A safe haven where he could live free of the dangers of the sun. Other vampires had come, of course, as had so many others seeking the refuge only this town could provide.

Young and old, rich and poor, human and supernatural alike, those with troubles and burdens the ordinary world couldn't understand came here. She welcomed them. It made her feel better knowing that while the love of her life might not be able to enjoy the place she'd created, it had become a home to many others.

That was something, wasn't it?

She exhaled a deep sigh, feeling a swell of self-pity rising up in her. Too often these days, she let herself indulge in it.

Thoreau turned his massive head to look at her and let out a whuff of breath.

She nodded as she clasped her hands in her lap. "I know. I shouldn't let it get the best of me, but I can't help it. I miss him." The sky forgotten, she cast her gaze toward the garden again as her heart ached with memories. "I miss him terribly."

Thoreau sank down, stretching his front legs out before him, his massive paws flexing once.

Behind her, one of the French doors opened. Soft footsteps announced Beckett, her majordomo.

Her warden.

"Brandy?" He held out a snifter on a silver tray.

She picked it up. "I suppose."

He tucked the tray under one arm. "Beautiful evening."

She sipped the brandy, letting it warm her throat and ease the stinging in her soul. "I hadn't noticed."

He let out a quiet snort. "The stars are really something tonight, too."

She swirled the brandy in the glass, inhaling the aroma and watching the amber liquid slosh around. "Yes, they are."

"You aren't even looking."

"I've seen the stars." She was in no mood for his pleasantries. If she wanted to sit here and feel sorry for herself, that was her right.

"Tonight?"

"Yes."

"In the last few minutes? That particular formation?"

With a sigh, she looked up. "Why would that—oh." She set the brandy down, her focus on the sky. "That can't be right."

Beckett shook his head. "I don't know what it is, but it looks ... significant."

It looked that way to her too. She stood, needing to be closer in any way possible. "It can't be."

"What is it? Aliens?"

Mouth pursed in exasperation, she cut her eyes at him.

He arched one brow. "It's a valid question."

She gestured at the sky. "You see the three stars in the center of the sky? How they're aligned? And how there's a halo of dimmer stars around them?

"Yes. That's what I was talking about. What is it?"

"It's a sign." And not one that had been seen for a very long time. She pulled her pashmina tighter around her shoulders.

"A sign of what?" Beckett asked.

She still couldn't believe what she was seeing. The question of what was coming had finally been answered. "The ancient Egyptians called them the Tears of Anubis. Other civilizations referred to them by different names, but in more secret circles they're known as the Aerarii."

"Which is what? A constellation?

"A meteor shower."

"Never heard of it."

She nodded and glanced at him. "That's because it's a very special meteor shower. One I have always hoped to see in my lifetime. One I always hoped might be drawn to a place like this." She narrowed her eyes as she studied the formation in the sky, making sure she hadn't missed anything.

Where would they fall? The Enchanted Forest seemed the most likely place. Aerarii were drawn to other sources of magic, and the forest had the strongest meridian lines. So did the Dark Acres. The citizens must be told. It wouldn't do to have them fear the occurrence. And there were plenty who could benefit from having a wish granted. *If* they could be the first to find a meteor after it fell.

She just had to make sure she was one of those as well.

Beckett crossed his arms. "They must not have anything to do with death because I don't know anything about them."

She rolled her eyes. Reapers thought death was all there was to life. "They have nothing to do with death and everything to do with living. The Aerarii are ..." She paused. "They possess cosmic energy. Deep, unfathomable magic. They spin through the universe collecting it as they go. Magic older and stronger than anything you can imagine. And when they fall to earth, that magic can be harvested. Or it can grant wishes. One wish per meteor."

Beckett smirked, his brows knitting, his skepticism plain. "Falling stars that grant wishes? Pretty sure that's just a children's rhyme. Twinkle, twinkle and all that."

"Think what you want, but it's true. Also, that song isn't about falling stars." Her heart began to beat faster with what the Aerarii could mean for her. This was exactly the kind of magic she needed to find out the truth about the two most important men in her life. Thoreau.

And Pasqual.

Chapter Two

Lexi Gardner strode through the woods with purpose, the sunlight filtering through the leaf canopy and giving her skin a dappled appearance. Her destination was still a number of miles ahead, but distance didn't matter. She could walk as long as was necessary. She had a few things in the bag that hung from her shoulder, but she didn't need much. Despite her long strides and sure steps, she made very little noise. Creatures such as herself rarely did. Humans were louder. Forest animals less so.

She was neither of those. She was a being of dust and air, age and magic, myth and a sprinkling of reality. The world and its inhabitants remained a curious thing to her, regardless of her years upon the planet. No matter how long she remained here, there was always something new to keep her interested.

Or at least there had been.

Lately, she'd found herself drifting away from her surroundings, less concerned with the humans who inhabited her shared space. Lost in thoughts of what might come next. What could be. That had been enough for her to understand her time here was coming to an end. Whatever lay beyond, she had no idea about, but she was ready to discover it. Ready to take the next step into ... whatever it might be.

But in order for her to move off this plane of existence, she would need a tremendous amount of magical energy. Not always the easiest thing to come by. She'd had to attune herself to the vibrations of earth and sky so that she might home in on the currents of power flowing through the cosmos.

That had taken a large amount of her already dwindling supply of power.

But that was also how she found herself headed to this new destination. This town that gave safe haven to those struggling with great burdens. Physical, emotional, mental, magical, it didn't matter. The town opened its gates and welcomed them in.

Lexi, however, was not seeking shelter. She wasn't headed to the town for anything resembling sanctuary. It was the deep stores of magic in the town she needed.

Her own store was in need of refilling. Her well of power wasn't exactly dangerously low, but there was no reason to tempt the fates by letting it decrease any further. And if she really was going to move on from her current state, she required as much magic as she could store.

It was her own fault for letting it get so low. She'd gotten cavalier about it. Used her magic as if there was nothing to worry about. Helped a few too many folks along the way. That was something that still brought her joy, and she'd been hoping that helping more of them would reconnect her to the world around her.

It hadn't. And now she desperately needed to refill her own store. She needed to bathe in magic. To let it suffuse her until she couldn't hold another iota of power.

Shadowvale had a lot of magic. It was built over energetic meridian lines that seeped power into the very ground on which the town was built.

But that still wouldn't be enough.

There was only one thing that could provide that volume of magic. An event of epic wonder that would not and could not be missed. It hadn't come to earth in hundreds of years, but it was coming to Shadowvale very soon. She would be there for it, and she would do everything in her power to get her fill.

Lexi stepped over a fallen log. The soft tingle on her skin told her she was getting close to her destination. She would stay only as long as necessary, but time was a fluid construct to someone like her.

Whether that meant she was here for a week or a year or a decade, she had no way of knowing how long she'd be here before she could move on. She didn't much care either. What was time to an immortal? What was time to a creature of starlight and ether?

Nothing she worried about, that was for certain. She already had a reason to be here, something she'd worked out in the days before she'd begun her journey. Humans asked questions. They liked to know things about newcomers. To understand them. To feel safe around them.

In the same way that Lexi had chosen her current name for herself, she would give those who asked the kinds of answers they wanted. Ones that would make them like her. Ones that would keep her secrets. It was better that way, to let them think she was one of them. Easier. For them.

She broke free of the trees and into a clearing, a small patch of tall grass and wildflowers that led to the town's entrance.

She smiled. Before her towered an impressive set of iron gates. They gleamed softly in the sun, the dark metal polished and perfect. Motes floated in the beams of sun, the last she'd see of that great star for a while, but she was at peace with that. The sun had never provided her with any power, so nothing to worry about.

"Hello, Shadowvale," she whispered.

With the quiet shush of well-oiled metal, the gates swung open. A hummingbird hovered nearby, its tiny black eyes fixated on her for a moment, seeing her for what she was—something other. It flew around her a few times, inquisitive. She lifted her hand. The jewel-colored bird came to rest on her palm, so light its touch barely registered. Animals never feared her the way they did humans. One of the many perks of her kind.

"Are you well, little one? Or do you need assistance?" She had *some* magic to spare if the bird required it.

But she could sense the bird was fine. It stretched, tipping its head to see her better. Then, after a moment, it took flight again, headed toward a patch of flowers.

She walked forward, onto the paved road that led through the gates. As soon as she crossed the threshold, the tingling on her skin softened and sank into her, becoming one. Magic recognizing magic.

Clouds hid the sun. She walked on, following the road into town. Her instincts and innate sense of direction guided her, too, but that had more to do with her connection to the earth than any real knowledge of east or west, north or south.

For a while, there was nothing but nature surrounding her. Trees and underbrush lined the road. She didn't mind the walk. She liked being outside, liked the fresh air and the sounds of the insects and animal life around her. She was connected to those things.

A smile curved her mouth. This was a good place. A town, with plenty of people, yes, but there was a wildness here in the way the forest seemed to encroach from every side. As though it was just barely being held back by invisible hands. As though it might take over again at any moment.

That was interesting. She liked that idea. Even more so, she began to wonder about the people she might meet here.

As the cloud-glazed sky dimmed and dusk approached, the town began to take shape ahead. She was on Main Street, which was convenient. The place she was headed was somewhere along this route. She kept walking, unconcerned with the time or the hour.

She walked until she reached the business. She glanced up at the sign, then over to the second story windows that looked out onto the street. The rooms beyond were dark.

Not for long.

She opened the door and went in. The Five Bells Pub was busy with people eating dinner. There were more at the bar, some of them also eating, some of them just drinking. Most at the bar were watching sports on the televisions that hung around the space.

The occasional desire for entertainment was something she shared with them, but most sports confounded her. Although she found rugby rather interesting. It was brutal and animalistic in a way that appealed to her coarser senses. The attractive men in shorts didn't hurt either. She might not be human, but she was not without an appreciation for the male of the species.

Generally, they weren't sturdy enough for her kind. Sad. But some of the rugby players she'd seen had promise.

She went straight to the bar. She didn't drink. She could, if she wanted to, but alcohol had very little effect on her so she saw no reason to do it. She also understood too much of it turned humans incapable of functioning properly, sometimes with disastrous results. Amusing to watch but nothing she'd ever want to experience.

A Sky Full of Stars

The man behind the bar came up to her with a warm smile. "Evening. What can I get you?"

She smiled back. "I'm Lexi Gardner. I'm the new owner of the building. Which makes me the pub's new landlord." Amazing what you could buy when money was no object. It had taken her a fair bit of magic to produce enough cash for this, but shelter was necessary.

He blinked, then quickly nodded, his smile fading. "Right. Teddy left everything you'd need in an envelope. I'm Trip Carston. He probably mentioned me. I'm the GM."

She tried to think of what that was and couldn't. She hadn't actually talked to the previous owner. Everything had been done via a secondary source. "GM?"

"General manager. You, uh, you planning on bringing your own people in?"

He was the boss. And he was nervous. She softened her expression. She needed him on her side, and she needed him to stay and keep running the place. She had no interest in that. "Not unless you think there's a need. Do you?"

"No, ma'am. We have a good team here. Be a shame to break them up, if you're asking me." He pulled out a large manila envelope from under the bar and handed it to her.

"I am asking you. And if you don't think there's a change needed, I won't make one. In fact, I don't plan on changing anything, unless I see a reason to. Business as usual is the plan."

"Sounds good, ma'am."

"Please, call me Lexi, Trip." She could tell by the weight and bulk of the envelope that the keys she'd need were inside as well as the paperwork that went with the sale.

"Okay." He smiled again. "Lexi it is. Nice to meet you. I didn't even know Teddy was selling."

Neither had he, but she'd made him a very good offer. She stepped away from the bar. "It's been a long day. I'm going upstairs to retire. I'll leave things in your capable hands."

He nodded. "Sure. What if I need to get ahold of you for something?"

"How would you get ahold of Teddy?"

"Cell phone."

She didn't have one. Electronics didn't work well with her supercharged system. "You won't need me, will you?"

His mouth came open, and he hesitated, as if looking for the right answer. "I guess not ..."

"If you do, I'll only be upstairs. But I don't expect you will. I'll see you tomorrow night then." Without waiting for a response, she took the envelope to drop off at her new living quarters, which she hadn't seen yet, but that wasn't of any concern to her. Spaces were adaptable. Although that would take more magic.

What she needed was time as close to the meridian lines as she could manage. That would give her a small recharge. She had a few things to gather before the stars fell and brought their power to earth. Things that would make capturing more magic easier.

But for both of those tasks, she needed to head into the forest.

CHAPTER THREE

He preferred the night to the day, but not by a large margin. Day was very nice too. It was just that at night, the magic in the earth seemed stronger. Easier to absorb. During the day, there was still magic to be had, but it was different. Not bad. Just different. A little less of what he needed to grow and become himself again.

Whatever that might mean. He wasn't sure about any of it really. How long it would take. Or if becoming himself was even possible. Did he really want that? Not the old him, certainly. Not the monster he'd once been.

The animals at night were more interesting, too. Their visits more frequent. They seemed braver. Not as skittish as they were during the day. A bigger variety came to the stream to drink, sometimes to bathe, sometimes to play. Sometimes they tried to catch fish.

Watching them was good. They were fascinating. He liked the animals. He wondered if that was what he'd been, once upon a time. He wasn't sure. His memories were only accessible in bits and pieces, and the fragments were often disturbing.

He also liked the night sky a lot. The stars and the moon were far better to look at than the clouds. Tonight there were a lot of stars and only a sliver of a moon. The sky looked like a painting come to life. Not that he could recall seeing many paintings.

Sometimes, at night, meowls came to rest in his branches. They were cute, even when they were eating freshly caught field mice and fish scooped from the stream. During the day, birds often visited him. Squirrels, too. None of them had stayed and made a nest in his branches, but then he supposed there was something about him that told the birds and squirrels he wasn't an appropriate place to make a home or raise their young.

For reasons that went beyond his memories, he thought they were right. It was a feeling that sat deep within him. A thing he couldn't shake in the same way that he couldn't remember his name or where he'd come from or how he'd gotten here.

Just that monster was once a word that had applied to him.

If only he could get free of his current state, he might be able to figure out who he was, but he didn't know how. It had something to do with strength, and he knew he wasn't strong enough. He wasn't sure he ever would be, either.

Then there was the question of where he would go if he could get free. He had no home outside of the forest. No friends. No family. He might have. He had a feeling there had been someone. But not anymore.

Despite the darkness that crept in whenever he tried to remember who he was or where he'd come from, it was better to be planted in the ground, alive and growing, than planted in the ground in a box, dead and gone.

He knew a few other things with certainty. His past was nothing to be proud of, nothing worth any merit. And he was lucky to still be here. Lucky to be anywhere, at this point.

And if this life in the forest was all there was ever going to be, he was all right with that. Lonely as it was.

Better to be alone than not to be at all.

His leaves took in nutrients that kept him alive, but his roots drew in energy. Magic from the earth he was planted in. He could feel himself growing and changing. Not just as a living thing but as a being built from magic. How he knew that was something else he had no answer for. He just did.

Just like he knew that growth happened constantly. It almost seemed like his purpose, even though he had no control over it. He wondered if that growth would stop soon. How much growing could he do? Would he be taller than the trees around him? Most of them towered over him. He didn't think that was his destiny.

A deer approached the stream from the opposite side, soft shadows striping its tawny hide. He watched, taking pleasure in the creature's delicate movements and graceful strides. How beautiful. How different than he had ever been.

Wary, the deer glanced around, pausing to take him in but obviously not judging him a threat. It planted its narrow feet and bent its head to drink. A moment later, it picked its head up again and stared down the length of the stream.

A woman approached. She was beautiful in the same way the deer was, lithe and graceful, clothed in a long, loose dress with an equally long sweater coat over it. A strand of beads hung around her neck, and slouched boots covered her feet. She looked very much at ease in the dark depths of the forest.

Every fiber within him took notice. He hadn't seen a human being since he'd come to consciousness. He thought eventually he would, but she was his first.

And she was impossible to look away from. Her hair fell in soft, dark waves that made her skin seem to glow in contrast. Maybe she was glowing. In fact, it was almost as if there was a light inside her. But he understood what he was looking at.

The presence of great magic. Not that unusual. Not in this place. He sensed it even in some of the animals. But it was something to see so much contained in one being. Whatever she was, she had power.

She was on his side of the stream, but she'd yet to notice him. She was focused on the deer.

"Hello, beautiful creature."

Her voice carried the same light timbre as the trickling water.

The deer regarded her with no fear, no trepidation. It went back to drinking.

The woman bent and picked something from the forest floor and tucked it into an unbleached sack slung over her shoulder. She straightened, took a few steps, and repeated the movement. She did it a few more times, bringing her closer to him.

He was mesmerized. If he'd had a voice, he would have spoken to her. What words he would have used, he wasn't certain. It was probably better he couldn't speak. He would have frightened her off, for sure.

So he contented himself to study her, trying to embed her in his memory so he'd have something new to think about other than the fragments of his past.

She crouched again, this time plucking a few small mushrooms that had only just grown up in the last day. He knew. He'd watched them.

She stayed close to the forest floor as she studied them, her gaze suddenly lifting and fixing on him.

Without taking her eyes off him, she put the mushrooms in her sack and rose to her feet. "Hello, curious tree," she said softly.

She saw him. She. Saw. *Him*.

Hello, he desperately wanted to say. But he couldn't. The best he could do was tremble his leaves.

She smiled. "I hear you."

Did she? Emotions ran through him. Need, want, longing, joy, sadness, desperation, nervousness, too many for him to process, so he made do with watching her and hoping she would come closer.

She did. Still smiling, she hooked her bag over her shoulder and moved toward him. Her eyes narrowed, and her smile turned into something more contemplative.

She stood close to him now, so close the strength of her magic was palpable. That alone drew him to her. Or would have, if he'd been able to move.

"What are you? You weren't supposed to be a tree, were you?" Her gaze raked him, and she shook her head. "Not with that kind of shape. It's almost ... human."

No, he wanted to say. *I wasn't supposed to be a tree. But it's not a bad life.*

"Are you well?" She reached out and put her hand on his trunk. She closed her eyes, and a warm, inquisitive prickle spread out from the point of contact. If he'd had the ability to breathe as he once had, the air would have caught in his lungs. It had been a very long time since anyone had touched him.

Her magic continued to course through him, then she took her hand away and stepped back. "You're not a tree. You're not a plant at all, are you? Not really. So what are you then? Who are you?"

With her magic gone, he drooped. Unable to answer, he just shook his leaves again.

"What did you do to be this way? Who put you here? What magic? It feels familiar."

He understood by the softness of her voice and the change in her tone that she was talking to herself now, not to him. All the same, he wanted to answer. *I don't know,* he wanted to tell her. *I only know I was a monster. And now I'm this. This is better. Safer. I don't mind it. But now, maybe I do, a little.*

She stared up at him. "You can call me Lexi."

Lexi. He had no voice, but he repeated it to himself, unwilling to lose the gift she'd given him. Names were important. Names meant something.

"Do you have a name?"

He had. Once. But that collection of letters had long ago left his consciousness.

"I don't have magic to spare or I'd give you some." She kept staring. Her eyes were a pale gray that seemed to reflect the stars.

She smiled again. "Well, maybe I could give you a little." She looked over her shoulder. "The meridian lines are strong here. I can feel them. Can you? Is that why you're here?"

He didn't know what she was talking about. All he wanted was to feel her hand on him again. To know that someone saw him. Someone understood he was more than he appeared.

She reached out again, and her hand flattened on his trunk. "Just a little. But I'll come back when I have more, all right?"

Then a burst of magic filled him, sparks of light and streaks of power, and everything else disappeared.

CHAPTER FOUR

Lexi had never seen anything like the tree in front of her before. And that was saying something. It was obviously not a tree. It also didn't seem like a plant that should have become a tree, and yet, it had. Why? Magic? There was no other explanation she could think of for this strange hybrid, mutant plant-tree.

But after touching it, she'd felt how much more it really was. There was, somehow, the spirit of a man inside that tree.

Whether he'd been put here as some kind of punishment or a spell gone wrong or some other strange occurrence, she had no idea, but she'd sensed how resigned to his fate he was. She didn't like that. It was a sad, lonely feeling.

What had he done to deserve such a fate?

Yes, there was darkness around him. It hung over him like smoke. It had emanated off him and traveled through her fingers when she'd made contact, too. But who didn't have some darkness within them? Humans and supernaturals alike all had their own issues. Their own demons.

She was not exactly a creature of complete light herself.

Her heart had been moved by what she'd felt, so she'd done something she shouldn't have and given him a little magic. Not with her reserves in need of refilling.

She stepped back. Magic crackled over his leaves and trunk, traveling across the strange, almost humanoid form the tree had taken. Little dancing sparks that flared and flamed, then vanished as they were absorbed.

He'd gone silent. She sensed it. Maybe she'd give him too much? Or not enough? Hard to tell with a thing like this. She hadn't done him any harm; she could sense that. But had she done him any good? That much she didn't know.

She sighed. "Rest, my friend. I'll be back."

For now, she needed to seek out the source of the magic she felt coursing through the earth under her feet. Earlier, when she'd just been gathering ingredients, she'd attempted to do it the easy way, but she knew better than to think that would work. She sat on the ground and tugged off her boots, then carefully tucked them into her sack with the plants she'd harvested and the other things she'd picked up.

She stood and wriggled her bare feet against the ground. She closed her eyes, and behind her lids, a map appeared.

The meridian lines. Subtly glowing like veins of cool lava in the earth, some thick, some thin, some strong, some faint. But so many. This town was the very essence of magic. She found the strongest line, opened her eyes, and followed it.

She traveled without a care, passing through the forest as if she'd done this a thousand times. She saw more wildlife. Or maybe they saw her. None approached her.

Then the forest went still and the landscape around her changed as the meridian line under her feet grew stronger. The trees went dark as soot and the air carried a sharper, ashy tang that she could almost taste.

The magic here was stronger but not as clean. For her purposes, that didn't matter too much. Magic was magic to some extent. Fuel to replenish her diminishing supply. Dark magic wasn't ideal, but she could manage it in small doses.

Light moved through the trees. A swarm of tiny, glowing red insects came toward her. She stopped moving and watched them. They snapped and crackled as if they were electrically charged. They ebbed and flowed like liquid, flying around her.

She sensed they were dangerous. Or would have been to someone else. She shook her head at them. "You cannot hurt me. But attack me and I will take your magic."

The swam hovered a few inches back as if considering her words. Then it tightened. And shot forward.

She put her hand up and exerted a tiny bit of power. As the lightning bugs hit her palm, she absorbed their magic and they fell dead to the ground, their light extinguished. She wiped her hand on her dress and frowned. "I told you."

That tiny bit of magic was only a drop in the bucket of what she needed, but perhaps she'd gone far enough for tonight. The meridian line beneath her feet was as wide as she'd seen it and pulsing with power.

She planted her feet firmly over it, closed her eyes, and let it fill her. She was careful not to take too much. She didn't want to disrupt anything by suddenly draining one of the town's sources of magic. But it was hard to stop.

Her head went back as the energy flowed through her, quickening her and replacing a portion of what she'd been missing. Another few seconds, just to give herself a little extra, and she stepped off the line, breaking the connection.

The line was half the size it had been and only pulsing faintly now. She scowled at herself. She hadn't meant to take that much. It should replenish itself soon enough. She hoped.

She put her boots on and headed back toward town and the pub.

Unconcerned with time, she returned to her new dwelling while it was still dark. The pub was open, but there were fewer people inside than there had been when she'd first gone in. She went up the steps at the rear of the building to access her living space, staying close to the wall. She didn't care for heights.

She dug the key out of her bag and went inside. For the most part, the apartment was empty. It was essentially one very large room, the same size as the pub below it, with a partial wall for the kitchen, which also housed a pantry with a washer and dryer. A bank of windows looked out onto the street and, she imagined, would let in plenty of natural light during the day. Such as there was in this town.

The floors throughout were wide planks of hardwood. They needed refinishing, but she could handle that. The bathroom was its own room. A good size but nothing fancy, all the usual fixtures. Sink, toilet, shower, and a separate clawfoot tub. It would do.

All she needed was the most basic bits and pieces to start with.

She set her sack on the kitchen counter and took out the things she'd gathered as well as a few items she'd brought with her, like a small chunk of marble and a few pieces of beach glass. In the forest she'd found plants, mostly, but also a few choice rocks. Several hunks of wood. A snakeskin. Three small bones, bleached by time. Half an eggshell from a robin's egg. A handful of feathers, large and small. A little ball of spider's web. Flowers in as many colors as she'd been able to find. And then the various plants and fungus she'd need.

She selected one of the chunks of wood, a piece of bamboo, some nettles, a couple of feathers, a few strands of spider web, and a forgotten wire coat hanger from the closet. She added pieces of silk and cotton that she'd brought with her, then carried it all to the other side of the space and set them on the floor. She fixed a picture in her head, then held her hand out over the items and dispersed a bit of her magic.

With a swirl of golden light and glittering sparks, the items lifted off the floor and twirled around in the tempest of energy. They transformed and shifted, their components pulled apart and put back together again at Lexi's pleasure.

She dropped her hand as the spell played out. A few moments later, the light disappeared, and in place of the objects she'd started with was a big, beautiful, four-poster bed, complete with mattress, sheets, comforter, and pillows. The posts were carved into spiraling twists that tapered to blunt points; the mattress, comforter, and pillows stuffed with cotton and down; the linens finely spun silk, bamboo and nettle thread, soft as a kitten's ear.

She sat on the edge and lay back. As comfortable as a cloud. She smiled and sat up again, envisioning the rest of the space. She would only use the smallest amount of magic, but she would do her best to make the apartment comfortable.

CHAPTER FIVE

Amelia woke, unsettled by an odd feeling she couldn't shake. But this time it wasn't the approaching meteor shower. This was different. This time it wasn't something that was coming but something that had already happened.

Her drapes were pulled tight, but the hour was early, and it would have been dark regardless. She looked at the time on her bedside clock. It was nearly three in the morning. She exhaled. Far too early to be awake, but there was no way she was going back to sleep. She was wide awake now. She closed her eyes and reached out with her power to see if she could find the source of the disturbance.

The image that appeared in her head was of the Dark Acres. That wasn't good. That part of the Enchanted Forest was a necessary evil in Shadowvale. The yin that balanced the yang. The shadow cast by the lightness of everything else. Didn't mean she wanted to go there.

Reluctantly, she got up and dressed in a caftan, a long silk cardigan, and silk slippers. She pulled a turban over her hair, then went down the hall to Beckett's room and knocked.

It took a moment, but he finally opened the door. "It's 3 a.m. woman."

He might have just gotten out of bed, but he looked as polished as ever. That irritated her for reasons unknown. "Drive me to the Dark Acres."

He scrubbed a hand over his face. "You have a driver."

"He's sleeping."

Beckett's mouth firmed to a hard line as his eyes narrowed. "So was *I*."

She raised her brows. "I thought death never slept." Truth was, she felt safer with him. Not that she couldn't defend herself. She had a great deal of magic. But she was still a woman of some age. And he was a reaper. Who better to protect the very soul he was here to someday claim?

He cut a look at her, his displeasure plain. "I'll get my coat."

She glanced at his striped nightshirt. Such an old-fashioned choice of sleeping apparel for a man. "Perhaps find some trousers, as well."

He disappeared back into his quarters without another word, returning fully dressed.

They were on their way shortly in the midnight-blue Rolls, a tank of a car that gave her another sense of security. Falsely, she knew. A few inches of steel would do nothing against dark magic, if that was indeed what was afoot.

But the perception of safety amounted to something.

Beckett looked at her through the rearview mirror. "Should I ask what this is about?"

"I don't know. But there's been a disturbance. I felt it. It woke me."

His eyes narrowed as he focused on the road. "Is this because of the Aerarii?"

"I wouldn't think so. That announcement doesn't come out until tomorrow's, that is, today's paper. Which has yet to be delivered. This is something else."

"No thoughts on what?"

She shook her head and stared out the window. It was too dark to see much beyond the exterior lights on the houses.

It grew darker when they entered the canopy of the Enchanted Forest.

"The Dark Acres?" Beckett confirmed.

She nodded. The odd sensation that had awoken her was growing stronger.

Another few moments and he pulled the car onto the shoulder and idled. "We're here. What now?"

She stared into the dark woods, knowing all too well what lay beyond. "Now I find what happened."

He got out and opened her door. "You're not going in there alone."

She exited the vehicle. The night air was cool, but there was no breeze. Even so, the sound of insects carried to them. "I was hoping not to."

He closed the door but left the car unlocked. Amelia

understood. No one would bother her vehicle. No one with any sense. "Which way?"

She gave a little shake of her head. "I'm not sure. Somewhere in there. I'll know more soon, I think."

"Lead the way."

She went forward at a slow pace, sending out strands of power like a magical metal detector, in search of something gone amiss.

Beckett stayed near her side. They were only about fifty yards from the car when he touched her arm. "Death. Close by."

She looked around and saw nothing, but then, the dark was nearly impenetrable. She flattened her palm in front of her and called up a small, glowing orb of cold fire. She moved her hand, casting the light about them.

"There." Beckett pointed. He took a few steps, crouched, and picked something off the leaf litter. He straightened and held what he'd found out for inspection.

"A lightning bug."

"A whole swarm of them," he said. "All dead on the ground."

She held her empty hand out. He deposited the dead bug into it. She lifted it to her nose and sniffed. "I don't smell any kind of pesticide. Or any kind of magic."

"So they just died?"

"No. I should smell *some* magic. The whiff of something dark and acrid. These are magical creatures, after all."

His eyes narrowed. "Are you saying there's no magic left in them?"

"It seems that way."

"Have you seen anything like that before?"

"Not that I recall, but this is Shadowvale. I long ago learned that nothing should surprise me."

"I guess you found your disturbance then."

She tipped her hand and let the insect fall to the ground. "I don't think I have. Whatever happened was more than just a handful of bugs having the magic drained out of them."

"Is that really what you think was done to them?"

"Do you have a better explanation?"

He shook his head. "No. You're the expert on all things magical."

"I need to do a little more looking." She extinguished the orb, leaving them in utter darkness once again.

She gave her eyes a moment to adjust, then crouched down and planted her hands on the earth and whispered, "*Magicae viratur*."

Quivering lines of glowing light spread out all around her, visible through the leaves and other detritus that covered the forest floor.

"What is that?" Beckett asked, stepping back.

"That," Amelia answered, "is what energizes this town. Those are the meridian lines that carry power and magic throughout Shadowvale. The same lines that protect us and make this place the safe haven it is."

Beckett let out a low whistle. "How do you like that."

Carefully, she got herself upright again. She brushed her hands off. "I don't like it. They aren't right. They're weaker than they should be. That one especially." She pointed at a thin, stringy-looking line. "That should be one of the prime lines. One of the big ones. It used to be."

"Why isn't it now?"

"I have a feeling it's because those lightning bugs weren't the only things drained of their magic."

"On a scale of one to ten, how much trouble is this?"

Amelia took a deep breath and did some mental calculations. "If this is a one-off, it's not much trouble. The line should replenish itself over time. If this isn't a one-off, then it's serious. But there's more to it than that."

"Such as?"

"Who or what is causing this? If it's a who, I can deal with that." At least she thought she could. "If it's a what … then I'm not sure. Because if this is happening because of some bigger problem—"

"Like Shadowvale is leaking magic?"

She hadn't wanted to put that into words, but she nodded all the same. "If that's what's happening, it's more than serious. It might be fatal to the town."

She glanced skyward, focusing on the stars visible overhead. "And if that's the case, the Aerarii can't come soon enough."

"Can you tell which it is?"

She'd tried, when she touched the earth, to ascertain the reason behind the disturbance. To get a sense if it was caused by an animal, a human, a supernatural, or something else entirely. As best she could tell, the answer had been something else entirely. That wasn't good. That was very distinctly bad. "I can tell it wasn't caused by anything or anyone that I can name."

"So ... some kind of leakage then."

"Maybe. Or there are powers at work here with greater magic than my own."

"Is that possible?"

She lifted her eyes to him, a pit in her stomach opening up. "Yes."

He let out another of those low whistles.

She started for the car. She had work to do. Spells to cast. Books to read. There had to be an answer somewhere. "We need those Aerarii more than ever. They might be the only thing that saves us."

CHAPTER SIX

He regained consciousness to a sky bright with clouds and the sounds of birdsong and the stream's quiet burbling. He felt stronger and more aware than he had since he'd found himself in this forest.

He could sense things in a way he hadn't before, too. The colors of the forest, once so muted and dim, were much more vibrant. The smells of the fresh damp earth, flowers, moldering leaves and rotting wood, the brightness of green, growing things, all of those and more came to him on the gentle breeze.

He could feel that breeze rustling his leaves. It felt good. When was the last time anything had felt good? He couldn't remember. Being out here in the forest wasn't bad. Even when it rained or stormed or snowed. It really wasn't much of anything.

He didn't get hot or cold, hungry or thirsty. If he felt tired, he slept after a fashion. Mostly he just felt lonely, and he'd learned to deal with that. Now, though, he could feel things in a brand-new way.

There was only one explanation for that.

The beautiful woman in the woods last night, Lexi. She had changed him. Or at least her magic had. It had caused him to grow faster than any of the magic he'd absorbed from the earth so far.

How was that possible? Was it just the amount of magic? Was it *her* magic? He didn't know and had no way of finding out.

He hoped she came back.

A squirrel jumped from the nearest tree and landed in his branches. He watched it, no eyes and yet eyes everywhere. Chittering and chirping, the little animal ran across one branch, down another, back up, and leaped again over to the next tree.

The day warmed. Birds came to rest in his branches. A woodchuck scampered by. More deer appeared at the stream. He watched them intently. Something was different about them, then he realized it wasn't the deer that were different.

The deer were drinking in the same spot the doe had been last night, and yet they were farther away, which was impossible. Which could mean only one of two things. The deer had gotten smaller. Or he'd grown taller overnight.

Obviously, he had grown. How powerful was Lexi's magic? There seemed to be only one answer to that question. Very.

More than anything he wanted to see her again. Not just because of her magic, although he wondered if she'd share it with him again. Mostly he wanted to see her because she was the first contact he'd had with anyone in a very long time.

And because she'd seen him. Actually recognized that he was something more than a tree. Some of the animals seemed to know. Or maybe they all did and only a few cared.

Could a person tell if they came by? Or did he just think no one else could see him for more than he was because no one else *had* seen him?

He had a lot to think about, but Lexi was at the forefront of his thoughts. Beautiful Lexi with eyes like starlight and skin that glowed. There were only a few women in his memories, but he knew what beauty was, even without much comparison.

If he were capable of laughter, he would have laughed at himself right then. He liked Lexi very much. Him. The monster trapped in a tree, because that was how he'd come to think of himself.

What strange things her magic had done to him. And he didn't mind them at all.

He focused internally, trying to determine if there was anything else new with him. Did he have more leaves? Had his bark hardened or changed color? How much taller had he grown? Was he—

A butterfly landed on one of his thinnest branches. A twig really, but it wasn't something he'd ever felt before even though it wasn't the first time such a thing had happened. But this time, the butterfly's light touch tickled him. Muscle memory, whatever that was worth, made him wish he could twitch enough to make it move.

His branches shook, and the butterfly fluttered away.

He went still. As still as a tree could. Had he done that? Had he caused his branches to move? That had never been possible before. He'd tried to many times in the early days of finding himself here. Nothing. Now the best he could do was gently shake his leaves, something that usually happened whether or not he meant it to.

Moving branches on purpose was something else entirely.

This time, with intent, he concentrated on one medium-size branch, about the circumference of Lexi's arm. He pushed everything he had into it, willing it to obey him, to move, to do *something*.

Wood creaked.

He'd moved the branch. He'd actually done it. Something he'd never thought possible.

Just how strong was Lexi's magic? It sent a shiver through him, causing a few leaves to drift toward the ground. Had she known what a valuable gift she was giving him? How it would change him?

She must have. Which might mean she'd given him the magic to see what he could do with it. And if that was true, she had to be coming back.

He hoped so anyway. He couldn't imagine never seeing her again. He wanted to thank her. If only he could find his voice again. He was sure he'd had one, once upon a time. Most creatures did.

In some of his memories, the darkest of them, the ones he didn't like to keep in his mind for too long, he'd had a voice. Been able to speak a few words. But he remembered thinking, too. Not the way he did now.

His thoughts, as best he could tell, had been more fractured. A lot like his memories were now. He'd had a lot of anger in those memories, too.

Why had he been so angry? Why had rage filled him that way? It had driven him. If his memories were true, he'd done a lot of things that brought him shame now. Caused hurt and fear and destruction. Terrible things. Awful things.

Monstrous things.

Had Lexi seen that in him? She couldn't have. She wouldn't have given magic to a monster, would she?

If only she'd come back. He thought she would.

Until then, he would practice his new skills and put her magic to good use. He'd make her proud.

Had he ever made anyone proud?

He didn't think so.

He very much wanted that to change.

CHAPTER SEVEN

Lexi had dreamed of trees walking through a forest and talking deer and a sky bright with stars. Being awake wasn't much different. Her thoughts as she got out of bed were all about the tree that wasn't a tree that she'd encountered in the woods last night.

Whoever was in that tree, or had become that tree, could definitely use more of her magic. She wanted to help him, too, but she only had so much to go around. Especially after the power she'd used up furnishing her place.

She would get more magic soon, though. Hopefully enough for her own needs and enough to help the man in the tree. She wondered about his story. How he'd ended up there. People didn't get turned into trees for no reason.

Curious, that. Curiouser still was what the consequences might be for helping him get loose of that tree.

Not that consequences had ever bothered her much.

Before she could visit him again, however, there were a few things she still needed to get for her apartment. Things that would make her new place seem more like a home. Maybe that was silly because she might not be here very long, but what was the harm in it?

There was a part of her that wondered if she might entertain the tree man here one day. Anything was possible.

She also needed food. Regardless of what she was, sustenance was still a necessity.

Both of those things would require money, however. That tiresome human construct. At least it wasn't hard to come up with.

She searched through her things and managed to come up with three wrinkled dollar bills. They would do very well. She set them out on the kitchen counter, smoothing them a little. Then she laid her hand over the first one and summoned a teensy bit of magic.

When she moved her hand, the dollar bill had become a hundred-dollar bill. She did that twice more. Generally, she didn't like to leave herself without a few single dollars on hand as a security measure, but she'd tuck a couple away as soon as she had change.

She got dressed, changing her gown from last night into a pair of jeans and a slouchy faded blue sweater that hung off one shoulder. She paired that with lace-up ankle boots and a slim ivory scarf draped twice around her neck.

Most women carried purses for things like their phone, ID, money, credit cards, lipstick, and ... honestly, she wasn't sure what else they carried in them. Some purses were enormous. Some tiny.

She didn't really need one as she had no phone, no ID, no credit cards and didn't need cosmetics, but she went with a small pouch of a purse, mostly as a concession to blending in. She put her three hundred-dollar bills in it along with her apartment key, then threw the long strap over her head and across her body.

She went downstairs to the pub. The food smelled really good, but she didn't want to waste time eating right now. Trip wasn't there, so Lexi went up to the woman behind the bar. "Hi, there. I'm Lexi Gardner. Did Trip mention me?"

The woman, a natural redhead with fine lines around her eyes, nodded. "Sure thing, honey. I'm Belle. How are you doing?"

"I'm good, thank you. Just getting settled in. Do you think you could give me some change? All I have are big bills." Lexi pulled out two of the hundreds.

Belle glanced at them. "I can do that for you. I'll do it out of petty cash in the back."

"Thank you." Lexi handed over the two bills.

Belle took them and went into the office, returning a few minutes later. She had a little stack of twenties. "This okay? You didn't say what kind of bills you wanted."

"That's great. I appreciate it." Lexi eyed the burger on a server's tray as she walked past.

"You want some lunch? Might as well if you're hungry. I imagine you'd eat for free, seeing as how you're the new owner and all."

Lexi smiled. She was hungry. She shook her head. "I

have a lot to do. Moving into a place makes you realize how much you have that you don't need and how much you need that you don't have."

Belle laughed. "Ain't that the truth. Well, you come back when you're ready and I'll make sure you get full."

"That's kind of you. Can you tell me the best place to get groceries? And also, where I might find a shop that sells lamps and other household items?"

"I can do that," Belle said. "Want me to write them down for you? Then you can look up the addresses on your phone."

Lexi shook her head. "I don't have a phone."

Belle's brows went up. "You don't?"

Lexi gave her standard response. "I don't think they're environmentally friendly."

"Ah, right. You're one of those." Belle laughed. "No judgment. Tell you the truth, if I could get rid of mine, I would." She looked under the bar and pulled out a folded newspaper. "Why don't you take this with you? It's the local paper, and the last couple of pages are mostly advertisements for the businesses around here. The Green Grocer has their sales insert in there, too."

"Maybe I'll take a seat at the bar and page through it now. If that's all right."

"Right as rain. You want a cup of coffee? Maybe some toast? It's not on the menu, but it'd be quick. We've got orange marmalade, too. I know because I've had it on toast here myself a few times. Goes in a couple of the

A Sky Full of Stars

recipes, but the cook doesn't mind if you want a little bit of it on the side."

Belle obviously wanted to feed her. Lexi nodded. "That sounds great. Thank you."

As Belle went to get the coffee, Lexi took a seat and opened up the paper. The *Vale Messenger*. The headline on the front page caused her jaw to drop. She stared at the words, reading them a second time to be sure she was actually seeing what she was seeing.

Epic Wish-Granting Meteor Shower Coming!

Belle put the cup of coffee in front of Lexi. "Isn't that something? Might have to head out and see if I can catch one of those falling stars myself. You know, it's kind of the unwritten rule around here that we don't talk about each other's troubles, but I don't mind telling you mine isn't too awful. I can't cry. Doesn't sound like a big thing, but it can be. Now, my husband, Fred? He's got some bigger issues, bless his heart. I don't share those 'cuz those are his to tell, but he could use that wish more than me."

Lexi just nodded and tried to act as if the news meant nothing to her. "You don't really believe these things can grant wishes, do you?"

With a look of utmost seriousness, Belle nodded. "That information came from Amelia Marchand herself. She wouldn't have given all that to the paper if it wasn't true."

"Who's Amelia Marchand?"

Belle glanced around. "The witch who founded this

town. Created it, really. And I know you're going to say witches aren't real, not in that kind of magical hocus-pocus sort of way, but I know for a fact they are. I've lived here long enough to understand that."

Lexi needed to read the article, but a sinking feeling had already filled her.

Belle looked at the kitchen. "Let me go check on your toast."

"Thanks." Lexi continued to stare at the article, most of the words blurring, but she picked out enough to see that everything had been made perfectly clear.

The meteor shower had been announced in the paper. It was coming tomorrow night. She hadn't known when, just that she needed to be here and be ready.

But this article changed everything. It meant the woods would be thick with people hunting for the magic that would make their wishes come true.

The forest would be mobbed. Her own chances of getting some of that magic for herself had just drastically been reduced.

There was only one way of bettering those odds. She needed help. Someone who knew the forest better than she did. Someone who could use a little magic themselves. Someone with their own stake in the game.

It was time to go visit her new friend again and see if he really was a friend or a foe. A friend she could use. Together they would be far more effective at finding enough magic when the meteors began to fall.

But if he was a foe ... well, that wouldn't be all bad,

she supposed. She'd still be on her own, so nothing gained, but she could take every ounce of magic he had in him and leave him to spend the rest of his life as he was.

A tree. And nothing more.

CHAPTER EIGHT

He'd managed to wear himself out practicing his new ability to move, but he'd definitely gotten better at it. Now, drowsy from his efforts, he was resting. The day had warmed some, but the breeze was still cool when it zipped past.

Another month and it would be plenty warm. He tried to think back to before he'd been here. Had he seen the sun then? He didn't think he had. Or maybe those memories just hadn't survived.

Drifting a little closer toward his version of sleep, he was suddenly brought back to consciousness by leaves crunching. Footsteps. Coming closer.

He was fully alert now. Then he saw her, winding her way through the underbrush and saplings, following the stream toward him. It was her. The woman with the glowing skin and the beautiful smile.

Lexi.

He shook his leaves to greet her.

She smiled at him, but the happiness didn't seem to find her eyes. "Hello again, my friend. How are you?"

How he wished he could answer her.

"You look well." She raised her gaze to his branches, following their lines with her eyes. "You look ... taller."

I am, he wanted to say.

"I guess the magic agreed with you." Her smile faded. She stared at the ground between them. "I want to help you further, but that means a lot of magic. Which I have now. But giving it all to you, because I think you're going to need vast quantities of the stuff to become whole again, means leaving myself without enough. Over time, this wouldn't be a problem, because I'm sure I'd find more, but it will make me vulnerable."

I will protect you. But the words had no sound. No voice. If only.

She wrapped her arms around her torso, raising her face to him again. "I know two places to get the kind of magic I need. But taking from the first one means destroying something many people rely on. And while I might be many things, I am not a destroyer."

He shook his leaves again, the closest he could get to a nod.

She tipped her head. "You agree with that, don't you? You don't want to be a destroyer either, do you?"

He didn't want that at all. He wanted to be good. Whatever that meant. Whatever it entailed. He wanted to be different than what his memories showed him. To be the opposite of those images. To not have people be afraid of him.

He just had no way of telling her that.

"I need to know for sure." She took a step closer. "I

need to know who you are. What you are. Can you tell me that?"

He couldn't. Not because he didn't have a voice but because he didn't know those answers himself.

"Of course, you can't. But you can let me find the answers for myself." She reached out and flattened her palm against his trunk. "You might not like the way this feels, but don't fight it. Let me in. Let me see what I need to see."

A moment later, warmth spread out from the point of her contact. It traveled through him, slowly but insistently. Digging in. Going deeper. The heat and the strength of moment intensified. It reached up into his branches and down into his roots.

It made him feel too big for the form that held him. Like he might split and crack under the onslaught. Her magic itched and prickled and burrowed into his being like an invasion of hungry insects. He wanted to push against it, to do anything he could to get it out of his system, but he didn't.

This was what she needed to do, and he didn't want her to leave.

He went as still as he could and did nothing to hinder her examination of him. Maybe she could figure out those answers for him. He hoped they were the answers she wanted. He hoped she would still be willing to help him after she found them.

Finally, Lexi stepped back. Her shoulders drooped and she exhaled hard. "Okay. I didn't see everything I wanted to, but I saw enough. You are a very interesting being. Or you were. What are you now is ..."

She just shook her head, sat down at the base of his trunk, and leaned against him. "I need to rest. And think. That took more out of me than I thought it would."

Very soon, her breathing changed. She slumped against him a little more, and he sensed she was asleep.

What had she found? Did she know he was a monster? It hurt him to think that was the answer she'd gotten. But if that was what she'd seen, would she really have stayed? Would she sleep at the foot of a monster?

He didn't think so.

Then again, he didn't know what to think.

Until she awoke, he tormented himself with every variation of what she might have seen and what her answer to him would be.

Thankfully, she didn't slumber too long. The shadows had deepened only slightly when she stretched and got to her feet.

She faced him again. "I will help you. I will use my magic to free you from your current situation. Make you whole again. Or as whole as I can. But I must ask something in return. That isn't how I like to do things. I prefer to help as often as I can and with no conditions—my way of creating a purpose for myself as well as balancing some of the injustices of this world—but I am in a rare position where I need help myself."

He would do anything for her. He already knew that.

He trembled at the idea that she had found enough good with her inspection to do this for him.

"If you agree to that, give me a sign."

He was so glad he'd practiced. He moved the small branch he'd moved earlier. It was almost easy.

She laughed softly, a sound that rivaled the stream for its pleasing quality. "Very good. I have to go and gather as much magic as I can. I'm still not sure it will be enough, but it will have to do. I can't leave myself with nothing. Either way, I'll be back at dusk. This is something better done at night, I think."

She was leaving? He didn't like that. He supposed he understood it, and he certainly believed her when she explained what she needed to do, but would she really come back? He hoped so.

"While I'm gone, just rest. You will need all of your strength for what comes next." She patted his trunk. "I'll be back. I promise. I wish I'd learned your name, but maybe soon, hmm?"

With that, she walked away and left him to await her return.

She'd told him to rest. But that wasn't so easy. She was going to free him. That gave him a lot to think about.

Like how much he hoped that the man she freed was not the monster of his memories.

CHAPTER NINE

Lexi couldn't go back to the same meridian line she'd already syphoned from. Taking any more would potentially erase the line completely, and that would not be good for her or the town. Taking an entire source of magic, even with something like the meteors that were soon to fall, could go very wrong.

Mostly for the taker.

The dark magic, the blackest, dankest, most twisted bits, were always the last to come through. Like the dregs of wine. Better left in the bottle. Too much of that could change her. Turn her into something dark and twisted herself.

Absorbing all the magic from the meridian line would destroy it, too, and while this town had a lot of them, there was no telling what kind of trouble losing a prime line might cause.

She would not be responsible for that.

Instead, she went back to town. She needed to think and prepare and make a plan. To begin with, she stopped the first person she crossed paths with and asked for directions to The Green Grocer.

If she was going to rescue her new friend, it was going

to take an incredible amount of magic. So much that she might be left without, at least until the meteors arrived and they were able to track down one of those.

No magic meant she would essentially be human.

That required a decent amount of preparation. She'd need serious amounts of food and cash and even some clothing because she wouldn't be able to conjure anything.

She walked toward the grocery store. Might as well start with food first. On her way in, she went directly to the customer service desk.

The older woman behind it, wearing a green The Green Grocer vest, smiled. "Hello there. How can I help?"

"I'm new to town and don't have a car yet. Is there a taxi service that could take me home when I'm done getting groceries?"

"Sure. I'd be happy to make that call for you. Sunshine Cabs, although it's really only Thomas Wilson and his daughter, Kacy, that drive the cars. One of them will come out and take you wherever you need to go. Anywhere in town is five dollars, crosstown is ten."

"Perfect." Lexi loved small towns. They were often easier to maneuver in than big cities, although those had their advantages at times. "I'll stop by again before I check out."

"I'll see you then." The woman nodded.

Lexi grabbed a cart and filled it up with all the essentials she'd thought she'd need plus a few more for her

A Sky Full of Stars

new friend. There was no doubt he'd need sustenance once he was freed from the tree.

She paused in the baking aisle after putting a bag of sugar in the cart. He would probably need a place to stay too. What were the chances he had a home waiting on him? Probably not good. Her apartment was big enough. She could easily craft whatever he needed.

Actually, she couldn't. She wouldn't have the magic.

She went back to shopping, filling the first cart and part of a second one before she thought she had enough. She went back to the customer service desk. "I'm ready for that cab now."

"Just a second," the woman said. She turned around and picked up the phone behind her and dialed.

Lexi took the opportunity to pull out several of the twenty-dollar bills Belle had given her in exchange for the hundreds earlier. Lexi turned four of them into hundreds again, hoping that would be enough to cover her groceries.

"He's on his way."

"Thanks." Lexi went to pay.

Thomas showed up just as the woman had said he would. He helped Lexi load her groceries into the trunk of his sedan, then offered to help her carry them upstairs when they arrived at the pub.

She let him help, giving him an extra twenty for his trouble. It never hurt to befriend the townspeople. She asked him to wait downstairs while she put them all away, letting him know she'd need his services once more.

The groceries filled her refrigerator, her freezer, and a lot of her cabinet and pantry space. Now she had to buy a few more things in anticipation of her guest.

By the end of the day, she had gotten everything she thought she might need. Except for the extra magic.

It was nearly dusk, and she still had no answer to that question. She was tired from all the work she'd done and in no mood to fix herself something to eat. That would take magic, unless she cooked, and she had no idea how to do that. She went downstairs to the pub. Trip was on duty now, Belle already gone for the day.

He greeted her with a nod. "Miss Gardner."

"Lexi, please." She took a spot at the end of the bar.

"Get you a drink?"

"Water. And a menu."

"Coming right up."

How was she going to get enough magic to free him from that tree? It wasn't out of the question to think it would take more than what she had right now. She had to get more magic.

Trip dropped off a tall glass of ice water and a menu. She only half looked at it, her mind occupied with her dilemma. She stared into the mirror that backed the bar, which enabled her to watch the patrons behind her.

Lots of smiling faces and happy conversations. Several of the tables had copies of the newspaper on them. People were talking about the meteor shower that was coming. They were excited about the possibilities.

So was Lexi. But getting to one of those meteors first was going to be a lot more difficult now that the event had been broadcast.

Trip returned. "Do you know what you want?"

She focused on him. "What's the name of the woman who started the town? Emily?"

"Amelia. Marchand."

"She's the one quoted in that article about the meteors, right? She's a witch?"

"Yes, and yes, that's pretty common knowledge."

"Where does she live?"

"Indigo House. Why are you—"

Lexi pushed the menu away. "Can you call Sunshine Cabs for me?"

His brows furrowed. "Sure, but—"

"Thanks. I'm going to wait outside for him."

Thomas arrived to pick her up in just a few minutes. "Hello again."

She climbed in the back. "Hello."

"Where to, young lady?"

She could see him smiling in the rearview mirror. "Indigo House."

His smile vanished. "You sure about that?"

"Yes. I need to speak to Amelia Marchand."

"She know you're coming?"

"No. Do you think that's a problem?"

He put the car into drive and shook his head. "Probably not. She knows people are coming even when they don't tell her."

Lexi sat back. She'd already suspected Amelia to be a very powerful woman. Anyone who had enough magic to create a town like this had to be. But now she was wondering if Amelia was more than just a witch. "What else can you tell me about her?"

Thomas exhaled before answering. "She created this town for her beloved, a vampire named Pasqual. But not long after, he upped and vanished. No one knows what happened to him. She's got a tiger, too."

Lexi leaned forward slightly. "Sorry. Did you say a tiger?"

"Mm-hmm. Big ol' thing. Size of this car, maybe bigger. I saw him one night, couple years ago, just walking through one of the parks like he owned the place." Thomas shook himself. "You don't forget a thing like that, no sir."

"No, I don't suppose you do." She stared out the window at the enormous live oaks that guarded both sides of the road. Spanish moss hung from the branches, softening the trees' appearance. So Amelia had a tiger. Witches had familiars. Nothing unusual about that. But they generally weren't enormous beasts of prey. Amelia had to be extraordinarily powerful.

"You still wanna go?"

She nodded, smiling a little. "Yes, I do. I'd like you to wait for me, too."

"You got it."

Indigo House was a majestic, two-story property that would have looked right at home in the French countryside. Perhaps as the ancestral manor home of an old noble family. A wrought-iron fence, reminiscent of the gates Lexi had first passed through, surrounded the extensive property. At a second glance, she noticed the swirling motif was actually a scowling tiger.

Other than that little reminder, the creamy white stucco and dark blue roof were welcoming and the landscaping crisp and attractive. All good, but Lexi wasn't letting her guard down just because the house looked like the monthly feature from *French Country Living* magazine.

Thomas pulled up the drive and stopped in front of the double doors. Two more tigers, these carved from glittering blue-black stone, flanked the entrance.

Laying it on a little thick, wasn't she? "Thanks. I don't know how long I'll be but just let the meter run because I know this isn't a standard trip. I'll take care of you, whatever the amount."

Thomas nodded and shifted the car into park, then turned off the engine. "You got it." He picked up a copy of the paper off the seat next to him and unfolded it. "I'll be right here."

Lexi took hold of the door handle, all kinds of second thoughts swirling through her head. Maybe she should have changed into something more presentable. Jeans and a sweater were awfully casual for this sort of meeting.

Thomas was reading his paper and not paying attention to her. With a quick flash of magic that she couldn't really afford, she transformed her jeans and sweater into a navy-blue shirt dress with a woven brown leather belt and low heels to match. Her jewelry became gold hoops, a strand of pearls, and an antique gold tank watch on a brown alligator strap. She quickly changed her purse to brown leather as well.

"Good choice," Thomas said without looking up.

Lexi flicked her gaze at him but said nothing. A good reminder that no one in this town was as they seemed.

She got out and went to the doors. They were wavy blue glass, impossible to see through. She lifted her hand to knock, but the door opened. Before her stood a man with salt-and-pepper hair that was more salt than pepper. He was barely an inch taller than she was with a barrel chest and the kind of sturdiness that spoke of past military experience, or a youth spent playing contact sports. Maybe both.

Neither of those things explained the aura of death about him.

He eyed her warily. "Can I help you?"

"I'd like to see Amelia Marchand, please."

"And you are?"

"Lexi Gardner."

"I'll see if she's available." He closed the door and left her standing there, his dark form receding into the house.

She lifted her fingers and made contact with the door

frame. The house hummed with magic. She could probably syphon what she needed from it alone. Tempting as that was, it would have far greater consequences than finding the magic elsewhere.

She didn't need to start a turf war with the town's most powerful resident. She dropped her hand. Maybe, if this didn't go as planned, she'd return and take the magic anyway. While being wary of the tiger.

If the creature actually existed. She was starting to wonder if the beast wasn't mostly magic and myth. Not that she doubted Thomas's account. But some spells looked as real as could be. That might have been all he'd seen. A magical show of power. Amelia reinforcing what she wanted people to believe.

The butler, or whoever he was, returned. "Ms. Marchand will see you. Right this way."

He opened the door wide, and Lexi stepped through.

She really hoped this worked.

CHAPTER TEN

Amelia had just taken a break from her research to sort through some of the choicer rough gems from one of the mines. She'd kept an imperial topaz of exceptional color and a stunning amethyst the size of a duck egg. She was rather partial to amethyst.

Both stones would be cut and polished to her specifications and returned to her. The rest would be cut and polished as well, but those would be sold to various vendors around the world. That money helped finance the town and make the citizens comfortable.

A reasonable cost of living benefited all of them.

The day was warm enough not to need a fire. She'd had the housekeepers open the French doors onto the patio as well. Fresh air in the house was a wonderful thing.

She sat in her favorite chair near the fireplace, wondering if she should have lit it anyway. Just for the look of it. But that was silly, wasn't it? Who was she trying to impress? Well, that remained to be seen, but she had some idea the being she was about to meet was one of significant power.

She waved her hand, and the embers glowed to life. Couldn't hurt.

Beckett stepped into the room. "Lexi Gardner to see you, ma'am."

"Thank you." Ameila stayed seated.

Beckett bowed, then nodded at the woman, who'd yet to enter.

Lexi walked in.

Amelia stood. She hadn't planned to, but it had been many years, in a time before Shadowvale, that she'd encountered such a powerful being. The magic radiating off this woman was palpable. "Hello."

"Hello," Lexi said. "Thank you for seeing me."

Amelia almost hadn't. Now, she was glad she'd decided differently. "You're new to Shadowvale, aren't you?"

"I am."

"I like to meet all the newcomers when possible." Amelia gestured toward the sofas. "Please sit. Would you care for something to drink?"

Lexi shook her head. "No, thank you." She took a spot on the sofa opposite Amelia's chair. "You have a beautiful home."

As Lexi sat, so did Amelia. "Thank you." She glanced at Beckett, dismissing him with a nod. He wouldn't go far, though. Probably just outside the door.

The magic surrounding the young woman, who was obviously only young in appearance, was ... familiar.

Amelia almost immediately understood why that was but said nothing about it. Yet. "What can I do for you?"

Lexi smiled almost self-consciously. "I am most definitely in need. I don't like meeting someone new with my hands out, especially not someone like yourself—"

"You mean a witch?"

"I mean a woman of such obvious power and influence."

Amelia allowed herself a brief smile. "You are rather powerful yourself, aren't you?"

Lexi took a breath, lifting her chin slightly. "I am."

Amelia sent a trickle of magic toward Lexi, just to confirm her suspicions. The answer was as she'd imagined, albeit still surprising. "You're a sylph, unless I'm mistaken. A truly rare being."

Lexi laughed. "I am. I haven't been called by my rightful name in a long time."

"I don't think I've ever met one of your kind. What do most call you?"

"Witch, if they call me anything. Sometimes fairy. Once, a long, long time ago, starchild. Most, nothing at all because they don't understand what I am."

"They wouldn't. Magic like yours is as old as the stars. That's why you're here, isn't it? The Aerarii?"

"Yes."

"You also helped yourself to one of our meridian lines."

Lexi pursed her lips. "I did. I took more than I intended. My apologies."

Amelia held the woman's gaze, keeping her own stern. "You don't plan on doing that again, do you?"

"Not unless I have to."

"I would prefer you not. You run the risk of hurting the town and by extension, the people who call this place home. It's a sanctuary for many of them. You understand that, don't you?"

"I am coming to. And it's not my intention to do anything against you, the town, or the people. But I am in need of magic. A great deal of it."

"The kind the Aerarii bring."

"That would be best. And I am hoping for that, although my odds have gone down since that article in the paper announced the meteor shower to everyone."

Amelia sat back. "Everyone deserves a chance at having a wish granted, don't you think?"

"Mostly." Lexi sighed, seeming a little frustrated. "I understand. I really do. But I need the magic in order to survive."

"And without it?"

"I will follow the path of most of my kind. I will slowly forget who I was, what I was, and become an ordinary mortal woman. Some of us go mad when that happens. I would hope that wasn't my fate, but ..." She shrugged.

"I see."

"There's more," Lexi quickly interjected. "I need some magic right now. To help a friend. Someone trapped in a situation they don't deserve to be in. Not any longer."

Amelia frowned. "Who is this person? Someone here in town?"

"I don't know their name because they no longer know it. And yes, it's someone here in town, but that's all I'm willing to tell you. I've promised to help him, but doing so will take all the magic I have."

Amelia sat quietly, thinking.

After a few minutes, Lexi spoke again. "I could have taken another meridian line. I could have taken them all. I didn't. I came to you for help instead."

"And I appreciate that. How much magic do you need?"

"At least as much as—oh. Hello there." Lexi's gaze had shifted to the patio.

Amelia took a look.

Thoreau was sitting there, staring back.

"He won't hurt you," Amelia said.

"I know." Lexi smiled. "Animals never do."

To Amelia's ears, that sounded like a rather brave statement. She trusted Thoreau's judgment when it came to people. She got up and went to him, glancing at Lexi. "Come meet him, then. Thoreau, this is Lexi."

Much to her credit, Lexi walked toward him without any sign of hesitation. She held out her hand for him to sniff. "He's incredible. Gorgeous. Just really something to see in the flesh, you know?"

"I do," Amelia replied.

Thoreau sniffed Lexi's hand, pushed his head against

it, then lay down and curled onto his side. He wasn't one bit bothered by her.

Amelia found that interesting and not at all what she'd expected. "I'll give you the magic you need on one condition."

Lexi's attention was back on Amelia. "And that is?"

"You swear on your own magic that you will not touch the meridian lines again. Regardless of the outcome of the meteor shower."

Lexi's eyes narrowed. "You're telling me that if I don't capture an Aerarii for myself, I just have to live with no magic."

"Your magic will rebuild itself eventually, won't it?"

"So long as it isn't completely used up, yes. But that could take a long time. Even for me, and I'm someone for whom time means nothing."

Amelia nodded. "I understand that."

"I'd have to stay here. Have to get a job. Have to live like a regular person."

"Would that be so bad?" Amelia suspected it might be for a being like Lexi. To live without magic would be a curse of its own for someone like her.

Lexi took a deep breath. "I don't know. I've never tried it. Not sure I want to."

Amelia looked down at Thoreau. His eyes were closed, and he seemed to be sleeping. She knew better. It was nearly dusk. He'd go out wandering soon. He usually did. "The choice is yours, but I suggest you decide quickly. My offer has an expiration date."

"And if I don't agree to leave the meridian lines alone?"

Amelia made eye contact with Lexi again. "I may not be as powerful as you in some ways, but my abilities might surprise you. This isn't a threat. Just a warning. I will protect my town and the people in it with everything I have."

Lexi suddenly smiled. "I like you. You don't back down. I find your offer acceptable."

"I'm glad we were able to find some common ground. I'll give you as much as I can spare. If you attempt to take more from me—"

"I won't."

Amelia chose to believe her. Losing a portion of her magic was a small price to pay to keep the town safe. She had more than enough, and she used it so rarely that it would replenish itself in no time. She held out her hand. "Give me your hand."

Lexi did as she asked.

Amelia let magic flow through her and into Lexi, who did exactly as stated and took only what was given. Touching Lexi confirmed everything Amelia had learned about her so far. Amelia knew that had Lexi wanted to, she could have taken every spark of magic Amelia had in her.

Sylphs were generally good, but they were not creatures to be trifled with, Amelia knew that much. But more than that, she wasn't sure of. At least this one seemed to be benevolent.

She tapered the flow and brought it to an end. "I hope that helps."

Lexi had closed her eyes. She opened them now, the soft gray irises sparkling with the new influx of power. "Thank you. That should be sufficient. Perhaps I'll see you again. Tomorrow night, in the woods?"

"Perhaps you will. I wish your friend all the best. It's kind of you to help him."

Lexi smiled. "I can see myself out."

"Until we meet again." Because Amelia had no doubt they would.

But before that happened, she needed to educate herself further on who she was dealing with.

Amelia followed Lexi back into the house. Beckett was already waiting at the door to see Lexi off.

Amelia waited for him to return. "I'll be in the library. I'd like my dinner served in there as well."

Beckett nodded. "Brushing up on our new arrival?"

Amelia glanced toward the foyer. "Seems a wise thing to do, don't you think?"

His brows lifted. "Absolutely. She could be the end of this place, couldn't she?"

Amelia didn't mean to shudder, but one ran through her anyway. "It's within the realm of possibility. So I need to know how to prevent that. Just in case."

CHAPTER ELEVEN

The sun had set, and it was nearly dark when he heard footsteps coming toward him. It was Lexi, and she was making no effort to be silent. She wanted him to hear her. To know she'd returned.

"Sorry I'm late," Lexi called out. "I had so much to do, but I'm here now. I hope you're not angry with me."

He could never be angry with her. She'd come back. He was happy. More than that. He was joyous. Or as close to that as he could remember being. He shook his leaves at the pleasure of her arrival.

"I hope you rested today like I asked you to do." She had the same glow she'd had earlier. Maybe it was a little brighter now. And the same cloth sack over her shoulder. There were things in it, but he couldn't tell what. "This is going to be very taxing on you, but there's no way to avoid that. I'm going to give you every ounce of magic I can spare. Even so, it may not be enough. You might not be as … transformed as you'd like. But I'll get you there. With your help. But don't worry about that now."

He was ready for whatever she needed him to do.

He gazed at her, amazed by her beauty and how she seemed to radiate light.

She rubbed her hands together. "All right. I suppose we might as well do this and see what happens. No reason to put it off. Are you ready?"

He shook his leaves again.

"I'm taking that as yes." She went within inches of him and pressed her hands to his trunk. She closed her eyes and said softly, "Here we go."

He braced himself, as much as he could. What he expected was something similar to the first time she'd connected with him. That hot, prickly sensation.

And it was a little like that, but more warm than hot and more tingly than prickly. The magic trickled in at first. A slow but steady stream that felt like light shining on him.

The stream increased. Parts of him began to ache. Just a dull throb initially, but as more and more magic entered his system, the throbbing became genuine pain.

If he'd had a voice, he would have cried out. The magic seared through him, dividing him from his home and changing him, the same way he'd been changing throughout the days he'd been here, but her magic was pushing it to happen in a matter of minutes.

His leaves shriveled up and died, falling to the ground around him like ashes. His branches dried and cracked, the sound like gunshots echoing through the wood. And still Lexi pushed more magic into him.

The earth bubbled around his roots as they pulled loose from the soil. The pain increased, blinding him to everything but the awareness of what was happening to him. The memories that had once been fragments returned, fully formed, his past becoming a moving picture he couldn't escape from. The horror of who he'd been and what he was played out before him in full nightmarish color.

He had a fleeting thought that Lexi was not here to save him, but to end him.

Maybe that was what he deserved. Undoubtedly, it was.

His trunk cracked from the bottom up. His branches snapped. He was nothing but pain, his world a black hole of hurt and anguish and regret. All of it black black black.

Time passed. How much, he didn't know.

But then he opened his eyes and stared up at a sky full of stars, glittering and brighter than he ever recalled seeing them. The face of an angel appeared, looking down at him.

Lexi. His angel.

She was pale and drawn, like she'd been wrung out. She smiled. "You did it." Her lids were drifting closed. "I ... need to rest."

Rest sounded good to him. She collapsed beside him, her head on his arm. He closed his eyes and joined her in sleep.

A little while later, something landed on his cheek. He lifted his hand and swiped at it. Instantly, he sat up.

He had a *hand*. He had two hands. And arms. And legs. And feet. He sucked in a breath. He could breathe!

His joints hurt, and his skin was rough and dry, but none of that mattered. "Lexi, wake up."

She'd even given him a voice. Those words had hurt, but it wasn't more than he could bear. He swallowed, eyes hot with unshed tears. He was overwhelmed with what she'd done for him. "I can talk."

Lexi mumbled something that might have been the word good or food. She still looked pale and very, very tired. She said something else. "My ... bag."

The bag she'd brought was lying beside her. He grabbed it and opened it up. There was a bottle of water, a large sandwich wrapped in waxed paper, some paper money, a key on a ring, and a folded swathe of white fabric. He didn't know what to do with any of it.

"Eat," she whispered. "Drink. Strength."

As if agreeing with her, his stomach growled. He twisted the cap off the water and lifted her head as he put the bottle to her mouth. "You drink."

She took a little water, then shook her head. "Rest. You eat."

He did as she told him, finding himself unimaginably hungry. The water soothed his throat, and the food filled part of his belly. He watched her while he ate. She'd fallen back to sleep. That had to be good. She certainly looked like she needed to rest. She was no longer glowing.

A piece of cheese fell from the sandwich. He glanced down to pick it up and realized he was naked.

Was that why she'd brought the sheet?

He finished eating, then took out the fabric and shook it. It seemed small. Or was he big? He was a little disoriented yet, and it was hard to tell. His joints ached. He wrapped the fabric around his waist, tying it tight to keep it secure.

Lexi remained asleep.

He looked into the sack again and found a slip of paper with an address on it. Main Street seemed easy enough to find. But he didn't really know which way to go to get there.

He sat down next to her again, content to wait until she was ready to move. He wasn't sure how much time passed, but when she opened her eyes again, the moon was in a different place in the sky.

"Are you okay?" he asked.

She breathed for a few seconds before answering. "I will be. We need to get back to my place."

"Okay. How do we get there?"

She lifted one finger and pointed through him. "That way. I'm going to need help."

"I will help you." He would always help her. She had given him new life.

"Did you find the sheet?"

So that's what that was. "I'm wearing it. Was that what I was supposed to do?"

Weakly, she smiled. "Yes. And you ate?"

"I did. Is the address on the paper where you live?"

"Yes." Her lids were drifting downward again. "Do you think you can get us there?"

"I will do my best." He thought he had enough information. If not, he had the address written down. Maybe he could find someone to help him. He put his arm through the straps of the sack, which now held the empty water bottle, the sandwich wrapper, the money, the key, and the address. Then he stood.

He wasn't quite as disoriented this time, and he realized he was tall. And large. Taller and larger than Lexi by a good bit. He bent and carefully lifted her into his arms, cradling her against his chest.

For the first time, he looked back to where he'd been for so long, his place near the stream. The ground was covered with leaves and ragged pieces of wood, the dirt disturbed and uneven, pocked with holes and divots.

Nothing remained that resembled a tree.

He made sure she was as comfortable as he could make her, then he walked in the direction she'd pointed, unsure what lay ahead for him, but that didn't matter.

Only taking care of Lexi did.

Chapter Twelve

Light filtered through Lexi's lids. She opened them to slits. She squinted against the brightness, squeezing them shut again. A shadow fell over her, taking the light away. She opened her eyes cautiously.

The shadow belonged to a mountain of a man. "You're awake."

So much of what had happened was a blur, but she knew the gist of it. "You're him, aren't you? The man in the tree?"

"I am. Thank you for freeing me."

She leaned up on her elbows and looked around. "We made it back to my place, I see. Good job."

He smiled, a beautiful, happy-to-be alive smile. "It took me a while, but it was smart to write Five Bells Pub on there. That helped a lot."

She lay back down, tired, but that seemed about right. Eating would help. Eating and rehydrating. Refilling her magic, too, but there was little chance of that until tonight. "Could you get me a bottle of water?"

"Anything. Yes." He went to the kitchen and came back with a bottle, cold from the refrigerator. He handed it to her.

"Thank you." She sat up and drank the whole thing.

"Do you want more? What else can I get you?"

She nodded. "Another bottle would be good. I need to eat, and—you're still wearing the sheet."

He glanced down at the sheet wrapping his hips. "I didn't know what else to put on."

"Right." She gave him a better look. He was a very large man. Six foot eight, maybe. And wide. The rugby players she'd seen looked small compared to him. But her magic hadn't been enough to fully transform him.

His skin was dry and rough like bark, and there was a stiffness in his movements as he went back to the kitchen that made it seem like his joints were literally wooden.

"We'll find more magic tonight. We'll get you fixed and me refilled and then we'll be fine. We'll both be fine."

She hoped. One meteor wasn't going to be enough. They'd need at least two. What were the odds of that? With the whole town out looking? Not good.

He returned with a second bottle of water. It looked tiny in his hands. "Why do you look worried?"

She took the bottle and drank half of it before answering. There was no point in keeping anything from him. He needed to know. "Because it's not going to be easy. Especially not with us in this kind of shape. I'll be fine when I get some food in me, but I can't do anything that requires magic. If I use any more, all of my magic will be gone and I'll be ..."

She didn't want to tell him she'd turn into an ordinary human woman. He was certainly no ordinary human

man, and he might not want her company otherwise. "It won't be good. That's all."

"Is that why you don't glow anymore?"

Interesting that he'd been able to see her magic. "Yes."

He put his hands on his hips and looked toward the kitchen. "I don't know how to cook. Is there something you can eat that doesn't require cooking?"

Standing there, draped in the sheet, he looked like the statue of some ancient warrior king come to life. He was a remarkable specimen. Rugged in a way that she couldn't recall seeing before. It excited her to think about spending time with a man like this.

"I'm sure there's something. I'm trying to remember what I bought. There should be fruit in the refrigerator. That will help. That sugar should help me get some energy back."

"I'll look." He returned with two apples and a bag of grapes. "Is this good?"

She nodded, holding her hands out. "It's a start."

She devoured the fruit, and as expected, the natural sugars gave her a boost. "I feel better." She put the apple cores in the grape bag with the stems and eased out of bed.

He was instantly at her side, offering her his arm. "Here. Hold on to me."

She took his arm. His skin was as dry and rough as it looked, and the wood grain was still visible. "You shouldn't be like this. I'm sorry I didn't have enough magic to make things right for you on the first try."

"Please, don't apologize. I'm fine. I don't need anything more. I am happy."

She stopped walking and looked up at him. "You are a beautiful man, inside and out. I want to make things right for you. And I will." They just had their work cut out for them.

"I am not beautiful. I was spelled into that tree for a reason. I was a monster." He got her to the kitchen where she could hold on to the countertops, then pulled away, pacing to the windows. His back was to her. "I was a monster, but for all I know, I still am."

"No, you're not. Just because you were something once doesn't mean you're destined to be that thing for the rest of your days. This is your second chance."

He didn't turn around, just heaved out a sigh that seemed to say he couldn't quite believe that.

"Do you feel like a monster?"

Silence stretched out between them while she waited for him to answer. Finally, "No."

"That's because you're not one anymore." A new thought occurred to her. "What's your name? Do you know?"

"Yes." His head hung.

"Do you want to tell me?"

"No."

"Then you don't have—"

"Edgar." He turned to face her but didn't make eye contact. "Edgar Hyde."

She thought a moment. "As in Dr. Jekyll and—"

"Yes." He was still staring at the floor.

Few things surprised her anymore. But this news came very close. "You're sure?"

He nodded.

"Maybe you're not Hyde anymore. Maybe you're Jekyll now."

"I'm not. He was a separate entity. He was ..." Edgar looked up finally. There was pain in his eyes. "He was the good one. I was his curse."

She hurt for him. She shook her head. "You're no one's curse anymore."

"I need to go see him. To tell him I understand and I forgive him for banishing me into that plant and that I will never bother him ever again. I want to thank him, too. For letting me live. He could have made a different decision."

Lexi blinked. "You mean he's still in Shadowvale."

"He was." Edgar glanced toward the windows that looked over the street. "I don't know if he's still here or not. Maybe he left once he got rid of me. I wouldn't blame him."

She sighed, still weak from everything she'd done. "Tell you what. Let me get my strength back and I'll get you some clothes, because you can't go out like that. Then we can find him together, all right? If he's still here."

Edgar nodded. "Thank you. You've been very kind to me. I owe you my life."

"You don't owe me anything. But I could use a little help in the kitchen."

He smiled and returned to her side. "Tell me what you want me to do."

With her directions and his work, they put together two sandwiches with the bread, cheese, and roast beef she'd bought. They had glasses of milk with it, and when she'd finished her sandwich, her energy levels were a lot better, but she still felt off.

There was nothing to be done about that. It was the lack of magic in her system. That feeling would be with her for a long time unless they found a meteor tonight. If they didn't, they'd have two more nights to try.

Three nights to capture the magic from at least two meteors. What were the odds they could actually do that?

She refused to calculate them. She didn't want to know exactly how impossible this impossible task was.

Just like she didn't want to think about spending the rest of her life as an ordinary human.

Chapter Thirteen

He was Edgar Hyde. The realization had come to him in a surge of difficult memories. He'd been right about being a monster. He truly had been one.

But was Lexi also right? That he wasn't that man any longer? He stood by the windows while she took a shower. He stared down at the world below. Remembering.

He'd been so angry then. Trapped in another person's mind and body. Unable to express himself or make anyone understand that all he wanted was to be free.

That inability to make himself understood had turned him into a tormented creature who'd expressed himself through rage and destruction.

The people in this town would remember that, too. They would be afraid of him. And with good reason. Henry wouldn't want to see him either. Henry probably believed that he was done with Edgar.

Maybe it would be best to just leave. To let everyone continue to think he was gone. That was what they wanted. He didn't blame them. No one would want to live near him. Even if he was different. Which he wasn't so sure of.

How could he know that the Edgar who'd terrorized this place, who'd torn trees up by their roots, who'd caused chaos and destruction, didn't still live inside him? He couldn't. Just like he had no way of knowing what might trigger that Edgar to return.

He was, in a sense, a bomb waiting to go off.

Lexi should have never freed him.

Where would he go? He had no idea and little memory of the world beyond Shadowvale. He couldn't go now, like this, dressed only in a sheet. He'd have to wait for Lexi to come back with clothes for him, then he'd explain there was no way he could stay.

She'd understand. Hopefully.

The bathroom door opened behind him. He turned and watched her emerge in a cloud of steam. Her hair hung in damp waves around her face. She was in jeans and a sweater. The same clothes she'd had on earlier.

She'd explained she couldn't use magic right now because she didn't have enough to spare. In a way, maybe that was good. It might keep her from trying to stop him. Or from coming after him.

Although leaving would mean not helping her find the magic she so desperately needed. He couldn't do that to her. Not after all she'd done for him.

"Good shower?" he asked.

She nodded. "I feel better. Well enough to go get us some clothes."

"Don't, uh, don't spend a lot on me. I only need one outfit."

With an odd smirk on her face, she pulled out a wad of cash from the pocket of her jeans. "Don't worry. I have plenty of money. I made sure of that before I returned to you last night. It should be more than enough until I have magic again."

"You've already done so much for me."

She walked over to him. "So you're good then? You don't need anything to wear? Happy in the sheet, are you?"

He smiled. "No, some clothes would be nice. I just feel like you've done so much for me and I haven't done anything for you."

"You're going to help me tonight, though, right?"

"Yes. I absolutely am."

"That's all I need. All I ask. What I did for you I would have done for anyone. I like to help. Makes me feel … useful." She touched his arm, giving it a quick squeeze. "When you've been around as long as I have, you start to question your purpose. And your worth. Why am I here if I'm not doing something valuable? My presence must have some function. Or else why do I exist?"

Those were questions he ought to ask himself. Although he suspected he'd be unable to answer them.

She laughed softly. "The lack of magic in my system has turned me awfully philosophical, but those are the thoughts that drive me. Those are the reasons I like to do good things when I can. To help people. Even though I don't fully understand humans. But then, who really understands much about this world?"

He nodded. That part made sense to him. "I don't."

She patted his chest. "I think you'll find your purpose soon enough. There is a reason you were spared. The man you were part of must have seen some good in you. He must have known there was more to you than just the monster in his head."

Edgar took a deep breath. Was that true? He had his doubts.

"Listen, I won't be too long. I'm afraid I can't say how long because time means very little to me, but I'll try to get what we need as fast as I can. I don't know what size you might wear either, so I should probably take your measurements."

She went into the kitchen, dug through a drawer, and returned with a measuring tape still in its packaging, a notepad, and a pen.

He stood still for her as she set the notepad and pen on the chair by the windows and opened the tape measure.

"I really need more furniture." She smiled at him. "I didn't know I'd have a guest though."

"It's fine." Beside the chair there was a small table with a little lamp on it, like a reading area. But otherwise, in this half of the apartment there was the bed with a nightstand on each side and a large chest of drawers. That was it. Unless you counted the big rug that covered most of the floor on this side, but he didn't think rugs counted as furniture.

"You need a place to sleep. Arms up." She looped the

tape around his chest, her fingers light as they grazed his skin.

"I can sleep on the floor."

"Why don't you nap in the bed while I'm gone? The floor won't be comfortable, and there's no reason for you to sleep on it when there's a perfectly good bed available." She wrote down a number, then dropped the tape to his waist. Her touch was warm against his rough skin.

"It's your bed."

"Edgar. Don't argue. I'm not having it." She read the tape, then wrote down another number.

He smiled, despite his less-than-happy mood. "You like to get your way."

She was measuring from his hip to his ankle now. "I'm used to being alone, which means I always get my way because my way is the only way. But seriously. Sleep in the bed. If you were up all night, you have to sleep sometime. Might as well catch a nap while I'm gone."

"All right."

She crouched, wrote down another number, then measured the length of his foot and wrote that down. She straightened and started to wind the tape up. "Maybe I should measure your neck too."

He lifted his chin, his joints creaking loud enough that she had to have heard.

She glanced at his neck. "That'll go away when I can give you more magic."

He moved only his eyes, trying to see her better. "What?"

"The difficulty with your joints. And the texture of your skin."

"I don't care about those things." He did. A little. His joints hurt. And his skin caught on anything he brushed against. But she needed magic more than he did.

"Well, I do. When I help someone, I like to help them as completely as possible." She put the tape around his neck. Then her hand flattened on his chest. "You're a very handsome man, you know that?"

"I don't think so."

She snorted and moved her hand off him. "You can't tell me my opinion is wrong. It's my opinion. That's how opinions work."

The tape fell away from his neck. He bent his head to look at her. "*You* are beautiful. I am ... not. I am a monst—"

"You *were* a monster. You aren't anymore." Sparks snapped in her eyes.

"Why does that make you angry?"

"Because." She glared up at him. "I know you don't think much of yourself, but if I'd sensed anything bad in you, I never would have helped you. What is it going to take to make you see that you're a good man? I felt that in you. I felt goodness. And a longing for life. This is your second chance to start over. Don't you want that?"

He stared at the floor. He hadn't thought of it that way. He didn't know how to answer. He did want a second chance. He just wasn't sure he was worthy. All he could think about was the monster he'd been. How long would his second chance last if that monster returned?

She exhaled, sounding frustrated. "Edgar?"

He looked at her.

She put her hands on his shoulders and went up on her tiptoes as she pulled him toward her. His mouth collided with hers, which was her intention, he realized.

She kissed him. Soft and warm and gentle. Then she let him go, her gaze searching his face. "Don't you want to see what that second chance could bring you?"

His mouth came open. He'd never been kissed before. His body was filled with new sensations. But at least she'd finally asked a question he could answer. "Yes."

Chapter Fourteen

Lexi used the phone at the pub to call Thomas for a ride. Landlines, thankfully, weren't affected by her. He showed up quickly. She climbed in the back.

"Morning, Miss Lexi. Where to?"

"I'm not sure. I need to buy some clothes. Men's and women's. I'd like to do it without breaking the bank either. Any suggestions?"

"Mm-hmm. I've got just the place."

"I thought you would."

"You don't need me to get there, though. It's only a handful of blocks down the street."

She liked Thomas a lot. "Take me anyway. I'll pay you to wait and bring me back, too." She took a hundred-dollar bill from her pocket and held it out to him. She'd turned every bill she had into hundreds before setting off into the forest last night.

He shook his head. "That's too much."

"You don't know how long I'm going to be inside."

He smiled. "True. But I don't really work that way. I charge by the trip."

"I know, but take it anyway. When it runs out, you tell me."

"All right." He took the money and drove.

The cab stopped outside a shop called Stella's Bargain Bin. Looked fancier than Lexi had been expecting, but if Thomas thought it was a good place to shop, she'd give it a try. She opened her door. "Thanks."

"Have fun. I'll be right here." He picked up his paper and settled back to read it.

She went inside.

A little bell jangled as the door opened. Lexi let it close behind her as she took the place in. The older woman behind the counter had fiery ginger hair and black cat-eye glasses with little rhinestones in the corners. She had a deck of cards spread out on the counter and was playing some kind of game. "Hello, honey. Welcome to the Bin. I'm the Stella on the sign. You need help finding something?"

"Do you have any men's clothing?"

"We've got some. Just got a new delivery of some big and tall stuff. Any chance you need big and tall?"

Lexi had sensed the magic in the place as soon as she stepped inside. A wry smile bent her mouth. "As a matter of fact, I do."

"I haven't unpacked it yet. It's all in three big boxes by the dressing rooms, which are straight back." Without looking up from her cards, Stella pointed. "You help yourself to anything you want in there. Shout if you need me."

"Thanks." She started for the dressing rooms. "Are the things in the boxes priced?"

"Not yet. But let's say four items for ten dollars."

Lexi stared at the woman. "Four items for ten dollars?"

Stella finally looked up, her lids heavy with glittery purple eyeshadow that matched the blouse she wore. "You're right. That's too much. Five for ten dollars."

"That's ... very reasonable." It was almost too cheap. But Lexi wasn't going to complain. She had no magic to use. And they needed clothing. Edgar more than her.

She went straight to the boxes and opened them up. The first box held pants and jeans, T-shirts, and some button-up shirts in various fabrics. She checked the slip of paper with the measurements on it. Almost everything in the box seemed suitable for Edgar. A couple of items were too large. She set those aside and selected a pair of jeans, two pairs of pants in tan and black, some sweatpants, three T-shirts in gray, blue, and black, and two long-sleeved flannel shirts, one red and black, one blue and green.

She moved on to the next box and found brand-new packages of men's pajamas, underwear, socks, and undershirts. Beneath them were some folded sweaters and fleece pullovers. She took a navy-blue sweater, a forest-green sweater, a charcoal pullover, and two packs each of pajamas, underwear, and socks, and one package of undershirts.

All in his size. What were the odds? She glanced over at Stella, who was still deeply engrossed in her card game.

Lexi moved on to the third box. She opened the flaps and sucked in a breath, unable to believe what she was seeing. Shoes, belts, and a black leather jacket. She looked at her measurements again. She didn't know how to determine shoe size from inches.

She straightened and looked at Stella again. "Do you have a chart that shows—"

"On the wall." Stella picked up a card and slapped it down again. "I knew that King of Hearts was hiding in there somewhere."

Smiling, Lexi glanced at the chart even though she already knew what she was going to find.

All the shoes in the box were Edgar's size. This kind of magic was something special. But then she was quickly learning that Shadowvale was a pretty special place, too. She selected a pair of brown suede sneakers that didn't look the least bit worn, black loafers, and two pairs of boots. One pair were black motorcycle-style, one tan leather work boots. Because why not? He needed shoes. Maybe the black ones weren't necessary, but they went with the jacket, which she was also buying.

She consolidated the remaining items into one box and put all the things she wanted to buy in another. She carried that large, heavy box to the counter and set it down on the floor. "I want what's in the box so far. Need to look for a few things myself."

Stella stood up to look over the counter. "Perfect. You've saved me a lot of work. Now I don't have to price all that stuff or find a place to put it. Just for that, every sixth item is free."

"That's too much," Lexi protested. She didn't want to take advantage of the woman.

Stella pushed all the cards together, tapped them even on the counter and shuffled. "It's my shop. I make the rules."

"Yes, ma'am." Inspired by the woman's kindness, Lexi went back to the boxes to make sure there wasn't anything else Edgar should have.

Somehow, she found a blue bathrobe she hadn't seen before. She added it to the box of items she was buying, then looked through the rest of the shop for herself.

She ended up with more than enough: jeans, leggings, dresses, sweaters, a long skirt, shoes, and some T-shirts. There were brand-new packages of women's underwear and bras in her size, too, something that Lexi no longer found so surprising.

Obviously, Stella was a woman of exceptional magical gifts. Lexi had never experienced this kind of situational magic before, but she loved it. She'd wondered if Shadowvale might fight against someone like her, someone who'd come to take magic.

Instead, she found herself feeling very welcome.

She picked up a few bits of jewelry and added them to the growing pile. "I think I'm ready."

Stella leaned over to have another look. "Fifty bucks."

"I don't think that's right. It has to be more."

"Does it?" Stella asked, arching her brows in a sly expression.

Lexi wasn't going to argue. "Your store. Your prices. Your rules."

"Now you're getting the hang of it."

Lexi pulled out a hundred. "I don't have anything smaller, sorry."

"I don't have change for that."

Lexi thought fast. "How about you give me credit then? Fifty dollars left to spend for Lexi Gardner."

Stella nodded. "I can do that. Let me get you some bags." She pulled a few from somewhere behind the counter and came out from around it to help Lexi get everything packaged up. Stella had on zebra-striped pants and chunky red platform heels with her glittery purple blouse.

She helped Lexi carry all the bags out to Thomas's waiting sedan, too.

Thomas hopped out when he saw them coming and opened the trunk. "Nice to see you, Stella."

She smiled at him. "Nice to see you, too, Thomas. I've got a fedora in there that would look like a million bucks on you."

"Yeah?" He scratched the side of his head. "Might have to take a look at that."

Lexi deposited her bags into the trunk. "Put it on my tab, Stella. If he wants it."

She went back inside to get the rest of her purchases.

Thomas drove her home wearing his new hat.

CHAPTER FIFTEEN

"This is too much," Edgar protested, although he was touched by Lexi's generosity. She'd overdone it. Probably the nicest thing anyone had done for him, outside of her saving him, but still more than he needed.

"No, it's not." Lexi shook her head. "You don't have anything. You need all of this. And more, but this is a good start. Besides, the woman at the shop practically paid me to take all this. Now get some clothes and go shower. When you're done and dressed, we'll go down to the pub and have something to eat, and we'll see if we can find out if Henry Jekyll is still in town."

A chill went through him for two reasons. The idea of facing Henry. And the thought of being out in public. "I don't think that's a good idea."

"Which part?"

"Any of it. I need to talk to Henry. You're right about that. It's not going to be easy, but I need to do it. But being out in public? Where people can see me? I don't think that's a good idea." The thought of being recognized as the monster he'd been didn't sit well.

"Why not?"

"Because if those people find out who I am, they will

be terrified of me. Which is probably the right response." He shook his head. "It's not a good idea."

"First of all, you have to go out in public sometime. Secondly, people come to this town because they have some kind of issue they feel is a curse, right?"

He nodded. "That's why Henry came here. Because of me. I was his curse."

"You *were*. Past tense. But the point is they accepted him. So why wouldn't they accept you? Especially now that you're no longer a monster? Because you're not, Edgar." She moved closer to him. "You have to know that."

He heaved out a deep breath. "But I don't. I can't. And neither do you. I appreciate your faith in me, but how can either of us know what still dwells deep inside of me? That monster could be there."

She stared at him, sympathy plain in her gaze. "I'll make you a deal. If the old monster comes out of you, I will use the last of my magic to neutralize him. I give you my word. That's how sure I am that it's not going to happen."

"I don't like that."

She put her hands on her hips. "I don't care."

Without meaning to, he laughed. "You are a very interesting woman, Lexi."

She grinned. "I'm good with that. Been called worse, I can assure you. Now go shower and get dressed. I put a fresh towel on the rack for you. I'm hungry."

"As you wish." He stared at the clothes she'd laid out

on the bed. "I don't know what to pick. What things go together." He looked at her, brows lifted.

She selected a pair of underwear, an undershirt, jeans, and the blue and green flannel shirt. "Here you go. Okay?"

"Yes." He took them from her.

"You know how to shower, right? Wash your hair with shampoo, wash your body with soap, rinse off, dry off, get dressed. Shampoo and soap are already in there."

"Of course." He wasn't going to tell her, but he had been wondering about the order of things.

"I probably should have gotten you some razors, but a little stubble is kind of fashionable these days, so you're good there."

He touched his face. His skin was so rough. "My face might destroy a blade."

Her smile deflated slightly. "We'll take care of that as soon as possible."

"It's fine." He headed for the bathroom.

He set his things on the counter and looked at the controls in the shower. Thankfully, there was a red H and a blue C, which he quickly figured out meant hot and cold. He turned the knob toward hot, and water sprayed out of the showerhead.

He stepped back to let it warm up. While he waited, he looked at himself in the mirror. She'd kissed him. On purpose. Why? There was nothing in that mirror worth kissing, was there? Or had she just done that to make him feel better?

That seemed most likely. She was that kind of person.

He ran his fingers over his mouth. The kiss had been very nice. It had filled him with sensations that seemed like serious magic. The good kind. The best kind.

Maybe she would do it again. Wouldn't that be something?

He untied the sheet and got into the shower. He had to duck down to get his head under the spray. He did exactly what she'd told him. Washed his hair, then his body, rinsed the suds off, got out and dried off with the towel she'd left for him.

The clothes she'd bought him fit perfectly. He studied himself in the mirror again before going out, wiping away the fog that clouded it. He looked ... almost human in the clothes. His skin gave him away, the rough texture that still very much looked like wood grain to him. Maybe once that was gone, no one would know who he'd been.

Or maybe that was wishful thinking.

He used his towel to dry his hair a little more, then went out to get Lexi's approval. She was sitting on the couch, looking through the paper. "Do I look the way I'm supposed to?"

She glanced up. Her mouth came open. Then she exhaled as her gaze swept him. "You wear clothes very well. Socks and work boots are by the bed."

He went and put them on, then returned. He was nervous about going into the pub. "People are going to stare at me, aren't they?"

She put the paper down and met him by the kitchen.

She fixed his collar. "Probably. People like to look at attractive things. Fine art, baby animals, beautiful women, handsome men. Add to that your size and height, and yes, they are probably going to stare."

He swallowed. Her answer hadn't helped his nerves. "What do I do?"

"Just smile back and let them look. Eventually, they'll get their fill and go back to their business."

"They will?"

"Sure."

He huffed out a breath. "Not being a monster is hard."

She snickered. "You'll get the hang of it." She smoothed her hand down his chest. "You ready?"

He wasn't. He didn't feel like he'd ever be ready. But she wanted to go eat. And they needed to find out if Henry was still around. So he nodded.

Her hand stayed on his chest. "I know you don't want to do this. I appreciate that you are. It's very courageous."

"I don't feel courageous." He felt foolish. He felt like he was about to make a big mistake. He felt—

She went up on her toes and kissed him again, pulling him down to meet her. He wasn't any more prepared for it this time than he had been before, but at least he knew enough to enjoy it. His hands found her waist, and he kissed her back. A little. At least he tried to.

She finally let him go. "How do you feel now?"

Her eyes were so pretty. Her mouth so soft. Her body warm under his touch. He blinked. "About what?"

She snorted. "Come on, let's go eat."

He held his breath as they walked into the pub. He smiled like Lexi told him too. A few people looked. Some definitely stared. But no one pointed at him or screamed or ran for the exits. And just like Lexi had said, after a few moments, most of them went back to their business. He exhaled, although his heart was pounding.

Lexi grabbed them a table by the wall. Not long after they sat, a young woman approached them. Edgar braced himself, prepared to be told they had to leave.

The young woman smiled and put a menu in front of each of them. "Hi there. Welcome to Five Bells. Do you know what you'd like to drink?"

"Water," Lexi answered.

Edgar nodded. "Water."

The young woman was still smiling. "Our lunch special today is fish and chips. Comes with a side of coleslaw. Our burgers are really good too."

"Thanks," Lexi said.

The young woman left. Lexi reached across and touched Edgar's arm. "You okay?"

"I thought she was going to ask me to leave."

Lexi made a face at him. "That's not going to happen. Relax. It's all good. What do you want to eat?"

Now that they were inside and apparently allowed to stay, he realized he was starving. The sandwich he'd had earlier hadn't made much of a dent in his appetite. He looked at the menu. "I don't know."

"Um ... can you read?"

He glanced at her. "Yes."

She shrugged. "I didn't mean anything by that. I just wasn't sure."

"I was both my own person and a part of Henry Jekyll. What he knew, I knew, to some extent. I could tell you the scientific formula for the hydrogen bomb, the specific weight of carbon, the names of every element on the periodic table, but then some things, like how to pick out clothes, don't come as easily."

"Interesting. I wonder if that's something Henry has trouble with too. Maybe we can ask him that."

"We?"

"Sorry. I shouldn't have assumed you wanted me to go with you. Don't worry, if you want to do that on your own, that is absolutely your right."

"No. I want you to come. I just didn't know you were going to. Thank you. I would like that." Just knowing she'd be there with him took the edge off. "Fish and chips."

She smiled. "I was going to get that, too."

Something about making the same food choice as Lexi put him at ease. He smiled back. Maybe meeting with Henry wouldn't be that bad after all.

Not so long as she was by his side.

CHAPTER SIXTEEN

Lexi could tell Edgar had been on edge, but when the food arrived and they began to eat, he seemed to lose the last of his worries.

"It's good, isn't it?"

He nodded, mouth full. He swallowed. "I like fish and chips a lot. I could eat another one of these."

"Then order one."

"You can do that?"

"Yep." She found their server and gave her a little wave.

The young woman came over to the table. "How are you doing? You guys need something?"

"Another order of fish and chips," Lexi answered. "And is Trip in yet?"

The girl looked toward the bar. "He is. I think he's in the walk-in getting fruit for the bar. Do you want me to get him?"

"No, that's all right. I'll go see him shortly. Thanks."

"I'll get that second order right in for you." The server left.

Lexi looked at Edgar. "Will you be all right if I leave you alone for a bit? I want to ask Trip about Henry."

He nodded, his expression serious again. "I will be fine."

She wasn't entirely sure about that, but they'd soon find out. "I won't be long."

With a quick smile to reassure him, she got up and went to the bar to find Trip. Didn't take long. He was coming out of the back with a bag of lemons for the bar.

"Hi, Trip."

"Lexi. What can I do for you?" He set the lemons on a big cutting board.

"I was wondering if you might have a phone book? Or some sort of citizen directory? I'm trying to find someone in town."

"A phone book?" He grinned. "I don't think we've had one of those since the early '90s. Maybe I can help? Who are you looking for?"

"Dr. Henry Jekyll."

"Oh, sure, he's around. If you're looking for health care, I don't think he takes on too many patients these days, although he does work at the hospital."

"No, I just need to speak to him."

Trip found a knife and started cutting the lemons. "I don't know the man personally, but you could probably find him at the hospital. That's where I'd start. He probably has office hours there. I'm just guessing, so don't take that as gospel."

"Okay. Thank you."

"Sure."

She went back to their table.

Edgar looked up, eyes filled with anticipation. "Is he still around?"

She sat down and nodded. "Yes. He works at the hospital. After we eat, we should go there and see if we can find him."

The server arrived with Edgar's second order of fish and chips. He gave her a brief smile but didn't touch the food. As she walked away, he frowned at Lexi. "I'm nervous about talking to him. It probably won't go well."

"It might not. But better to seek him out and let him know what's going on with you than to run into him accidentally, don't you think?"

"Yes. True." He sighed.

"It won't be as bad as you think. You're a different person now. You're in a different place." She snagged one of his fries.

They got to the hospital by way of Thomas, who gave Edgar a brief look of consideration but said nothing about his size or appearance. He dropped them at the main entrance. "You want me to wait?"

"Yes, please," Lexi said. "I don't know how long we'll be."

"That's all right. I still have the crossword to do." He patted the folded newspaper next to him. "I'll go find a spot to park, but I'll watch this entrance for you."

"Thanks."

She and Edgar went inside, went through security, then straight to the information desk, where they were given stickers to wear that said Visitor. "Can you tell us where Dr. Henry Jekyll's office is?"

The woman looked at her computer. "Fourth floor, Neuroscience." She pointed down the corridor. "Elevators are that way."

"Thank you." Lexi shot Edgar a look.

They rode up in silence, but the tense expression on Edgar's face said it all. He didn't want to do this as much as he knew he had to.

As the doors opened, she took his hand. "It's going to be all right."

He nodded but didn't say anything.

A directory across from the elevators listed office numbers. Dr. Jekyll was in 412. They walked to it but stopped outside the door.

Edgar stood there staring at it but made no move to go in.

She watched his chest rise and fall with his breathing. "Do you want me to talk to him first? Tell him what's going on?"

"Yes. But no. If I am going to be a man, I need to act like one." He exhaled, stepped forward, and opened the door.

A small, empty waiting room greeted them. Across from them was another door that simply said Office on it.

He paused, then walked to that door and knocked.

"Just a moment," a man's voice called out.

Edgar stepped back. He swallowed hard.

The door opened, and a man who looked very similar

to Edgar stepped out. He wore a white lab coat. "Can I help you?"

Henry's mouth came open, and he went very still. Then he shook his head and laughed. "My apologies. You look like someone I used to know. Do we have an appointment?"

Edgar said nothing. His hands clenched and unclenched, and Lexi had the distinct feeling he might bolt.

She stepped up to stand beside him. "You're Dr. Henry Jekyll?"

"I am."

"This man is who you think he is. Edgar Hyde."

Henry shook his head, brow furrowing. "That can't be."

"It is. I freed him from a tree growing in the forest. He wants you to know that he's in town and means you no harm. He just thought it would be best that you found out from him, not some other way."

Henry continued to stare. "How is this possible?"

Edgar took a deep breath. "I'm sorry for all the terrible things I did. For the way I plagued you. For all of it."

Henry blinked a few times and said nothing, then he stepped back and motioned toward the interior of his office. "I think you should both come in."

CHAPTER SEVENTEEN

Edgar sat on the leather couch in Henry's office because the chairs in front of the desk were too small to accommodate him. "I know you must hate me."

Henry went around and sat behind his desk. "I don't. Not at all. You could no more help being a part of me than I could help having you in my head."

Lexi gave Edgar a little smile.

Edgar frowned. "You don't hate me?"

"No. I mean it." Henry sighed. "If I could have caused things to have had a different outcome, I would have."

"Meaning what?" Lexi asked. "You wouldn't have put him into that tree?"

"It was a houseplant," Henry explained. "And I thought that would be a better place for him than just disappearing him into the ether. I never imagined anything would come of it. I see my mistake now. I feel I'm the one who owes you an apology, Edgar."

Edgar had never imagined he'd hear those words from the man he'd tormented most of his life. "You don't need to. You did what you had to in order to survive."

Henry nodded. "My entire life had been dedicated to

eradicating the curse of the men in my family. It was my entire work at the time."

"You mean the curse of me. And those like me."

"Yes. I'm sorry. But that's what you were to us. You must understand that? You seem very different now, though. Completely different, as a matter of fact. Can I ask how that happened?"

Edgar looked at Lexi and felt comfort that she was there. He smiled at her. "Lexi happened. She saved me. Gave me her magic. Gave me life again."

Lexi shook her head. "Wait now. That's only partially true. Yes, I freed him from the tree, but I didn't change him. He was like this when I found him, which is why I freed him. He was already a good man."

"How did that happen?" Henry asked again. "Something changed somewhere."

"The growth process?" Lexi suggested. "Or maybe it was the way you removed him from your mind? You're the brain doctor."

Henry seemed to ponder that. "Edgar, would you be willing to let me run some tests on you? To see if I can find out what happened. Maybe how it happened? Nothing intrusive, I promise. Some brain scans. Things like that. I know it's a lot to ask. You've obviously been through a lot. But it might teach us all a great many things. Might even result in something groundbreaking."

Edgar took a deep breath. "I don't know."

"I can understand if you want some time to think it over." Henry smiled. "This is honestly amazing. I never expected any of this. As hard as it was to have you as the other half of me, I am truly glad nothing bad happened to you. I would love to just sit and talk with you sometime." He held his hands up, palms toward Edgar. "No strings."

Was this man who'd been the subject of Edgar's destructive behavior actually offering him friendship? How was that possible? Maybe he was reading too much into it. Maybe this was just Henry's way of getting answers. Edgar didn't know how to respond. Friendship would be all right. "Lexi and I are very busy for the next few days."

"We are," Lexi said. She seemed willing to go along with whatever he wanted. Not that he'd anticipated anything different from her.

"Let me guess," Henry said. "The meteor shower?"

Edgar glanced at Lexi. He didn't know how much she was willing to reveal, and he didn't want to say something she'd rather be kept a secret.

She smiled at him before looking at Henry. "It took almost all of my magic to free Edgar, and as you see, that still wasn't enough to completely transform him. We're hoping to find at least one of the meteors, yes."

A serious expression overtook Henry's face. "So you believe with more magic you can transform him into what? A more typical-looking man?"

"I think I can erase the remnants of the tree from his skin and joints, which are still stiff." Lexi glanced at him. "They are still stiff, right?"

Edgar nodded. "They are. They ache a little. Not too bad." He hated to complain. It felt like a criticism of what Lexi had done for him, and he didn't mean that at all.

"Interesting," Henry said.

Edgar couldn't leave it at that, though. "Lexi needs the magic for herself more than I need it. She gave up a lot to help me. She deserves it."

Lexi reached out to him and took his hand. "Thank you, Edgar. But I want it for both of us."

He could spend the rest of his days exactly how he was, but he knew the same wasn't true for Lexi. She needed that magic. And he was determined to get it for her. He held her hand but spoke to Henry. "I was nervous about coming here. Lexi got me through that. I would like to talk to you again someday. I'll think about the testing. I just don't know yet."

Henry nodded. "I understand. Listen, about the meteors ... would you like some help? Finding one, I mean? I know the forest is going to be mobbed with people on the hunt. Why wouldn't it be? It's an incredible opportunity. But Izzy and I weren't planning on going out. Neither of us really needs a wish granted. We could help you, though."

Lexi sat up straighter. "Izzy?"

Henry smiled. "Isadora. My wife. We got married a couple of months ago. She's wonderful. Helped me with Edgar when all of that was going on. She was a big part of getting him out of my head."

Edgar thought about all the memories that had come and gone. "I think ... I remember her."

Henry leaned back in his chair. "I know she'll remember you."

Edgar swallowed. "Did I hurt her? My memories of that time are fragmented."

"Doesn't surprise me," Henry said. "And no, you didn't hurt her. You were surprisingly good with her for the most part."

For the most part meant there had been parts that weren't good. Edgar didn't want to know about those. Not now, anyway.

Lexi cleared her throat softly. "Help would be amazing. We could really use two meteors' worth of magic, which I know is asking a lot, but that's what it's going to take to fully restore both of us. So if you're serious ..."

"I am," Henry said. "I'll talk to Izzy when I get home. I'm leaving in an hour. I'm sure she'll be up for it. Just give me your number and I'll text you and let you know."

Edgar shook his head. "We don't have phones."

"Oh. Um ..." Henry seemed to be wracking his brain, thinking of an alternative.

"I can't use electronics," Lexi explained. "My magic isn't compatible with such things. But I'm sure if you called the Five Bells Pub and left a message for me, they'd get it to me. I live in the apartment upstairs."

Henry looked at Edgar. "And where are you staying?"

Edgar glanced at Lexi. "With her. Until ... I don't know." He hadn't thought about it until now, but Lexi wasn't going to want him there forever. But he had no money and no way of getting any at the moment.

Lexi squeezed his hand. "Edgar is welcome to stay with me for as long as he likes. Leave us a message at the pub. We'll get it."

"Okay," Henry said. "I'll call by six. But I'll give you my numbers too, just in case. We'll have to figure out something, otherwise how will Izzy and I let you know if we capture a meteor?"

Edgar hadn't thought about that. "I don't know."

"You could get a phone," Henry suggested. "They sell some at Morton's Pharmacy that you don't need a plan for. You'll have to buy some minutes for it, but that's no big deal."

Edgar looked at Lexi. She shrugged. Then she let go of his hand and held up a finger. "I bet Thomas can help us with that."

She nodded at Henry. "Give us your information, and I'll make sure Edgar gets a phone. I may not be able to use one, but I'm sure he can."

"Good enough," Henry said. He smiled at Edgar as he took a card from the holder on the front of his desk. He flipped it over and scrawled a number on the back. "I can't believe it's you. This is amazing. Wait until I tell Izzy. I'm sure she's going to want to meet you. Maybe after the meteor business is sorted, we can all have dinner together sometime."

Edgar nodded, but his head was spinning. This was all going so fast. It was too much. He wanted to go. He didn't belong here. He wasn't sure he belonged anywhere. He stood suddenly, causing Henry to jerk back.

Lexi jumped up too. "Are you okay?" She put her hand on his arm. "You're overwhelmed."

He nodded.

She held his gaze. "It's okay. You don't have to do anything you're not ready to do." She gave Henry a tight smile and grabbed the card he'd written his number on. "Thanks. We'll be in touch soon."

Edgar already had the door open and was headed for the elevator. She caught up to him. "Hey, I know it's a lot. But it's okay. I'm right here with you."

The elevator opened, and he got on. "I don't belong here. I'm not like other people."

She walked in and tapped the button to close the doors, then she put her arms around him. "No, you're not, and that's why I like you so much."

He closed his eyes. Somehow, her embrace and understanding made things better. But she wasn't always going to be around.

How was he going to live without her?

CHAPTER EIGHTEEN

Lexi held on to Edgar. She wasn't surprised he had gotten overwhelmed. She wondered if Edgar might have handled the interaction better if Henry had reacted differently. Maybe if he'd refused to see Edgar or cowered or yelled or *something* more along the lines of what Edgar had been expecting.

But Henry's surprising friendliness could have thrown Edgar. It seemed to her that he hadn't been prepared for that. "It's okay," she whispered. "You're okay."

She felt him take a deep breath.

"Yes," he finally said.

The doors opened. She let go of him and took his hand. His skin scratched hers, but she didn't care. Nothing mattered but that Edgar was all right. In some ways, he was like a newborn that needed looking after. A newborn that could probably lift a bus over his head, but there was something about him that brought out her protective side.

They walked out of the hospital. "You're sure?" she asked.

He nodded, his gaze downward. "I overreacted. Henry won't help us now."

"I think he will. All you did was get a little freaked out. That's not a big deal."

He lifted his eyes to her. "You don't think he was mad?"

"No. I think he was and still is very curious about you. And I really do think he wants to help."

Edgar glanced back at the building. "I'm not good at interacting with people."

She shrugged. "That's a pretty common problem for a lot of folks. Regular people and supernaturals alike."

"You don't have that problem."

She grinned. "I'm not a regular or a supernatural."

He smiled even as his eyes held questions. "What are you then?"

"A sylph." She wasn't quite sure how to explain that to him, so she changed the subject. "You know what we should do?"

"What?"

Thomas had seen them, and his car was headed toward them now. "We should get you that phone, then we should find a place to get ice cream."

His brows bent. "I don't think I've had ice cream."

"You're going to love it."

She told Thomas they needed to get a phone, the kind you could buy minutes for. Then they wanted ice cream.

"Sure," he said. "I know just the place."

He took them to Morton's Pharmacy, which was where Henry had suggested. And because Lexi had asked, he came in with them to make sure they bought the right thing. Once they were back in the car, Thomas showed Edgar how to add numbers into his contacts, starting with the one for Sunshine Cab.

Of course, Edgar only had one other number to add in. Henry's. He looked at Lexi. "Should I call him now? I should apologize."

"Wait until he's had time to talk to his wife. Besides, we need to get ice cream. Thomas, where can we get some of that?"

"You buckle up and we'll be there before you know it."

He was right. Wasn't long before he was pulling into a place with a sign out front that read The Creamatorium. "Best ice cream in town. Although the Sunshine Diner ain't bad either if you want some pie to go with that ice cream. But this place does things right."

"What kind do you want, Thomas?"

He twisted in his seat to see her. "You buying me some?"

She nodded. "My treat." He'd been nothing but helpful, and she liked him very much.

"Well, that's real nice of you. Thank you. In that case, lemme get out and see what they have. Flavors change all the time."

The three of them stood in front of the menu board, contemplating the wide variety of flavors.

A Sky Full of Stars

Edgar looked befuddled. "I have no idea."

Thomas adjusted his fedora. "I'm having a scoop of the black raspberry cobbler."

"That sounds good," Lexi said. "I'm going for the peanut butter banana fudge ripple. I like all of those things so they should be even better together."

"Maybe I'll just get vanilla," Edgar said.

Thomas looked up at him. "Son, you can get vanilla anyplace. Isn't there something you think you'd like more?"

"Yes, but there are too many choices."

"Which ones are you trying to decide between?"

Edgar rubbed his chin. "The other ones I was thinking about are the dark chocolate with candied orange or the pecan maple waffle swirl."

"Okay. What if I told you they're out of both of those flavors?"

Edgar frowned. "They are?"

"No, but which one were you most disappointed to miss out on?"

Edgar smiled, understanding in his eyes. "Dark chocolate with candied orange."

"Then get that one."

"That's a good trick," Edgar said. "How did you get to be so smart?"

"You live long enough," Thomas said, "which I have, and you figure a few things out."

"What if you don't figure things out?"

Thomas shook his head. "Then you probably ain't gonna live that long."

Lexi laughed to herself. Thomas was a wise man and a special human. She could sense some magic about him but nothing strong. He might not even be aware of it. She went up to the counter and ordered for all of them.

Once they'd collected their ice cream, they went out to sit on one of the benches. There weren't too many other people around, giving them some privacy.

Her ice cream was rich and delicious. She finished a spoonful of the creamy goodness. "What brought you to Shadowvale, Thomas?"

He cut his eyes at her. "Is that your way of asking what my curse is?"

She quickly shook her head. "No. I know that's not something anyone's supposed to ask about. Just wondering how you ended up here. That's all."

He ate another bite of ice cream before answering. "No way to tell you about that without mentioning my curse. But that's all right. Same curse my wife had, same curse my daughter has. Can't sleep. Maybe an hour or two couple times a week but otherwise I'm just awake all the time. It's why I started the cab company. Might as well make myself useful if I'm gonna be up. I've made peace with it, you see. But my daughter ..."

He sighed. "Came here because the curse took my wife, and I thought Kacy would find some relief here."

"Your wife has passed on?"

He nodded. "Twenty-eight years now. Not sleeping

made her brain hurt. She couldn't take it. Finally took so many sleeping pills her body had no choice but to give in."

"I'm so sorry. You must miss her very much." Lexi felt for the man, moved by the pain in his eyes.

"I do."

"Are you going out to look for a meteor tonight?"

He shook his head. "I don't think there's much chance of us finding one of those. I'm too old to be traipsing about in those woods anyway. Not everything that lives out there is friendly, you know."

Lexi nodded as a thought came to her. "But your daughter would like to be rid of her curse?"

He looked at her. "You know something, say it."

"I don't. But I have an idea. No guarantees. No promises. But if you're interested—"

"I'm interested. How soon?"

Lexi finished another spoonful of ice cream. "We can go as soon as this is gone."

Thomas nodded. "I'll text Kacy." He got up to throw his empty paper cup away.

Edgar watched him. "He's a nice man. What are you going to do?"

Lexi blew out a breath. "I hope I'm going to help his daughter. And maybe myself a little bit, too."

Edgar finished his ice cream next, but Lexi quickly did the same, eating her last few spoonfuls faster than she would have liked. But it was all for a good reason.

Thomas drove them to his house, a small bungalow in

a neighborhood that looked like a nice part of town, but Lexi had a feeling Shadowvale didn't have any bad parts.

He parked in the driveway, and they all got out.

Edgar looked around. "I've been here before." He took a few steps toward the street, glancing in both directions. He nodded slowly. "The monster was here."

"It's okay," Lexi said. "That's all behind you."

He turned toward the house. Thomas was going inside. "Do you think he knows who I am?"

"Probably not. If he does, he doesn't care or he'd have said something." She took his arm. "Come on. Let's go in and see if this works."

Thomas had left the door open for them. They stepped into a cozy living room area, the only real foyer space designated by a throw rug and the door to a coat closet on the wall to the right.

Standing beside Thomas was a slender young woman. Even with how visibly tired she looked, she was very pretty. Her braided hair was wrapped up in a blue and yellow silk scarf that helped brighten her face. She smiled, and it went all the way to her big brown eyes. "Hi. You must be Lexi and Edgar."

Lexi nodded. "We are."

"My dad said you think you might be able to help me sleep."

It was a statement, not a question, but Lexi answered anyway. "I told him there are no guarantees, but I'm willing to try if you are."

"I'm always willing to try," Kacy said. "What do you need to do?"

"I need to touch you," Lexi said. "I need to get a read on the magic you have inside you."

Kacy shook her head. "I don't have any magic. Just this curse."

"Magic, curse, whatever you want to call it, the origins are the same."

Thomas went to his recliner and sat, then gestured to the couch as he spoke to Edgar. "Have a seat, please."

Edgar sat, carefully, like he wasn't sure the couch would hold him.

Kacy stayed standing. "Whatever you need to do is fine with me."

Lexi went to her and cupped the young woman's face in her hands. "It might not be the most comfortable experience."

"Try not sleeping." Kacy laughed weakly at her own joke, then shook her head. "It's all right. I'll be fine."

Lexi closed her eyes and focused on the magic she could feel radiating off of Kacy. It wasn't good magic. It was chaotic and disruptive just like all dark magic, but that didn't matter to Lexi. She could handle small doses of dark magic. Her body would just need a little time to process it.

She slipped tendrils of power into Kacy, hoping she could accomplish this with what little power she had left. Already she could feel the sourness building in her stomach, a sure sign that her own resources were nearly depleted.

Then Lexi found what she was looking for. Kacy let out a soft whimper. Lexi knew there wasn't a lot of time to do this gently. She grabbed hold of the energy tormenting Kacy and drained it as quickly and efficiently as she could.

Kacy yelped. Lexi opened her eyes in time to see Kacy's eyes roll back in her head. She grabbed the woman as she passed out, cradling her with little effort. Thomas was gripping the arms of his chair, his expression tense. Lexi smiled at him. "All done."

Edgar got up. "Put her here."

Lexi laid Kacy on the couch.

Thomas stood. "You sure she's okay?"

Lexi could feel the new magic coursing through her. It was good. Even if the magic wasn't the best kind. "She's great." She put her hand on Edgar's arm to stabilize herself, but she was thrilled that her experiment had worked. "She just needs to sleep it off."

Thomas stared at his daughter. "She's ... sleeping?"

Lexi nodded. "She sure is."

Kacy's soft, even breathing seemed proof of that. She looked profoundly peaceful and happy.

Thomas put his fingers to his mouth as a tear slipped down his cheek. Then he hugged Lexi.

CHAPTER NINETEEN

Edgar was impressed. With the touch of her hands, Lexi had removed Kacy's curse. No one said a word until they were outside the house.

Thomas locked the door, then turned to face them, still plainly emotional. "What do I owe you?"

Edgar went down to the car.

Lexi shook her head as she came too. "Nothing."

Thomas came down off the porch to meet them in the driveway. "I have to give you something."

"No, you don't. Kacy already paid me with her magic."

Thomas's brow furrowed. "I don't know what that means."

"Don't worry about it, basically," Lexi said. "We're good. You know, I could take your curse, too."

"I'm just fine with mine," Thomas said. "Lets me do my job and keeps me connected to my wife. Still seems to me like we owe you, but if you're happy with how things went, then so am I. Where can I take you?"

"Back to the pub, I guess." She looked at Edgar. "Unless there's somewhere else you want to go?"

He was exhausted. The ice cream had helped a little,

but that boost of energy was fading fast. He hadn't slept much since Lexi had freed him from the tree. He felt like he might fall asleep very soon wherever he was. "Back to the apartment works for me."

With a nod, Thomas headed for the driver's side of the car. "You got it. One trip home coming up."

Edgar opened the door to the back seat for Lexi, then squeezed in after her.

Thomas drove them straight back to the pub, the hum of the wheels on the road and the motion of the car nearly knocking Edgar out. When they arrived, Thomas refused the money Lexi offered him. "You ride free from here on out. That's the least I can do."

She made a face. "Thomas..."

He shook his head. "Nope. Your money is no good with me."

Lexi reached forward and gave his shoulder a squeeze. "That's very generous of you. Thank you. You take care now."

"You too. You all gonna want a ride to the forest later?"

Lexi glanced at Edgar. He shrugged, his energy low. "We are going."

"I'll have Edgar call you if we need a ride," she said.

"Works for me. Thanks again. Anytime you need a ride, I've got you."

"Bye, Thomas." Lexi waved as he drove off.

They went upstairs. Edgar was glad to be back. He

was tired physically but also tired of wondering what people were thinking about him. If they knew who he was. If they were scared of him. Maybe someday that would go away, but it was going to take time. Meanwhile, it only added to his mental fatigue.

Lexi got herself a bottle of water from the refrigerator. She held it up. "You want one?"

"All right."

She tossed the bottle to him, then grabbed another.

He drank about half of it. He never seemed to be able to get enough water. "How are you feeling? How much magic did she have?"

Lexi's smile was half-hearted. "Not much. And the kind of magic that causes troubles in people isn't high-quality. But it's still helping. I don't feel quite so drained. How are you feeling?"

He wasn't going to pretend to be fine. "I'm tired."

"You looked like you were drifting off in the car. And who could blame you? You've barely had any rest. Take the bed and get some sleep before we head out to hunt or you might not make it. Trust me, you'll feel better."

He wanted to sleep, but he didn't feel like he could just yet. "What about Henry? I should probably call him and give him my number so he can let us know what they're going to do."

She nodded. "That's a good idea. Then you can rest undisturbed and not have to worry about it."

The idea of calling Henry made Edgar anxious.

Henry might have come to his senses and realized he wanted nothing to do with Edgar. Or his wife might have talked him out of helping. Anything was possible. He dialed anyway. Better to know than to guess.

It took three rings before Henry answered. "Hello?"

"Hello. It's Edgar. I have a phone now."

"Oh, excellent. I was hoping you'd call. I talked to Izzy, and we would love to help you tonight."

"You would?"

"Yes. Izzy is very interested to meet you."

Edgar swallowed. "Okay."

"What time are you heading to the forest?"

"Lexi says dusk." He looked at her, and she nodded that was correct.

"We'll head out then too. I guess we should divide and conquer, huh? If you two take the east side of the forest, we'll take the west. We'll call this number if we have any luck capturing a meteor. Sound good?"

It sounded as good as any other plan. "Yes. And thank you."

"You're welcome. This is exciting. I hope we're successful."

"So do I."

"See you later, then."

Edgar nodded, realizing that was ridiculous because Henry couldn't see him. "Later then."

Henry hung up, so Edgar did too. He filled Lexi in. "They're taking the west side of the forest. Starting at dusk like we are."

"Great," Lexi said. "Now you can nap for a few hours."

He glanced at the bed. It looked very inviting.

"I did get you pajamas, if you're wondering what to wear to sleep in. Probably more comfortable than what you have on now."

"Oh. Right. Pajamas." He was just going to lie down, but she was right. His clothes wouldn't be comfortable to sleep in. He got the pajamas out of the box of stuff she'd bought him and went into the bathroom to change.

When he came out, the blinds were drawn and the apartment was much darker. Lexi was stretched out on the couch, hands resting on her stomach.

He felt bad. This was her apartment, and she'd already done so much for him. "Are you sure you don't want the bed?"

"Nope. All yours."

He'd already learned there was no use in arguing with her. "Thank you."

"You're welcome."

He appreciated it. He wouldn't fit very well on the couch. And the floor definitely wasn't as comfortable. He lay on the bed. It was so soft. He sank into it slightly, making him feel like he was in a nest. And there was plenty of room for him if he angled himself from one corner to another.

He tucked a pillow under his head and thought about his life in this moment. He'd gone from a strange, trapped existence to having ice cream and making new friends. He turned just enough to see Lexi. And now he was sleeping in the bed of a beautiful woman who had kissed him more than once.

He'd inherited a lot of Henry's intelligence, but at the same time, Edgar knew very little about a great deal of things. Like love.

But the way he felt about Lexi felt like love. He had a deep desire to protect her. He wanted to be with her. Near her. All the time. Being around her made him happy. Just watching her be happy made him happy.

He wasn't so blind as to think she reciprocated those feelings. His intelligent side understood that she saw him as a project. A person in need that she could help. And help him she was, magnificently. But when he was as fixed as she could make him, she would probably move on. Wouldn't she?

He hoped she would at least stay in Shadowvale. That they would be able to remain friends. Anything less than that made him ache inside. He couldn't imagine his life without her. But was that what was coming?

Would she leave once she got the magic she needed?

That thought hurt.

"Lexi?" He said her name very softly, in case she was sleeping.

"Yes?"

"What are you going to do after you get your magic?"

"I'm going to make sure you get the magic you need, too."

Always looking out for him. "And after that?"

"I ... I don't know yet."

That meant she was leaving. She just didn't want to tell him.

The pain in his chest was his heart breaking. He rolled over and tried to go to sleep.

Chapter Twenty

Lexi listened as Edgar's breathing evened out. It was a nice sound, like waves on a distant shore. It made her happy he was finally getting some rest. She was a little tired, but nothing like him. She'd had some sleep last night after freeing him.

Getting the small influx of magic, despite the less than desirable quality of it, had given her some new energy as well. Once her body processed it, she would be fine for tonight's hunt. The anticipation would keep her keyed up and ready to go, too.

Even so, a little nap wouldn't hurt. It was going to be a long night. The meteors would arrive in the greatest numbers as the planet turned into the onslaught. That wouldn't happen until the earliest hours of the morning.

She closed her eyes and attempted to sleep, but the thrum of her body adjusting to the new, chaotic magic made settling down difficult.

She turned to her side, which had the benefit of putting Edgar in her line of sight. He was sprawled on the bed, deep in sleep. Good for him. That bed was very comfortable. It was no wonder he'd passed out so quickly. Of course, he had to be utterly exhausted, too.

Time passed as she lay there, not sleeping, watching him. After a while, she got up and padded quietly to the bed.

He looked so peaceful. Almost angelic in sleep. The creases of worry from his brow were gone, the wariness in his eyes hidden behind his lids.

He was so unsure of himself and his place in this world. She hoped she could change that. He deserved to be here as much as anyone did. Maybe more. He hadn't asked to enter the world as someone else's monster.

Time with Henry would help, she thought. It would allow Edgar to understand that who he'd been was not who he was now and no one with a brain would hold his past against him. The very idea someone might do that made her angry.

He was worthy. Even if he didn't think so yet himself. And if Henry could forgive him and move on, no one else had an excuse.

She sat on the edge of the bed, wondering if the small movement would wake him. It didn't. He slumbered on. She lay down, fitting herself into the space next to him, her back to his side. He was warm, and the sheer size of him made her feel safe.

An odd feeling that. She hadn't felt unsafe on the couch. Or anywhere. There was no real danger to her outside of losing her magic completely. But being next to him like this was pleasurable and comforting in a way she didn't often experience.

She closed her eyes and listened to his breathing and

the softer, rhythmic beating of his heart. It lulled her to sleep, and she drifted into the kind of dreams she only had when her magic was running low.

Dark, chaotic images that had no rhyme or reason. Fears brought to life in short bursts, scenes playing out like snippets of nightmares. Falling with nothing beneath her but a black abyss that threatened to consume her. Falling, falling, falling—

"Lexi. *Lexi.*"

She came awake, breathing with her mouth open, heart pounding.

Edgar leaned over her, brow furrowed with concern. "It's just a dream. You're all right."

A moment passed before she could shed the last images and regain her grip on reality. She nodded. "I'm okay."

"You're sure?"

"Yes." She exhaled. She hated feeling like that. Like she'd lost control. He lay down next to her again. She turned into him and closed her eyes. At first, he didn't move. Then he slowly put his arm around her.

"Thanks," she whispered. "I have bad dreams when my magic gets low."

"We'll fix that tonight."

"Yep." But that answer was for him. She wasn't at all confident they'd get a meteor tonight. There would be so much competition. The odds weren't great.

He drifted off again without much effort. She did her

best, but sleep didn't return. Just as well. Nothing about those nightmares was restful.

She adjusted her position and watched the little bits of light coming through the blinds. When it lengthened and dimmed, she got up and took a shower, changing into jeans and a sweater from the selection of things she'd gotten at Stella's store.

When she came out of the bathroom, he was sitting on the side of the bed, yawning.

"Feel better since you slept?"

He nodded. "Yes. But I could sleep more."

"You can sleep all you want when we get back." She went to the kitchen to put some supplies in her bag.

"I will too." He got up and took his turn in the bathroom, changing back into his clothes. When he came out, he had his phone in his hand. "Should I call Thomas?"

The forest wasn't that far, but they might spend a lot of their night walking and possibly running if they were trying to be the first ones to a downed meteor. "Yes, please. We can wait in front of the pub for him."

Edgar dialed. "Hello, Thomas. Yes, it's Edgar. Yes, we're ready. Okay." He smiled. "That's very good to hear. See you soon."

He hung up, still smiling. "Thomas said Kacy is still sleeping. He'll be here in a few minutes."

"That's great about Kacy." She hoisted the straps of the bag over her shoulder. "I've got some bottles of water, granola bars, meat sticks, chocolate bars, apples, oranges, and a bag of cookies. That should keep us from getting too hungry, don't you think?"

"It should keep everyone from getting hungry."

They went down the outside steps and walked around to the front of the building to wait, but they weren't there long before Thomas showed.

Thomas greeted them as they got into the car. "Which part of the forest would you like to go to?"

"The west side," Edgar answered.

"West side it is."

Thomas had them there quickly. When he parked, he twisted in his seat and held out his hand, fist clenched to them. "Take this with you. It's for good luck. It was my grandfather's. He brought it over with him from Nigeria. He gave it to me when I was just a little boy, but I never put much stock in it. A couple days ago, I started carrying it in my pocket."

He smiled. "Right after that, I met you, Lexi. And you helped Kacy. Now you need help. Take this." He opened his hand, palm up. In it sat a little tortoise, carved of black stone, worn around the edges with the caresses of many hands over many years.

"That belongs in your family, Thomas. Not with me."

"You get your meteor and then you can give it back."

She smiled and took the little carving. "That's very sweet of you. Thank you."

"You're welcome. Good hunting." He looked at Edgar. "You keep her safe."

Edgar nodded, as solemn as if he was promising his life. "I will."

They got out and headed into the forest. Lexi tucked the tortoise deep into her pocket, then adjusted the straps of her bag.

Edgar stuck his hand out. "I can carry that."

"No, it's okay. I've got it for now. If it gets heavy, I'll let you take it for a while."

The sky grew darker by the moment. Here and there, stars twinkled through.

Edgar walked next to her when there was enough room, behind her when there wasn't. "How long before the first stars fall?"

"I don't know. None of us do. We just need to find a good place to watch. And wait."

"I know a place."

She looked at him. "You do?"

"Yes."

"Then let's go."

He led her through the forest with enough confidence that it was clear he knew his way. How, she wasn't sure. Maybe it was a memory?

But before long, they were walking along the stream.

"This is near where you were."

"Yes."

They passed the exact spot, the dirt still churned up from where Edgar's roots had torn themselves loose from the ground. A few more yards and he pointed. "It's just ahead."

Lexi didn't see anything but trees. They kept walking, but it wasn't long before a massive tree trunk blocked their path, easily as wide as Thomas's sedan.

"Which way?"

Edgar stopped walking. "We're here." His gaze traveled up the trunk. The tree seemed to disappear into the sky.

Lexi shivered at the very idea of what he intended. She dug her fingers under the straps over her shoulder and clung to them. "Listen, I'm not afraid of much, but I don't like heights. If you're suggesting we should climb this tree …"

Edgar looked at her, tipping his head like he didn't understand. "You're afraid of heights?"

She frowned. She hated admitting such things, but this was Edgar. He wasn't about to use the information against her. "Yes. It's silly, I know, but I am."

"Don't be afraid. I will climb. And you will ride on my back."

Chapter Twenty-One

Edgar took off his flannel shirt, leaving just his T-shirt, but he wasn't cold. He'd had a long time to get used to the night air when he'd lived beside the stream. A little chill was nothing.

He held the shirt out. "We can use this to tie you to my back. You'll be secure, and you won't have a thing to worry about."

She looked unconvinced. And more than a little scared. He wasn't used to seeing that in her. "I know you're very strong, but ... I don't know about this."

"I would never let you fall." He dropped his arm, letting the shirt hang from his hand.

"I know." She glanced up the tree. And swallowed. "How far up are you going to go?"

He shrugged. "Far enough to get a good view of the sky."

"That might be kind of high up."

"It probably will be. But you'll be safe. I swear it."

She exhaled, the breath shuddering out of her. "Maybe you could just go up by yourself?"

He stepped closer to her. "Are you really that scared?"

She frowned. "I'm being an idiot. I'm sorry. Normally,

I could get past this, but without enough magic to save myself, heights are suddenly a lot more terrifying than they were before."

"I can understand that. But I really will do everything possible to keep you safe."

She nodded. "And two pairs of eyes will be a lot better at spotting a meteor than one." She exhaled and gave him a quick smile. "Okay. Let's do this. I might just keep my eyes closed until we get to the top."

"Good plan." He smiled, even as his heart went out to her. "Once you're on my back, wrap the shirt under you like a sling, then I'll tie it in front and we'll be good to go."

He turned and crouched down, making it possible for her to reach his shoulders. She hugged his neck, then got her legs around his waist. "Don't move yet. I'm going to get the shirt into position."

Soon, she handed him the sleeves. He tied them as tight as was comfortable. "How do you feel?"

"All right. Secure. I have the bag looped over my head so that it hangs on the right. If you want me to move it, I can."

"No, it's fine there. I'm going to stand now."

"Okay. I might need to readjust once you do."

He pushed up right. "How's that?"

"Hang on."

He felt her move a little, making some slight modifications to her position. He smiled, liking her arms around his neck. When she turned in a certain direction, her hair brushed his neck, and her warm breath tickled his skin.

"I think I'm good. No way to tell but for you to move a bit."

"I'll walk around the tree once, just to see how it feels for you."

"You sure I'm not too heavy?"

"I can barely tell you're there." It was the truth. She didn't seem to weigh much at all. He could feel her weight because his joints were stiff, but it wasn't enough to make a difference to him.

"I find that hard to believe, but if you're sure, then all right."

He walked around the giant trunk. "I'm ready to go if you are."

She inhaled. "I'm as ready as I can be. Tell me when we're there."

He found a good spot at the base to start climbing. "Are you really going to shut your eyes?"

"I think so. I don't want my fear to get the best of me."

"Maybe you should just focus on the sky then. On our goal."

She hugged his neck a little tighter and kissed his cheek. "Good thinking."

"Here we go." He got a toehold in the craggy bark, reached for the nearest branch, and up he went. Although he could have dashed up the tree pretty easily, he climbed slowly and carefully. Not only was it more comfortable for her, but it was easier on his joints. Too much movement aggravated their tightness.

He made sure each toehold and each hand grip was firm and sure. He enjoyed the climb even though his body protested. The breeze zipped past with a little more force as they ascended, but it still wasn't cold. To him. "Are you warm enough?"

Her head was buried against his neck. "I'm fine. Are we almost there?"

"Soon." They were just now cresting the forest canopy.

He found a good spot in the heart of the tree's branches where there was a lot of area to stand on. He walked out onto one of the thickest branches where there was a clear view of the heavens and another good-size branch behind him that she could rest against. He ignored the aches the climb had caused and looked out at the sky. "You might want to open your eyes now."

Her movements were followed by a soft gasp. "Wow. I feel like I could reach out and touch the stars."

He smiled. "They do look close, don't they?"

She relaxed her arms a bit. "So now I guess we just wait."

"Are you comfortable?"

Her arms rested lightly on his shoulders. "I feel like I could stay this way forever. How about you?"

He loved having her so close. "I am very good." He glanced down, the height not a factor for him. Every so often a glimmer of light showed through the canopy of leaves below them. "Those must be fireflies."

"Are you saying that to make me look down?"

He laughed. "No, sorry. Don't look."

"Too late." She moved her hand to brush back her hair. "I don't think those are fireflies. Too big. I think they're people with flashlights who are also on the hunt for a meteor."

"Oh." He scanned all around them. There were more spots of light than he'd originally noticed. "That's a lot."

"That's less than I expected. Although there are probably hunters out there who don't need flashlights. Supernaturals who can see perfectly well in the dark or well enough with the light provided by the phosphorescent moss."

"Like us."

"Like us."

He tipped his head back and focused on the sky. "We'll get one. Don't worry."

"I hope so," she sighed.

They stayed like that for a long while, watching the sky in anticipation of the show that was to come. Thoughts tripped through Edgar's mind, one after the other. There wasn't much else to do while they waited. Below them, more lights appeared beneath the leaves. He wondered if Lexi saw them too. She must.

Finally, he spoke. Mostly to distract her but also because he wanted her input. "I don't like my name."

"You don't like Edgar? I do. It's solid and masculine and instantly gives me trustworthy vibes."

He turned his head to see her. "It does? To me, it just reminds me of the monster."

She petted the hair on the back of his head. "Let me tell you a secret about life. There's nothing wrong with people being a little intimidated by you. In fact, it can often give you an advantage."

"I don't want people to be intimidated by me. They already are because of my size. I see them look at me. They might not react too much because the people here are more at ease with the strange and unusual, but what if I want to go beyond Shadowvale someday?"

"Are you saying you want to leave?"

"Not right now. Just maybe someday."

"So you want to change your name? To what?"

He hadn't come up with anything he liked better. None of the options he'd thought of sounded right. "I don't know."

"Edgar." She spoke his name distinctly, like she was tasting it on her tongue. "How about Eddie? That's a little lighter, more fun. Do you like Eddie?"

"I don't know. Maybe. It sounds odd applied to me." Everything but Edgar did. He just didn't like how that made him feel either.

A streak of light across the sky caught their attention. Shouts of "There!" and "Look!" drifted up from below them. The first meteor.

"Are we chasing it?" Edgar asked. He was ready to go. All she had to do was give him the word.

"It's not going to land anywhere near us."

"We could still go after it."

"No, let's just wait. Where there's one, there's more. This is a shower that will last three days. We need to be patient and pick the right ones. Ones we actually have a chance of getting to."

"We'll still be up against everyone down below."

"I know. We just have to be faster than they are."

"I can be fast." He didn't know how he knew that; he just did.

"Good. This is a situation where intimidating people will work in our favor. If you can get to a meteor before me and guard it until I arrive, then by all means, do that."

"Okay."

She petted his hair again. "I like your size. And I don't find you scary at all. In fact, I find you endlessly fascinating."

He smiled. Was she just saying that? He didn't think so. She wasn't the kind of person who said things she didn't mean.

"I like you too."

"You know, a lot of people find me intimidating."

He nodded. She intimidated him a little, but that was because he understood just how powerful she was. "I could see that. You're beautiful and smart, and there's something about you that speaks of your fearlessness."

"Except when it comes to heights."

"No one's perfect." Although she had to be as close as anyone could be.

"Thanks, *Eddie*."

He grinned. "Maybe I could get used to that."

Another meteor streaked across the sky. It looked like it was coming right for them.

"This one," Lexi hissed. *"Go!"*

CHAPTER TWENTY-TWO

Lexi held on for dear life, eyes closed, as Edgar descended. He did so by dropping from one branch to another. After she realized that was how they were going down, she shut her eyes and held her breath. There wasn't much chance she'd die from a fall, but she didn't want to recover from the injuries such an accident would cause.

She might be immortal, but that didn't mean she couldn't feel pain or bruise or break bones.

She knew when they'd landed because he didn't sway after the last drop. The branches had give. The ground did not. She opened her eyes.

"Which way?" he asked.

She could feel his pulse beneath his skin, beating away in a rapid staccato. "I should get down."

"No. Stay. This is faster."

Not something she wanted to argue about since he probably was. She remained on his back and pointed toward the direction the meteor had been taking. "That way."

He took off, maneuvering through the trees with a surprising amount of grace and agility. She doubted a man half his size could move that well. How much quicker would he be when she could give him enough magic to complete his transformation?

Even the sound of them crashing through the forest didn't hide the soft clicks and creaks of his stubborn disformed joints. He had to be hurting, and yet he kept going with machine-like endurance.

Ahead of them, a brilliant light burst through the trees, like a flash of lightning but longer and more focused.

"It's landed." Her own heart was racing now, caught up in the adrenaline of the moment. "Hurry."

Somehow, he picked up speed. Thin branches whipped at his arms and legs as they sped through the underbrush. Thorns caught on their clothing. A soft glow appeared through the trees ahead. It intensified as they grew closer.

Magic crackled in the air, so close Lexi could feel it on her skin and taste the honeyed sweetness of it on her tongue. She wriggled free of the shirt tying her to Edgar, pushed up on his shoulders to get loose of it and jumped to the ground.

Together they ran into the clearing and found a woman kneeling beside the meteor, her hands on the glowing orb, eyes closed, the light bathing her as she claimed the magic inside as her own, no doubt making her wish while they watched.

In complete and utter disappointment, Lexi fell to her knees and let out a single sob of frustration. She'd known this would happen. Known how stiff the competition would be. But she'd let herself foolishly believe they were going to get this one.

Edgar stood beside her, looking as dejected as she felt. "I ran as fast as I could."

"I know," Lexi whispered. "It's not your fault. It's no one's fault."

The woman opened her eyes. Her mouth curved in the most serene, grateful smile. "It's gone. My curse. I can feel that it's gone. The meteor granted my wish. The magic is incredible."

"That's great," Lexi said, even though she was sick to her stomach. Happy for the woman but so deeply disappointed she could have just lain down and given up. She wasn't going to—she had to keep hunting—but she had no drive left in her at the moment.

"It's all right," Edgar said quietly. He held his hand out to her. "The next one will be ours."

She kneeled on the forest floor a moment longer, then took his hand and let him help her up. She had to go on. She nodded, not feeling anything but failure. "Right. The next one."

He put his arm around her and kissed the top of her head.

The woman who'd gotten the wish stood. "I'm sorry. I guess you wanted that one too. There will be more. You'll get one. I know it."

Lexi nodded and tried to smile. "You're right. There will be. And one will be ours."

With a quick smile, the woman walked away, headed back to the road probably. Lexi waited until she was gone, then went to the cold, dark remains of the meteor, crouched down, and put her hands on it.

"Anything?" Edgar asked.

She shook her head. "Just the faintest hum of magic. Not even magic, just the echo of it really. The signature of what was here." Even so, she was captivated by it, by the strength of it. This much cosmic power would have done wonders for her.

"I know you're disappointed. I am too. But I know we'll get one. I know it."

She stood and brushed off the knees of her jeans. "We need two. One is not going to be enough. Not for both of us."

"I don't need more magic. I'm fine."

"No, you're not. When you were running, I could hear the popping and clicking of your joints. That speed cost you, didn't it?"

He frowned and looked away. It was plain he didn't want to answer.

She persisted. "How much pain are you in?"

"I'm fine."

He wasn't, and she knew it. He'd suffered for her. She put her arms around him. A second later, he embraced her too. "I will make you whole, Eddie. I promise. I will make us both whole."

She wasn't sure how, but she wasn't going to stop trying.

A chirping sound came from his pocket. He let go of her and dug into it, pulling out his phone. He answered. "Henry?"

She dug into her bag for a bottle of water, took the top off, and handed it to him.

He took it and gulped some down before speaking again. "No, we didn't get to it in time. I know. It was close. Next one. You too."

He hung up, then drank the rest of the water.

She didn't need an explanation to understand what the call had been about. She took a bottle of water out for herself and drank some, then grabbed a bar of chocolate. The sugar would soothe her a bit and give her a much-needed rush of energy. She unwrapped it and took a bite. "I guess we need to decide if we're going to stay here or try a different spot."

"Do you think it's less likely another meteor will fall here since one already has?"

"There's no rhyme or reason with these things. For all I know, another one could land right next to this one."

"Then I say we stay here."

She held out the chocolate bar. "Want some?"

"Not yet. What else have you got?"

"Apples, oranges, granola bars—"

"Apple, please."

She dug in, grabbed one, and tossed it to him.

He caught it one-handed. "Thanks."

"You want to sit and take a rest?" He had to be hurting. And there was no point in them going anywhere until they spotted another meteor.

"Okay." He looked around, then pointed. "There."

A fallen tree stretched across the ground a few yards away. They both took seats on it, although it groaned when Edgar settled his full weight on it.

All around them in the distance, lights flashed. More hunters. She sighed and took another bite of chocolate. Next to her, Edgar crunched through his apple in a few big bites. Then the sky lit up overhead.

She jumped up. "It's going to be close."

Edgar stared determinedly at the blaze of light streaking through the dark. "Close is all we need."

CHAPTER TWENTY-THREE

Three more *close* meteors and three more misses. Edgar was sorely disappointed, but he knew that probably couldn't touch what Lexi was feeling. She hadn't said a word since they'd lost the last one, and now dawn was arriving. She walked beside him back to town, head down, clearly lost in her own thoughts.

His phone chimed. He looked at it. Not a call. A message. From Henry. *Headed home. Maybe better luck tomorrow night? Talk soon.*

Edgar put the phone away. Henry and Izzy had stayed out all night to help, and even that hadn't made a difference.

He didn't know what to say to make it better, but that didn't matter because words couldn't fix this. Only magic could. And they hadn't gotten any.

He stayed quiet and let Lexi be. After all, she hadn't even wanted him to call Thomas for a ride. She'd just shaken her head and started walking.

He'd been no help tonight. No matter how fast he'd run, no matter how much he'd pushed himself, they hadn't been the first to arrive at any of the landfalls. At the second one, they'd been fourth to arrive. The forest had been filled with people out hunting for their chance at a wish.

So many had gotten them, too. But not Lexi. No matter how hard he'd tried.

All that speed had left him achy and tired. He couldn't imagine how Lexi felt, though. She had to be heartsick. She actually seemed a little broken. He hated even having that thought, but there was no other word to describe her appearance.

The competition was tough. And while he felt for those people, his heart and loyalty belonged to Lexi. She *needed* the magic. He supposed the others did too, but Lexi's situation seemed ... dire.

She was moving slower now, and he had to wonder if it was because she was growing weaker. That brought him sorrow. And made him worry. Could he lose her if her magic stores ran out completely?

He touched her arm very gently so he didn't startle her. "Lexi? Are you okay?"

She sighed before answering, her gaze still on the path ahead. "I don't know how to answer that."

"You can tell me the truth. I can take it."

She glanced up at him. "No. I'm not okay at all."

Light reflected off her cheeks. They were shiny. Wet. She'd been crying.

In one swift motion, he bent and scooped her into his arms, cradling her against his chest. "We need to sleep. Tomorrow night will be different. Better."

It had to be.

She pressed her face into his neck and wept. He walked as fast as he could without jostling her. By the time the pub came into view, she was asleep in his arms. He walked down the alley and carefully up the steps. At the landing, he held her with one arm so he could find the key in her bag.

It was tiny in his fingers, and it took concentration to get it into the lock, but he finally got the door open. He set her bag aside, laid her on the bed, then went around and closed the blinds so the morning light wouldn't disturb her.

He took off her shoes and covered her with a blanket, then he sat on the couch. He wished there was something he could do.

Would Henry have any ideas? He was a doctor. He'd spent his whole life dedicated to helping people. Edgar took out his phone and looked at the message Henry had sent. There was no way he could send one back. His fingers were too big to manage it.

He didn't know where Henry lived either. But he could call. He stepped outside and went halfway down the steps before he called.

Henry answered. "Edgar?"

"Yes, it's me. Thank you for your help tonight."

"You're welcome. Sorry we didn't have a better outcome. How's Lexi?"

"Not good. She needs magic. Do you know how I might get her some? Other than the meteors, I mean?"

"I'm not sure. There's a lot of magic in town, but I

don't know how she'd access any of it without there being a problem. My understanding is that the town relies on that magic. Maybe she could talk to Amelia Marchand. She's the woman who founded Shadowvale. Very powerful. If anyone would know where there's magic to be had, she would."

"How would I find her?"

"I can text you her address and phone number."

"Thank you. You are very kind."

There was a smile in Henry's voice when he answered. "You're welcome. I never thought in a million years we could have this sort of conversation. Well, any conversation, really. Happy to help. Keep me posted, all right?"

"I will. I hope you get some sleep."

"You, too, my friend." He hung up.

Friend. Henry had called him friend. For a moment, Edgar could do nothing but contemplate the astonishment of that. Then his phone chimed again with the promised message from Henry. Amelia Marchand's address and phone number.

The idea of calling her left Edgar numb with anxiety. If she'd founded this town, there was no way she didn't know who he was. She wouldn't want to see him. Maybe it would be better if he just showed up and pleaded his case.

There was someone else he could talk to. Someone who gave good advice. He called the only other number programmed into his phone, knowing at least he wouldn't be waking Thomas up.

"Morning, son," Thomas answered. "I bet you just got back from your hunt and you're calling to tell me the good news."

"We did just get back, but I have no good news."

"No joy in the forest, huh? How's Lexi doing?"

"She's sleeping now. She was very upset."

"I bet she was. Something I can do to help?"

"I don't know. Maybe. But that's why I called. To ask your opinion."

"Tell you what. I was just going to get some breakfast. Why don't I swing by and pick you up, then we can talk over pancakes. You like pancakes?"

"Are you asking me to have breakfast with you?"

"I am."

"I don't have any money." He wasn't about to take any of Lexi's either.

"My treat. What do you say? Pancakes on me. Or whatever else you want to eat."

Edgar smiled. "That is very kind of you. I don't know if I like pancakes, but I'm willing to find out."

Thomas laughed. "Everybody likes pancakes. See you in a few minutes outside the pub."

"Okay. Thank you." Edgar hung up and went back inside. He found a pen and paper and left a note on the kitchen counter. *Gone to breakfast with Thomas. Back as soon as I can.*

He made sure he had the key, then turned the lock so it would secure the door after he went out.

Thomas was arriving as Edgar came around the corner. He reached over and opened the passenger door next to him. "Sit up front with me."

"All right." Edgar got in. It was a little roomier than the back seat.

Thomas drove them to a place called the Sunshine Diner. "I love this place. I love it so much, I borrowed the name for my cab service." He parked and shut off the car, then looked at Edgar. "You don't have a problem with sun, do you? UV light, I mean."

Edgar shook his head. "Not that I know of."

"Good, because you're going to get some in here. They did that on purpose to give a boost to anyone who needed it seeing as how we don't get sun here in Shadowvale."

"Interesting. I guess no vampires eat here."

"You guessed right."

They got out and went in. There were sunflowers all over. The place smelled great, and Edgar's stomach growled loudly.

Thomas waved at one of the waitresses. "Morning, Lola. We gotta get this boy fed."

She waved back. "Grab yourself a booth. I'll be over with coffee and menus."

Edgar followed Thomas to a booth, and they each took a side.

Lola came as promised with two mugs in one hand, a pot of coffee in the other, and menus tucked under her arm. She set the mugs down, then handed them each a menu while she filled the mugs with coffee. "I'll be right back with creamer. Specials this morning are the Hungry Man plate, which is three eggs any way, two sausage links, two slices of bacon, home fries or grits, side of pancakes or French toast, and toast or a biscuit. We also have apple pie pancakes today."

She left them, and Edgar looked at Thomas. "That special sounded good."

He nodded. "It did. I'm going to get my usual. Stack of peach pancakes with a side of bacon. You get whatever you want."

"Peach pancakes?"

"I grew up in Georgia." He smiled. "Gotta have my peaches."

"How's Kacy?"

His smile widened. "She's a new woman since Lexi took her curse. Slept like a cat last night. Bright and happy all day, too. She's about as good as a person can be, and I am so grateful."

"Slept like a cat?" Edgar had thought the expression was "slept like a baby."

"You ever see a cat sleep? Tell me a creature that does it better."

He had a point.

Lola returned and put a small silver pitcher of creamer on the table. "You boys know what you want? Thomas, the usual or something new today?"

"The usual." He handed back his menu.

"I'd like the Hungry Man plate," Edgar said. "With home fries and pancakes. Could I have the kind with peaches like Thomas?"

She took his menu. "You sure can. I'll get that straight into the kitchen." She left them again.

Thomas tipped a little cream into his coffee and added two packs of sugar, then gave it a stir. "Tell me what's on your mind."

Edgar copied Thomas and made his coffee the same way. Lexi was on his mind, but first he had a question for Thomas. "Why aren't you afraid of me?"

"Is there a reason I should be?"

Edgar quickly shook his head. "No, not at all. But I know what I look like."

"Lola didn't seem scared of you."

"She might have been if I'd come in alone."

Thomas sipped his coffee. "Just because a person looks different doesn't mean they're something to be scared of. People in Shadowvale probably know that better than most. As for me, I like to judge people on their deeds and their actions. You know that saying, actions speak louder than words? That's true. And I've seen nothing to give me a bad opinion of you."

"Thank you."

"That's not really why you called me, though, is it? You want help with something. With Lexi. Right?"

Edgar drank some of his coffee. It didn't taste as good as it smelled, but it wasn't bad. "I want to talk to Amelia

Marchand. Lexi needs magic, and Henry told me Amelia would know where Lexi could get some."

Thomas picked up his mug. "Lexi's already been to see Amelia."

"She has?" He had no idea when that had happened, but it had to have been before Lexi freed him.

"Yep. But if Lexi needs more magic, I have an idea. If you're interested."

Edgar leaned forward. "Very much. What is it?"

"Well ..." Thomas pursed his lips. "Better see if it's something that can even happen before I say too much more. You leave it to me, and I'll let you know what I find out."

That wasn't what Edgar had been hoping to hear, but it was something. And he trusted Thomas. Now all he could do was wait.

CHAPTER TWENTY-FOUR

Lexi woke up feeling better physically. Mentally and emotionally, she was still drained, but that wasn't something sleep could help with. Magic would. She just had to hope tonight went differently. There was a way to increase her odds, but that would mean using a good portion of the small amount of magic she had left, and she wasn't sure it was worth it.

Maybe it was, but she still had tonight and tomorrow night to get those meteors she so desperately needed. Using her magic tonight might be premature.

She sighed and blinked a few times, clearing the last of the sleep from her eyes. Still lying down, she turned her head to see where Edgar was. She found him asleep on the couch, his large form contorted to fit. One arm hung off the side, and his knees were bent at such an angle that she knew the position had to be aggravating his already tortured joints.

She frowned. If she'd had a full supply of magic, she could have very easily made another bed for him. Or a bigger couch. Actually, if she'd had a full supply of magic, she could have just made him whole, then his joints wouldn't be a problem.

She sat up. She was still in her clothes. She wasn't sure how that had happened, but her mind wasn't cooperating. She took a moment as she realized she'd been wrong about feeling better physically. She didn't. Not entirely. She felt weak, and that made her feel vulnerable. It wasn't something she was used to at all, and she didn't like it.

That vulnerability made her feel mortal.

Feeling like that wasn't a good sign, but it certainly seemed to fit with how last night had gone.

She got up, grabbed a change of clothes, and went into the bathroom for a long, hot shower, which helped a little. Nothing would make her right except for magic, no matter how good it felt.

When she came back out, Edgar was awake, sitting on the couch, rubbing his face. Even in his current state, he was incredibly handsome. Rough and rugged and yes, a little intimidating. But she found that intriguing. She found all of him intriguing. No human had ever held her interest for so long, although Edgar definitely wasn't human. She wasn't sure how to classify him. Maybe that was part of what made him so captivating. She couldn't imagine growing tired of him, either. "Morning. Or afternoon. Or whatever time it is."

The very fact that she was now concerned with time meant she was declining.

He looked at his phone. "It's afternoon. So good afternoon. How did you sleep?"

She'd had a few nightmares but nothing as bad as the

night before. She didn't want to worry him, so she just shrugged and smiled. "Fine. You didn't look very comfortable on the couch. You should have just shared the bed with me."

He shook his head. "Not my place. Besides, you needed to sleep, and I wasn't about to do something that might wake you."

She could have crawled right back into bed, but again, more sleep wouldn't help.

He got up and stretched carefully, the grimace on his face confirming that his joints were no better. "We have about three hours until dusk. Is there anything you want to do before we head out again?"

"We should eat. I'm starving."

He nodded. "I could eat again."

"Again? Did you already have something?" The kitchen showed no signs of food preparation.

"I had breakfast with Thomas right after we got back."

Her eyes narrowed. The last thing she remembered was Edgar picking her up. "I don't actually remember getting back. You must have brought me."

"I did."

Which meant he'd also put her into bed and taken her shoes off. He was so kind. "Where did you eat?"

"At a diner in town. It was good. Thomas is a nice man. He paid for me. Kacy is doing very well."

"That was nice of him. And I'm glad to hear that about his daughter." She went into the kitchen and got some water, drinking deeply before speaking again. "I wish I knew where all the meteors came down last night. If we could map that out, we might be able to better guess where they'll land tonight. Maybe. It's so hard to know."

"We could walk the forest and look for the landing sites, but that's a lot of area to cover."

"Right. That's too much to do." She thought harder. "Any chance you picked up a paper when you were out?"

"No, but I could go out and get one."

"It's all right. They'll have one at the pub. Let's go down there and eat, and I'll see if I can borrow one. I'm hoping there will be an article about the shower last night. That might give us some clues."

"And everyone else who's hunting one."

She nodded. "I know." She stared at the kitchen counter. "I don't know why I thought this was going to be easy. Well, not easy. But easier than this."

"Are we doing something wrong?"

"No. Things just haven't gone our way yet." She did her best to smile. "Maybe tonight's our night, though, huh?"

"Yes." His smile looked a lot more genuine. "Tonight. Henry and Izzy will help us again."

"That's a lot for them to commit to. That means staying up all night. Again."

He shrugged. "They wouldn't do it if they didn't want to."

"True." She hesitated. "If we can make an educated

guess about where a meteor might strike tonight, I could set up a beacon of sorts to draw it in."

He nodded. "That sounds like a smart thing to do."

She drank a little more water. "Except it will require me to expend some magic. And I'm not sure I have it to spare."

He came over to her, eyes full of concern. "Is that why you've gotten weak?"

An alarm tripped inside her. "You can tell that?" If he could tell, others could too. She might be more vulnerable than she realized.

"I'm not sure you would have made it home last night if I hadn't carried you. I didn't mind. At all. But I hate that you're going through this." He looked away. "I hate even more that it's all my fault."

"It's not your fault."

"It is," he growled. "You used too much of your magic to free me. You should have left me there. I've been no help to you. In fact, I've been a hindrance to—"

She grabbed him, pulled him down to her, and kissed him. Then she leaned her forehead against his chest. "Don't. You're not a hindrance. I don't regret using my magic on you at all." She looked up at him. "Do you understand? I don't regret it one bit."

There was an argument brewing in his head. She could see the clouds forming in his gaze. "Lexi, I—"

She put a finger to his lips. "I mean it, Eddie. You are the best, most interesting thing that's happened to me in a very long while. Now go get ready so we can eat."

He sighed like he knew there was no point in arguing with her, which was good. It meant he was figuring her out. A tiny hint of a smile curved his mouth. "I like when you call me Eddie."

She smiled back, genuinely happy that worked for him. "Then I'll do it more often."

"Will you help me with what to wear?"

"I would be happy to." Never in a million years would she have imagined that such a small distraction could be so welcome.

By the time he was showered and dressed in the jeans, T-shirt, flannel shirt, and work boots she'd picked out for him, and they'd found a table at the pub, the light behind the perpetual cloud cover had begun to sink toward the horizon. Dusk wasn't far off, and they'd soon have to head for the forest if they had any hope of a meteor this evening.

They each ordered the dinner special, which was cottage pie, a large crockery dish filled with ground beef and vegetables in a savory brown gravy, covered with a thick layer of whipped potatoes. Edgar asked for his with the optional cheese on top.

While he stayed at the table, she went to find a newspaper. Trip had one behind the bar, as usual. "Bring it back when you're done. There's a few things in there I haven't had a chance to look at yet."

"I will. Thanks." She unfolded it as she walked back to the table and took her seat. She laid the paper out flat so Edgar could see it, too, and glanced up at him. "I guess it's the biggest news in town, hmm?"

The headline on the front page read *Thirteen Wishes Granted!* Underneath that was a long article about the meteors.

Thirteen. And they'd been close to four of them.

"We'll get one tonight," Edgar said. "I just know it."

He was trying to make her feel better, and she appreciated that, but their odds were no better this evening than they had been last night. Unless she used another portion of her magic.

Did she dare? She wasn't sure. But if she didn't, and they came up empty-handed once again, she'd regret it. Getting a meteor would change everything. So would losing more of her magic without replacing it.

Of course, they did have one more night.

She started to read the article, trying to figure out what to do.

But by the time their food arrived, she still hadn't made up her mind about what to do, and the article hadn't helped. She set the paper aside and picked up her fork. Maybe taking care of her hunger would allow her brain to come up with a new idea.

Anything was worth a shot.

CHAPTER TWENTY-FIVE

Edgar hadn't said anything about Thomas's potential idea because Thomas hadn't given him the details and wasn't sure it would work anyway. There was no reason to get Lexi's hopes up about something that might not come to fruition.

He wanted to, of course. He would have done anything to give her a ray of hope. But Thomas's idea, whatever it was, wasn't Edgar's to share.

His profound sadness at being unable to help her was compounded by his lack of knowing what to say. Small talk wasn't something he excelled at. "Anything interesting in the article?"

"Not really." She poked at her food, eating without any real enthusiasm.

"Did any of the people who got a meteor do anything special?"

"Nope. Just lots of right place at the right time sort of thing."

He ate another big forkful of his cottage pie. It was delicious, but his mood was taking the edge off the flavor. Lexi had gotten quiet and a little morose, too, which he understood. "How much magic would you have to use to set this beacon?"

She finally looked up at him. "That's the thing. In theory, I should use as much as I can to make the beacon strong and steady. Irresistible. But I don't have much magic to spare. So maybe even trying to create one is a waste of time. I might not be able to put enough power into it to make the thing even worthwhile. And if that's the case, why waste the magic?"

He nodded.

She went on, clearly spilling out everything that had been going through her head. "But then if I don't do it and we still don't get a meteor, I'll be forever wondering what would have happened if I had."

She groaned and put her fork down. "I don't know what to do."

"It's the proverbial rock and a hard place."

She nodded. "Yes, it is. And it's a wretched spot to be in."

He ate a little more and tried to think. She needed magic. Where could she get some? Minutes ticked by in silence before anything came to him, and when it did, he knew before speaking it out loud that she wouldn't go for it. "I have an idea."

There was a spark in her eyes. "You do?"

He nodded. "Take back the magic you gave me and use it. Once we get a meteor—"

"No." She shook her head adamantly. "Eddie, you can't ask me to do that. It's very generous of you and completely within character for you to even offer, but I can't. I need you by my side. I can't do this without you. I wouldn't have said that a couple days ago, but ... you've become really important to me."

"You've become really important to me, which is why I offered in the first place. You need magic, Lexi. You don't even have enough to set up this beacon that could help you, and that's because of me. If it means I go back to being a tree—"

The couple at the table across from them glanced over. He lowered his voice. "I'm okay with that because I know it'll only be temporary until you get what you need."

She grabbed his hand. "Thank you. No one has ever cared about me like this. But I meant it when I said I *need* you with me. I can't do what you're asking."

He sighed. "The offer stands if you change your mind."

"I won't." She gave him a quick, grateful smile. "But thank you." She looked past him at the windows. "Light's going down. We should get moving so we can get out there and find a spot. Let's finish up and call Thomas."

"Okay." He was all for that. Maybe by now Thomas would have come to some conclusion about his idea.

Edgar finished his food while she paid the bill, then he dialed Thomas. She ran back upstairs for her bag of supplies, promising to meet him out front.

"I figured you'd be calling about now. Ready to hunt some more?"

"We are," Edgar answered. He stood on Main Street. "We're by the pub."

"Be there real soon."

"Thanks."

Lexi returned, her bag over her shoulder. "Thomas on his way?"

"He is."

She took Edgar's hand. "Thanks again for what you said in there. Means a lot to me. But tonight will be different. We'll get one tonight. I feel it."

He hoped more than anything that was exactly what happened.

Thomas arrived then, and they climbed in the back. "Evening, my friends. Off to the forest, yes?"

"Yes," Lexi answered.

"Sorry my lucky tortoise didn't help you folks out."

Lexi stuck her hand into the pocket of her jeans and pulled it out. "Do you want it back?"

"Not yet," Thomas said. "Tortoises move slow. Might need a little more time to work. You hang on to it a while longer."

"Thanks, Thomas." She put it back in her pocket.

Edgar's phone rang. The name on the screen made him answer quickly. "Hello, Henry."

"We're on our way out. Same spot as last night, unless you tell us differently."

"I'll ask Lexi." He put the phone by his shoulder. "Henry wants to know if them being in the same spot as last night is all right with you."

"I think so. We have as much chance in our same spot as we do anywhere else."

Edgar went back to the call. "Same spot is fine."

"All right, good. Hopefully I'll be calling you again soon with great news."

Edgar smiled. "That would be wonderful. Thank you for doing this again."

"You're welcome. And listen, Izzy and I would like to have you and Lexi over to the house for a meal when this is all over. Talk to her about it."

"I will."

"Later then." Henry hung up.

Edgar was about to mention the invite when Thomas spoke up.

"Listen, I don't mean to eavesdrop, but I think you might have better luck catching yourself a falling star in a different spot."

Lexi inched forward. "You do? Where?"

"Well, seems to me that like attracts like."

Lexi nodded. "Yes, absolutely."

"Then you ought to be where the meridian lines are the strongest. Most people won't venture into that part of the forest, but if you're willing to take the risk, you could try the Dark Acres."

She sat back, mouth open. "Of course. You're absolutely right. I don't know why I didn't think of that. You're a genius, Thomas."

He grinned and tapped the brim of his fedora. "This hat has made me smarter, I think."

"What's the Dark Acres?" Edgar asked.

Thomas's expression went serious. "It's a little more dangerous part of the Enchanted Forest. There are things there better left alone, which is why, if you're willing to go there, you might have a better shot at one of these things. Lot of people won't risk it. You might even find the remnants of meteors that fell last night and were never found."

Lexi looked at him with obvious excitement in her eyes. "What do you think? I've already been there once. I know what he's talking about. We'll need to be more aware of our surroundings, but you're probably the one who needs to decide this. Nothing out there can really harm me. I don't know if that holds true for you."

It didn't matter to him if he could be hurt or not. What was a little pain? His joints already ached. If going to the Dark Acres meant getting Lexi her meteor and maybe getting a second one for himself, he was in. "I'll be fine. We should definitely go there."

Thomas looked at them through the rearview mirror. "There are things that sting and bite. Plants that can raise a fiery rash just from brushing past them. It's no joke out there."

Edgar rapped his knuckles against his bicep, making a *thunk thunk thunk* like wood on wood. "I don't think much can get past the skin covering me now. I want to go."

Thomas drove through the entrance to the Enchanted Forest. "All right. Just a few more minutes then."

What little light remained was quickly fading, but it disappeared altogether as the green, leafy canopy overhead blocked out the rest of it.

Before long, the forest around them changed from thick and lush to dark and foreboding. Edgar stared out the window. "It looks haunted."

"Might be," Thomas said as he pulled onto the shoulder and idled the car. "Don't spend a lot of time out here myself. You two be careful now, you hear? And you call me if you want a ride out. I don't care what time it is. I'm up anyway."

Lexi leaned forward and kissed his cheek. "Thank you."

Edgar nodded. "Yes, thank you. You're a good friend, Thomas."

Thomas smiled. "Take care of her, son."

"I will." Edgar opened the door and got out, then waited for Lexi to slide out after him. He closed the car door and tapped the roof.

Thomas drove up the street and turned around, waving as he came back by them. His taillights faded quickly, leaving them all alone in the dim gray glow of dusk. In the distance, things rustled the underbrush, and the soft light of a different kind of phosphorescent moss could been seen dotting the stark interior of the woods.

Lexi took a deep breath and looked up at Edgar. "Ready?"

"Yes." He would have gone anywhere with her. "Let's go find a meteor."

CHAPTER TWENTY-SIX

Lexi and Edgar walked slowly through the forest, no real direction, no real plan until a meteor presented itself. A few lightning bugs zipped past at safe distances, but none came toward them. For that, she was grateful. Just because Eddie had thick skin didn't mean he wasn't vulnerable to those things.

She wrinkled her nose. There was an acrid odor to this part of the forest that Lexi wasn't fond of. She much preferred the green, loamy scent of the proper part of the Enchanted Forest. It was a good smell. Like the essence of life and creation.

The Dark Acres smelled of death.

But that was a small thing to endure for a better chance at getting a meteor. She had a gut feeling Thomas's intuition about this place was spot-on. The average Shadowvale citizen wouldn't come here. It was too dangerous. Even for such a great reward. And that was definitely to their advantage.

"There's something eerie about this place," Edgar said. "I'm glad I didn't end up as a tree out here. But I guess Henry wouldn't have planted me in a place like this. He's not that kind of guy."

"He doesn't seem to be." She stared up at the night sky. The stars were out and easily visible since this area didn't have the same kind of thick leaf coverage. That might be another advantage.

"That reminds me about my phone call with him. He and his wife, Izzy, want us to come to dinner when this is all over. He wanted me to ask you. What do you think?"

She looked at Edgar. "They want to have us for dinner?"

He nodded, his gaze turning skyward now. "Yes. Will you go with me?"

She thought about it. A dinner party was the most oddly normal thing she would ever do. A very human, domesticated kind of evening and not something she did often. Or ever. Might be interesting. "Do you want to go?"

"Yes." He glanced at her. "Do you not?"

"I'll do whatever you want. At the very least, it will be an interesting way to pass an evening."

"I'm sure it will be." He hesitated. "Don't you like Henry?"

"I do like him. The fact that he's willing to help you speaks highly of his character. And even if he's why you ended up in the forest, I understand. He had his reasons. I will gladly go to dinner. Aren't you curious about his wife? I am."

"So am I. Henry said she remembers me. And she's still helping him, which is helping us, so she must be a nice person, too."

"She must be." Or Henry was making her help,

although that wasn't the impression Lexi had gotten from Henry. He hadn't come across as dominating or controlling.

A streak of light brightened the sky, but it was headed in the wrong direction.

"Was that the first one?" Edgar asked.

"First one I've seen." Anticipation built in her belly. "There will be more."

"Are you sure you don't want to set that beacon?"

"I'm sure. That will be our last resort for tomorrow night."

"Okay."

Somewhere in the distance, a horse whinnied. The scent of woodsmoke drifted past. She looked through the trees around them as they walked. "There must be homes out here. Smells like someone has a fire going in their fireplace. Although the whole place has that kind of smell, really."

"I think there are some homes out here. Mostly people who want to be left alone."

She glanced at him. "Would you live out here?"

He shook his head. "I would rather be around people. If I knew they were okay with that. I wouldn't want to be somewhere I wasn't wanted. But I like being in town. I like the activity of it."

He must have been so lonely by that stream with only animals and other growing things for company.

A little tingle rippled over her skin. They had to be

close to one of the major meridian lines. She put her hand out to stop him. "Here. We're close to a good spot. Let me walk this area and see if I pick up any stronger vibrations."

"Okay. I can hold the bag."

She handed it off to him, then walked in a big, slow circle as she paid close attention to the magic prickling her skin. It got stronger as she went, but then she was blocked by a large thorny section of underbrush that made the way between several trees impossible. It was so big she couldn't see over it.

She went around, but the magic faded after a few steps. She turned around and followed the signal again, which brought her back to the thorny brush. Either the plant had grown over a meridian line and had syphoned some of that magic into itself or there was a source of magic inside it. Either way, she couldn't investigate further without some help. She leaned to look around the brush. "Eddie? I need you."

"Coming."

He joined her, looking very happy to be called. "What can I do?"

"Lift me up. I want to see the top of this thorn bush."

"Okay." He went behind her and picked her up around the waist, lifting her several feet. "Good enough?"

She stared down into a hole that had been burned through the center of the brush. "That is very good. Can you lift me a little higher?"

"Sure."

She went into the air a few more inches. She grabbed one of the nearby branches and used it as a counterbalance to lean forward and look into the hole. It was dark and hard to see much of anything, even with her eyesight, but she could just make out a shape. A round, faintly glowing shape. She smiled. "I'm done."

He brought her back down to earth. "What did you see?"

She was still smiling. "I'm pretty sure there's a meteor hidden inside those thorns. Had to have landed last night and like Thomas said, there was no one out here chasing them, so that's where it stayed."

His eyes lit up. "That's excellent. And you can still get the magic out of it?"

Her smile disappeared with a shake of her head. "There's probably very little, if any, magic left in it. The magic has to be collected or used right away or it just drifts into the atmosphere and returns to the universe."

"But there might be some?"

"It's possible."

He looked at the brush. "Stand back."

"Eddie, it's all thorns."

"Doesn't matter. I doubt they'll penetrate my skin."

She got out of his way.

He crouched down and thrust his hands into the brush. Thorns scraped his rough skin, catching and cutting white grooves into it. He grabbed hold of the two thickest parts and pulled the whole thing out of the ground, roots and all.

He tossed it away, then brushed his hands off, looking proud of himself.

She grinned. She was proud of him too. "That was pretty impressive. Thank you." She pointed at what had been revealed. "Look."

In the center of where the brush had been was a craggy, black rock with the palest blue glow. Slightly round and half-buried in a crater, the meteor glinted with a glassy, metallic shine where the moonlight touched it.

"You were right," he said. "Do you want me to get it for you?"

"No. If there's any magic left, the next disturbance will release it."

He took a step back. "Then you should be the next one to touch it."

"Yes." She kneeled down in the agitated soil. She carefully placed her hands on the meteor and used the tiniest bit of power possible to absorb whatever cosmic energy was left in it. It came to her in a trickle and ended almost as soon as it began. Her shoulders slumped, and she sighed, leaning back on her heels. "Almost nothing."

"But there was a little."

For his sake, she nodded as she stood and brushed herself off. The magic left was maybe enough to turn a couple of dollar bills into hundreds, that was it. But it was something. Barely a drop in the ocean of her need, but he'd made it possible, so she didn't want him to be disappointed.

A streak of light ignited the sky over their heads.

She gasped at the suddenness of it. "Eddie, we've got a live one."

CHAPTER TWENTY-SEVEN

Edgar led the chase after the meteor so that he could clear any brush that might be in their path. Lexi trailed after him. She didn't move as fast as he did, but that was okay. All that mattered was that he get to the meteor before anyone else. Then he could protect it until she arrived.

That was his solitary goal. He tore through the forest, indifferent to the branches that whipped at his clothes or the thorns that scratched his skin. He brushed against something that left a welt of fire on his cheek, but nothing was going to stop him.

He caught glimpses of other things moving through the forest, but they were all headed away from him and Lexi, so that didn't raise any alarms.

He leaped a fallen tree and stormed through a curtain of glowing red vines, coming out into a small clearing. At the center was a glowing orb.

His heart pounded like it was trying to break free of his chest. They'd done it. He could hear Lexi catching up with him. He stood as close to the meteor as he dared. Close enough to make it clear he'd taken possession of it but not so close that he might accidentally touch it.

Something buzzed past his ear. He swatted it away, his full attention on the orb. It was beautiful. The meteor pulsed with heat and light, its surface crackling with magical energy. This was no ordinary meteor. That much was plain.

The buzzing thing was back. Sharp pain bit the side of his neck. He slapped at it, then looked at his hand. Some kind of glowing bug, but its red light was fading as the insect's life went with it.

He wiped his hand on his jeans. Another one, red and gleaming, darted past the corner of his eye.

Lexi came through the trees, her gaze fixed on the meteor. "You did it. You found it."

"We found it." Another sharp zap on his shoulder, then one on his calf. He turned to brush them off and Lexi gasped.

"Eddie, don't move. You're covered in lightning bugs."

"I know. They're biting me, and they hurt."

"I don't think it's a bite. I think it's actual electricity. I'm hoping if you stay still, they'll get bored and leave you alone."

A zap on his arm. He cringed. The pain was excruciating, even through his thick skin. One landed on his hand. "I can't believe my skin isn't protecting me."

He blew at the one on his hand, trying to get it off without causing it to sting him. Didn't work.

A bolt of pain went through him, making his muscles contract. Light sparked over his skin, leaving little scorch marks behind. A little panic went through him. Electricity could set fire to wood.

He might be in more trouble than he realized. "Lexi, what should I do?"

One landed on his ear, the snapping and buzzing amplified by the closeness. Instinctively, he pulled away. The creature stung him. He swatted at it. More pain erupted on his back. They were all over him now.

The tang of woodsmoke returned, but it wasn't from anyone's fireplace. It was coming off of him. His head spun, and his body ached with the pain. His skin felt like it was on fire. In some places, it was.

He fell to his knees, waving his arms to try to disperse the bugs.

"No," Lexi gulped. She ran past him.

He had no idea what she was doing. The creatures swarmed around him, stinging and sparking him until he could barely see because of the pain. He went down onto his hands. He was close to blacking out. The urge to vomit was strong.

Smoke spiraled off his skin, and tracks of electricity danced over his body. He couldn't breathe or see or hear. His world narrowed to a thin strand of pain and smoke. Was this death?

Lexi's hand closed around his wrist. A huge flash of light turned the night into day, then everything went black again.

He opened his eyes, confused by what was going on. It was no longer night. He was no longer in the forest. He was in a soft bed that smelled of Lexi. He groaned softly. Was he dead? He was pretty sure he was dead.

"Eddie?" Lexi walked into view. "Are you awake? How do you feel?"

"Am I dead?"

She laughed. "No, you're very much alive."

"What happened? Where am I?" His memories were murky. The last thing he remembered was intense pain and feeling like death was closing in on him. How had he gotten here?

"You've been asleep a while. You're back in the apartment." She sat on the edge of the bed and pressed her hand to his forehead. "Are you well? I was so worried. I thought you were ..." She swallowed. "Your skin was on fire. Smoldering in places but actual flames in others. It was terrifying."

The memory made him shudder.

A tear rolled down her cheek. "I thought you were dying. I was sure of it."

He nodded. "So was I. What did you do?"

She wiped at the tear. "What I had to. I gave you the magic you needed to save your life."

His eyes narrowed as his memories came back in bigger pieces. "The meteor." He smiled. "You got your magic!"

She sniffed. "I did."

He reached up to touch her face, but his hand caught his attention. His skin was smooth and even, all traces of wood grain gone. And his joints no longer ached. The realization of what she'd done crushed him. "You got your magic and used it all on me, didn't you?"

She smiled brightly. "It was worth it. You're alive, Eddie. And you're whole."

Whole. No longer half-man, half-tree. She had done what she'd promised she'd do. But at what cost to herself? The realization crushed him. "But you ... you needed it more."

She laughed, but the sound came out like a sob. "I need *you*. The magic will come some other way. I couldn't let you die, Eddie. I care about you far too much. And what kind of being lets another die so they can be whole?" She shook her head, sniffling again. "I did what needed to be done."

"You gave up all that power for me?"

She lifted her chin slightly. "And I would do it again. No regrets." More tears spilled.

His heart broke for her. She'd used *her* magic, magic he knew very well she needed, on him. He would never be able to repay her. She'd saved his life. Twice. He would spend the rest of his life trying to make it up to her. "Thank you. I love you."

She managed to whisper, "I love you, too."

Then he pulled her into his arms. She lay on his chest and wept.

CHAPTER TWENTY-EIGHT

They both fell asleep, but Lexi woke first. She stared at the ceiling, numb with everything that had happened. Even though there was one night of the shower left, her bid for a meteor was essentially over.

Not only had she gotten her shot at a meteor already, but she was back to having barely enough magic in her system to set a beacon, if that's what she decided to do. Was she willing to risk the last of her power on that one slim chance?

She felt like she didn't have a choice. Not using the last of her magic would leave her wondering what might have happened otherwise. She groaned softly. How had she let things get to this point?

For a brief moment, she'd had all the magic she needed and more. It had been glorious. But saving Eddie was all that had mattered. Nothing else was acceptable. He was in those woods because of her. She'd made him help her in exchange for his freedom from that tree. Even if he'd gone there willingly, that was the deal that had been struck. She'd been truthful when she'd told him she had no regrets. She didn't.

Yes, she wished she had that magic for herself, but

not at the cost of his life. She turned her head slightly so she could see him. He'd been fascinating before but now, made whole, he was breathtakingly beautiful. His body still displayed the hard, sculpted lines of his previous form, but now those solid muscles and carved angles were no longer covered in rough, bark-like skin. His skin was as perfect as the rest of him.

Now he resembled the statue of an ancient warrior god come to life. No one would ever look at him and think *monster* ever again.

That alone made giving up the magic worthwhile. She'd saved his life, but she'd also fulfilled her promise to him. She hoped he would stay with her for a while, even though he no longer had a reason to.

His declaration of love was no guarantee. She understood that. She wouldn't hold it against him if he wanted to explore the world. To see what existed beyond the gates of Shadowvale. He could do that now that he was completely transformed and no longer had to be concerned with people being afraid of him.

She couldn't go with him. Without magic, she was too vulnerable. Her best plan was to stay here, where she'd be protected. And hope a new source of magic could be found. Maybe Amelia would allow her to take small sips of power from the meridian lines once in a while. It was worth talking to her about it.

But not now. Lexi needed some time. She needed to mourn the loss of her magic. That was how she felt. Like she was grieving for the life she'd once had.

It was her own fault for letting her magic get so low. For thinking it was no big deal. If she were more practical, she never would have helped Eddie. Never would have given up so much power like that.

Forget the fact that she'd fallen for him. She liked to help. It gave her purpose. It made her existence make sense. She put her hand on his chest. No matter the consequences, he was worth it.

He shifted and yawned, his eyes coming open. He looked at her. "Hey," he said softly. "Are you okay?"

She wasn't. Might never be. She smiled and nodded. "I'm all right. How are you?"

"I feel ... better than I ever have."

"Good. I'm glad."

"We should get moving, right? Figure out where we're going to start tonight? Get something to eat and make a plan."

He was right, but she had no heart for it. The whole hunt seemed so hopeless. "I guess."

He sat up, displacing her a bit. "You guess? You don't seem like you want to go."

She took a deep breath and pushed upright. She had to tell him the truth. "I don't feel like there's much reason to."

"There's a huge reason. You still need magic."

"But I got my meteor last night. What are the odds we'll get another one?"

"I don't know, but we have to try. You can set your beacon tonight. That will give us an edge."

"If I do that, I will be out of magic completely, unless we can get a meteor." She shook her head, staring at her hands. "I don't know if I want to take that chance."

"What will happen to you if you run out of magic completely?"

She exhaled, not wanting to speak the words of that reality. "I will become mortal. Human, essentially. My magic and my abilities will no longer be a part of me."

"Is that really so bad?" He shrugged. "I don't have magic. And I'm pretty sure I'm mortal."

"Eddie, you are filled with magic. You might not realize it, but you are. I don't know about you being mortal either. You're a rare and amazing individual. Your size aside, just because you look like everyone else doesn't mean you are."

"If I really have that much magic, why can't you take some of it back from me?"

"In this case, it doesn't work that way. Yes, you are a being made possible by magic, but a lot of that magic was used up in your transformation. It made you into this new version of yourself. It's no longer available the way you think."

"Magic is confusing. Science is easier."

She smiled. "Sometimes, it is."

"I wonder if Henry might have any ideas about how to get you some magic. Or how to get you a meteor. Do you think it would be better if we worked as a group?"

"I don't see how. With them in another part of the forest, we at least double our chances."

"So we are going back tonight."

She wasn't feeling nearly as glum as she had earlier. Being around Eddie made that impossible. "Yes, we are. I have to."

"I'm not letting you go alone. Although I would prefer not to go the Dark Acres again."

"No, we're done there. It was a great idea on Thomas's behalf, but it's just too dangerous."

"What if …" His mouth bunched to one side like he was trying to decide whether or not to finish his statement.

"What? Go on. Say what you were going to say."

"I don't like this idea, but what if you and I split up too? You could safely go to the Dark Acres, and I could be in another part of the forest. That would up our odds even more."

"It would, but how would you let me know if you had a meteor? I can't use a phone, and I don't think smoke signals are a good idea." She also really didn't want to be without him. She'd never felt that way about anyone, human, supernatural, or otherwise. But being with Edgar was all she wanted.

He grunted softly. "I forgot about that. Do you think that's still true even with your reduced level of magic?"

"There's an easy way to find out. Where's your phone?"

"Charging over by the sofa."

She got up and went to it, unplugging the cable so she

could bring it back. "Here. Turn it on, then hand it to me and I'll show you."

He took the phone from her as she sat beside him on the bed. "I thought it was on." He pressed a button on the side, and the phone lit up. He held it a moment, then nodded. "Okay, it's ready."

She held out her open palm. He placed the phone in her hand. The screen blipped, then went fuzzy before fading to black. She offered it back to him. "Just like I thought. Looks like we're not splitting up."

"Looks like it." He smiled. "I'm good with that. I'd rather be with you."

Her heart did a little leap. "You would?"

"Yes. Did I make you think otherwise? Because if I did, I didn't mean to. When I said I loved you, I meant it. Or have you forgotten what I said? I'll say it again. I love you. You saved my life, Lexi. Twice now. All I want to do is spend the rest of mine trying to repay you."

Her throat knotted with emotion, but she managed to get out a few words. "You don't have to repay me." She leaned into him, and he put his arm around her. She cleared her throat softly. "But I like the idea of you being around. I like it very much. I hope that never changes."

"Unless you tell me to leave, I'm not going anywhere. I know I don't have any money, and we'll need it, especially if you don't have magic, but I'll find a job doing something. We'll make it work."

She straightened slightly as she realized something.

"You're right. We will need money. But I own this whole building." She looked at him. "I should be getting rent from the pub. That ought to take care of some of our expenses. I need to read through that paperwork the realtor left me. Are you really serious about staying with me?"

He nodded. "Very much so."

"Good. Because I want you to stay." A lightness came over her. She did *not* want to lose her magic entirely. But maybe things wouldn't be as bad as she'd imagined if that actually came to pass.

Not with Edgar around.

CHAPTER TWENTY-NINE

All the talk of money made Edgar reluctant to eat out. That would mean Lexi had to spend some of the cash she had left. Whatever that amount was, he didn't want to deplete it further. Besides, there was food in the apartment. No reason for them to go out, so he talked her into staying in.

Of course, he didn't know the first thing about cooking, and Lexi said she wasn't great at it either because she always used her magic to conjure up dishes from her groceries, but together they decided to make an easy meal with ingredients she'd already bought.

They followed the directions on the box of spaghetti, cooking it exactly as directed.

While waiting for it to cook, he put two bottles of water on the table along with forks and paper towels for napkins. He'd never set a table in his life, but he had a faint memory of it, so Henry must have at some point.

When the timer went off, he carried the pot to the sink, drained the pasta into the strainer, then put it back into the pot and returned it to the stove.

Lexi took over then. She added a jar of sauce, making sure to empty the whole thing in. She stirred the sauce and pasta together, her expression uncertain as she gazed into the pot. "Looks pretty good, I think. It at least looks the way spaghetti usually looks."

"Smells good." He wasn't going to say a bad word about the meal no matter how it tasted.

"There's cheese in refrigerator. We can grate that on top. You want to get it?"

"Sure." He found the cheese in the drawer marked Meat and Cheese, which was convenient. "Where's the grater?"

She scrunched up her nose. "I'd usually do that with magic. I don't think we have one."

He smiled. "I'll look." Lexi with magic was amazing. Lexi without it was oddly endearing. He opened cabinets and searched drawers. The best he could do was a knife. "Let me see if I can slice some very thin and chop it up."

She laughed. "I'm not good at being domestic, am I?"

"It's okay. We're figuring it all out. And you haven't needed to be good at it."

She sighed, her amused expression staying put. "I haven't, but that's no excuse." She watched him get out a cutting board and work on the cheese. "I really hope we get a meteor tonight. I've already decided I'm going to hold a tiny bit of magic in reserve. I'm not sure I'll be able to take care of myself otherwise."

There was a lost, slightly scared look in her eyes that made him stop slicing. "You won't have to. I'll take care of you. I owe you that much. And I want to."

She blinked and flashed him a quick smile before

leaning up to kiss his cheek. "Using my magic on you was the best decision I've ever made."

With a grin, he went back to slicing. "I'm glad you think that. I'm going to try to keep you thinking that, too." He would do everything he could tonight to get her that fallen star.

He chopped up the slices of cheese, running the blade over them again and again until the pieces were as tiny as he could make them. Then he showed Lexi the results. "What do you think?"

"I think we're ready to eat." She served up two plates of pasta, his much larger than hers, and carried them to the table.

He used the cutting board to carry the cheese over, and they sat. They each sprinkled cheese on their spaghetti. Lexi picked up her fork.

He stared at his plate. "I've never done this before."

Her forehead wrinkled. "Done what?"

"Helped make a meal. Sat down to eat it with someone I cared about." It felt like the most real-life experience he'd ever had. Thoughts of his past were miles away. That was nice. "If this is how ordinary people live, I like it very much."

"Do you? You don't think it's boring? You wouldn't rather be out in the world, seeing what else there is?"

He gazed at her beautiful face and shook his head. "Maybe someday. But not unless you're with me." He picked up his fork, thinking about what his existence had been like before when he'd been Henry's curse. "My life was nothing but chaos and destruction. If this is boring, I'm okay with that. It's peaceful and calm."

She gave his hand a quick squeeze. "I can see why that would appeal to you."

"Have you ever lived a life like this?"

"You mean this kind of human life? Or do you mean have I lived with someone else?"

He hadn't considered that she might have been involved with anyone else. "I guess … either. Both."

"No." She smiled. "And no. I've had relationships with men but nothing serious. Human men don't interest me, to be honest. And they tend to be a little … fragile for my needs. They'd never understand who I am anyway." She looked away. "Who I was."

"You still are that person, but I know what you mean. Your magic would be very hard for them to grasp." Did she think he was fragile? That wasn't a way he'd ever have described himself, but Lexi was a very different kind of being.

"So would yours, I suspect." She twirled pasta around her fork and ate it. She smiled. "Hey, this is good."

He ate some of his, nodding right away. It was good. "We make an excellent team."

"Yes, we do. But like I was saying, if you tried to explain yourself to a regular person living in the middle of some regular town, they'd probably have you committed." She gestured with her fork toward the windows. "But here? Nothing is really that weird, is it?"

"People have been far more accepting of me than I thought they'd be."

"Shadowvale is a very strange but very cool town."

"You could see yourself staying here then?"

She wiped at a smudge of sauce at the corner of her mouth. "I could." She looked directly into his eyes. "I love the company an awful lot."

"Thank you. But when you get your magic back, won't you want to leave?"

She didn't say anything for a moment, making him think she was trying to find a way to tell him the truth as gently as possible. She put her fork down. "You know, I've never really had a home base. Probably because I never had a reason to. I've never had anyone to come home to either." Her fingers twined with his.

She took a breath, the exhale coming out in a little shudder. "It scares me."

"As much as heights?"

She laughed. "Close. But it's a different kind of fear. I can't really explain that, but … maybe I'm afraid of being hurt? That seems like such a human emotion."

"Is that so bad?"

"No, I guess not."

"Do you think I would hurt you?"

"No, not deliberately." Another inhale. "But what if I did something to drive you away? Without even meaning to. What if you got tired of me? Or decided you wanted something different?"

He shook his head. "I wouldn't—"

"You might." Her fingers stayed laced through his. "This life is new to you, Eddie. I wouldn't blame you for changing your mind about things in a couple months or a year or even tomorrow."

He wasn't going to do that. He'd tasted this life with her, and it was good. It was calm and peaceful and wonderful. It was everything he'd ever wanted. Why would he ever leave it? But he also knew he wasn't going to convince her otherwise except by showing her, over time, that this was exactly what he wanted. "I don't want to be apart from you. But you might just as easily decide those same things."

"You're right. I might. But I'll tell you something very private. I came here to get enough magic to move beyond this plane. To ascend, as my kind does, to something new. It was what I thought I wanted." Her fingers tightened on his. "I don't want that anymore. Now I just want you."

"Then stay with me. Make a life with me. Here. An easy, simple, peaceful life. And if someday you want to go, I'll understand." He'd be heartbroken, but he'd understand.

"You really would be okay with that?"

"Okay with you leaving? No, probably not. But it would be better to have you for a short while than not at all."

She smiled. "Maybe we could take some trips together? See the world side by side. What do you think about that?"

If he was being honest, the idea of going beyond the

safety of Shadowvale gave him pause. But that was him going alone. Not coupled with this amazing creature.

He brought her hand to his mouth and kissed her knuckles. "I think as long as you're standing beside me, anything's possible."

She grinned. "Then our plan is settled. We're making Shadowvale our home. The rest we'll figure out as it comes."

"Good plan." He nodded as they went back to eating. "I already have tonight figured out."

"You do?"

He swallowed the bite of spaghetti he'd just taken. "Tonight, you're setting your beacon and we're getting you a meteor."

Chapter Thirty

Lexi stood in the middle of the forest, surveying the beacon she'd just arranged. She'd used every possible thing she could to create a strong magical pull. Bones for strength, rocks for endurance, a lit candle in the middle because fire drew fire, ferns to represent the land, salt to represent the sea, feathers to represent the air, and cobwebs to hold the magic once it arrived.

She arranged all of the many pieces in perfect symmetrical spirals, the whirling patterns specifically designed to support the spell they would hold.

Now all she had to do was infuse it with real magic. That would activate the spell and turn the beacon on.

But doing that would also leave her utterly without magic, because if she was going to do this, she needed to give the beacon as much of a boost as she could. That meant using all the magic she had left. No reserves. It was really the only way. Thinking she could hold a portion back was like setting herself up for failure.

Eddie put his hand on her shoulder. "You okay?"

She almost nodded, then shook her head. "No. Not really. I am willingly about to rid myself of every shred of remaining magic in order to hopefully get more. I will be human—and mortal—until that happens. *If* that happens."

"It will. Even if we don't get a meteor tonight, we have the rest of our lives to find you another source." His arm went around her shoulder, and he kissed the top of her head. "Don't be afraid. I won't let anything happen to you."

"I know. Still hard." She appreciated his commitment to her, but all the certainty she'd felt on the walk here had evaporated.

"Hard things are often the ones most worth doing."

She looked up at him. He'd done a lot of hard things in his life, and he hadn't shied from them, had he? Being human and with him was still better than being fully powered up and alone. She put her hand over top of his. "You're right. I need to do this."

"You can want to not do it and still do it, you know. It's okay to not like something while still getting it done. You conquered your fear of heights that way."

"I wouldn't say they were conquered, but I understand what you're saying." The difference when they'd climbed the tree had been he'd been with her during the entire journey up and down the tree.

Emptying herself of all available magic was something she had to do alone.

She took a breath. She was wasting time. "All right. I'm ready."

As if sensing she needed space, he stepped back. She approached the beacon. The candle's small flame flickered in the dim light of dusk. It would soon be completely dark, and the last of the meteors would follow.

She kneeled beside it and held her clenched hands over the beacon. For a moment, she did nothing, once again wavering. She looked skyward. This had to work. And if it didn't, at least she'd know that she tried.

She opened her hands, palms flat toward the beacon, and accessed the last stores of magic left inside her. Like turning on a faucet, she let it flow out of her and into the beacon.

Blue-green ripples of power spilled over the ground. It gathered in a pool and began to wind its way over the rocks and bones, stretching out over the fronds of green, dancing along the lengths of cobweb. It picked up speed, turning into a whirlpool of energy that followed the patterns she'd laid out, pulsing with soft light and undeniable power.

The last of her magic left her and joined the rushing swirl. She felt empty and a little sick. She sat back on her heels.

The spinning magic began to focus itself around the candle. The flame no longer flickered but stood straight and true. The flame lengthened, reaching toward the sky in a thin stream of blue-green fire.

Then the magic shot up, up, up, creating a twisted, whirling thread of energy that unraveled into the heavens.

"It's done," she said quietly.

She stayed where she was.

Eddie approached, his footsteps crunching the leaves. "Are you okay?"

"I don't know." She'd never felt this before. Never experienced being mortal. She was suddenly aware of her body in a new way. She could feel her joints and muscles. Her skin was different. Her eyesight not as sharp. Her hearing dull.

He offered her his hand. He looked bigger than she remembered.

She tucked her head. If her body felt this way, her appearance must also reflect it. Was she hideous to him now? Gray and wrinkled? She had no idea how much of her age would show.

"What's wrong, Lexi?"

"I don't want you to look at me. I must look awful."

He kneeled beside her, getting closer. Not what she'd been hoping for. "Lexi, you look as beautiful as ever."

There was no guile in his voice. She supposed he was capable of lying without it being obvious, but his words soothed her. She risked a glance at him. He looked like he was speaking the truth. "I do?"

He nodded, his face lit by the soft light of the beacon. "You do."

"I feel ... old. I can feel my bones and muscles and joints in a way I never have before." Her hands went to her face. She touched the skin around her eyes. Had those lines always been there? "I was sure my age was showing."

"I guess that's being human, huh?"

"I guess." She sighed. "I don't like it. My hearing and my eyesight aren't what they were either."

"I've heard that getting old is not for the weak."

She laughed, despite her mood. "I believe it. And thank you."

"For what?"

"For being you." She took his hand. "Help me up?"

He got to his feet and gave her a lift up. "How long do you think the beacon will take to draw in a meteor?"

"I have no idea. I don't even know if it will work. I might not have had enough magic to power it properly. I suppose we'll know by the end of the night if I made a mistake or not."

"No mistake." He shook his head. "Trying something worthwhile is never a mistake. Even if you fail. It just means you learned something."

She tipped her head. "You're awfully good at saying the right things."

He smiled. "I think I get that from Henry."

"I look forward to seeing him again." She glanced toward the sky, feeling slightly dizzy. She stayed upright, holding on to Eddie and hoping it would pass. The sky was fully dark now, the stars visible overhead. "All we can do is wait. I might sit again, though. I'm a little low on energy."

"You should eat something."

"Not a bad idea."

"How do you feel?"

She held on to him. "A little dizzy. Probably low on something." Like magic. But no amount of talking about it was going to make it come back. She had to get on with things. This was who she was now.

"Hang on." He whipped off his flannel shirt and spread it on the ground up against a good-size tree. "Sit on that, then you can lean back."

"Are you going to sit with me?"

"Yes." He gave her his hand again and helped her get comfortable. "Better?"

She nodded. "Definitely need something in my system." She breathed out, mouth open, trying to expel the weirdness she was feeling.

He grabbed a bottle of water and a granola bar from her bag, then sat next to her. "Here. Eat this and have something to drink. Lean on me if the tree is too hard."

She smiled. He was so incredibly sweet. She took a long drink of water, then tore the foil off the granola bar and ate a bite. As she chewed, she leaned into him. Definitely more comfortable than the tree.

They sat in silence while she refueled, both of them keeping watch on the patch of sky visible through the trees. An hour or so ticked by with no meteors.

The food and water had made her feel somewhat better. Not as good as magic, but she wasn't dizzy anymore.

"Should we change spots?" Eddie asked. "Watch from somewhere else?"

"We could, but if the beacon's going to work, it'll draw

them to us." She didn't really want to go anywhere. Sitting here with him was nice. And while she wasn't going to say it out loud, she was pretty sure there was no meteor in their future.

Eddie got out his phone and tapped at the screen. A few moments later, he sighed in frustration.

"What's wrong?"

"My fingers are too big. I wanted to send Henry a text and ask if they were seeing anything, but I can't hit any of the right letters."

She held out her hand. "I can probably do it now that I'm human."

"Oh. Right." He gave her the phone. "Thanks. Just ask him if they've spotted any. Then at least we'll know if the shower's begun."

The phone stayed on in her hands. Proof of her humanity. She tapped at the keyboard on the screen to input the message, then hit send. "I guess one perk of being human is the phone thing. I suppose I could get all kinds of electronics now. Maybe I'll even break down and buy a watch."

She snorted as she handed the phone back to him. "Once I get a job."

He set the phone between them. "What kind of work would you like to do?"

"I have no idea. I've never worked before. I don't have any idea what I'm good at."

"You're good with animals. I've seen that. Maybe you could do something with them."

"Maybe I could. I think dog walker might be all I'm qualified for, though. I don't even know how to take care of an animal. No one should trust me with their pets until I know what I'm doing."

He looked at her. "We could get a pet."

She was about to respond when his phone chimed. He looked at the screen. "Henry says they haven't seen any yet so it's not just us."

"That's comforting. But back to what you said. What kind of pet?"

He shrugged the shoulder she wasn't leaning on. "Once, when I was a tree, a cat climbed me." He chuckled. "I remember it being very soft. Not the claws, but the rest of it."

She wrapped her arm around his. "If you want a cat, we'll get one." Making him happy was the least she could do.

"Well, you have to want one, too."

"I think it would be interesting. I'm willing to give it a go."

The sounds of branches bending and leaves rustling made them both go quiet.

A tiger emerged from the brush.

Eddie leaped to his feet, putting himself between Lexi and the great beast. "That is *not* the kind of cat I had in mind."

Chapter Thirty-One

An older woman came out of the brush behind the tiger. She was in a colorful robe and a jeweled turban. "Good evening."

Eddie just stared. He had no idea who she was, but if that was her tiger, she'd better keep it away from Lexi. Humans were vulnerable.

Lexi got up. "Amelia. And Thoreau. Good evening."

Amelia nodded. "Lexi." She came closer until she was even with the tiger. She put her hand on its head and gazed curiously at Eddie. "You must be Edgar."

He swallowed. If she knew who he was, she must also know what he'd been. "I am. And you are Amelia Marchand." This was the woman he'd wanted to go see. The one Thomas had told him about.

"That's right." She smiled, her eyes shifting to the beacon still sending its thread of magic into the night sky. "I sensed strong magic. I thought perhaps I'd found a meteor no one had claimed. Now I see I was wrong."

Lexi, who oddly didn't seem to have any fear of the tiger, stepped alongside Eddie. "I was trying to give myself a better chance at getting one."

Amelia nodded. "Smart. Takes a lot of understanding

of the old ways to create a thing like that. A great deal of magic, too."

Lexi exhaled a quiet breath. "It took all I had."

Amelia regarded her again. "You used the last of your magic on this?"

Lexi nodded. "Probably not the smartest thing to do but—"

"I disagree," Amelia said. "You gave yourself the best possible shot at getting what you needed. Smart and courageous. I applaud you."

"Thanks. I wish I could tell you I thought it was going to work, but we haven't even seen a meteor yet."

"They're always thinnest near the end of the shower. I've had no luck either."

Lexi seemed surprised by that. "You're looking for a meteor? But you already have a lot of magic."

Amelia scratched the tiger's head. He sat down next to her. "I do, but there is something I need a great deal of magic for. Are you sure you gave up all of your magic?"

That was a quick change of subject.

Lexi nodded. "Yes."

"Stay, Thoreau." Amelia stepped forward, hand outstretched. The tiger remained where he was. "May I?"

Lexi hesitated. "O-okay." She met Amelia in the middle of the small clearing.

Amelia rested her fingers on Lexi's cheek for a moment, then dropped her hand and nodded. "The signature of magic is still in you, but it is most definitely gone. How incredibly brave."

Lexi said nothing, but she took a step back, putting her closer to Eddie again.

Amelia looked his way. Her intense gaze seemed to pierce right through him. She touched the long strand of sparkling purple beads around her neck. "You carry the same signature. She gave a great deal of her magic to you, didn't she?"

He nodded. "Yes. She saved my life. Twice."

Lexi shook her head. "I didn't—"

"She did," he said. "She's a remarkable person." He wanted Amelia to know that Lexi was special. Even without magic.

Amelia tilted her head in Lexi's direction. "Then it must be true what I heard about you, Lexi. You cured Kacy Wilson's troubles, didn't you?"

Lexi took Eddie's hand. "Yes."

Amelia gave a little smile. "How interesting." She looked over her shoulder. "Come, my darling."

The tiger got up and came to stand beside her. She petted his head while keeping her focus on Eddie and Lexi. "Have a pleasant night. I have a feeling we'll meet again. I hope you get your meteor."

"You, too," Eddie said.

Amelia walked past them, the tiger at her side. Neither looked back.

When they were out of sight, he exhaled. "That was weird. She knows I used to be a monster."

"Maybe. But if she does, she doesn't care. Didn't seem to anyway."

"No." Odd. Had Amelia sensed something about him that made her believe he wasn't a threat? She hadn't touched him like she had Lexi.

"Do you really think we'll see her again?"

Eddie shrugged. "It's a small town."

"I know, but the way she said it ..." Lexi shook her head. "Just made it seem like she knows something we don't."

"Maybe she does. You went to see her, didn't you?"

"Yes. How did you know that?"

"Thomas mentioned he took you there. Is that why you weren't afraid of the tiger?"

"In part. But also because I met him at her house and he showed no signs of aggression. There's something about that tiger. A deep magic something."

"What's that mean, deep magic? And how do you know? Did you sense it?"

"Deep magic just means that tiger is under some kind of enchantment. I know because just like Amelia touched me, I touched him when I was at her house. Right away I could sense magic in him. More than one kind too. Like layers of spells. I don't think I've ever run across that before except for a vase I discovered a couple centuries back in the Moroccan kasbah. Turned out to have a genie in it." She put her hands on her hips. "Boy, I could use one of Khalid's wishes right now."

Eddie blinked. "I would very much like to hear the rest of that story."

She grinned. "It's a good one. And we've got time."

His phone chimed. He took it out and read the screen. "Henry said they spotted a meteor, but it was headed toward the Dark Acres."

"The Dark Acres can have it," Lexi said. She tipped her head back to see the sky. "But at least we know they've started. Hopefully one shows up here soon."

He went back to the tree where his shirt was still spread out. He sat, then patted the area next to him. "Come tell me all about the genie while we wait."

She joined him and sat down. "It was 1768, and Muhammad Ibn Abdallah was the Sultan then. I'd been to the palace for dinner. You should have seen the gardens. They were spectacular. Unlike anything I'd ever seen before. And the food."

She put her hand to her stomach. "I've never been to another feast like that again. Anyway, the next day, I went to the casbah to do some shopping and—"

A spark of light overhead interrupted her.

She jumped to her feet. "Eddie, I think we've got one."

Chapter Thirty-Two

Lexi's heart was pounding. The light grew brighter as it got closer. The meteor seemed to be coming directly toward them, but at the same time it was moving far too slow for her liking. The forest around them was almost as light as day.

Eddie was next to her. "We're going to get this one. We're going to get it. I can feel it."

She wasn't that sure, and saying anything felt like putting too much out there. She stayed quiet, remained focused on the burning meteor coming toward them, and tried to breathe.

A man ran through the woods and into the small clearing. He wasn't looking at them. He was focused on the meteor.

"We were here first," Eddie said.

The man jumped in shock. "I didn't realize. Please. I need this. You don't understand. The wish isn't for me; it's for my son. His troubles make him very sick and—"

As the light grew brighter, two young women burst through the other side of the clearing. One of them immediately frowned. "We're too late, Sara. Look."

Sara grabbed her friend by the arm. "Come on, let's get out of here. We're wasting our time."

"No," her friend said. "I at least want to see it."

With a blinding light, the meteor fell into the clearing, landing just shy of Lexi's beacon. It rippled with magical energy, sending shivers of power over her skin. This was it. This was all the magic she needed.

The man who wanted the wish for his son took a few steps toward it and dropped to his knees. He clasped his hands together and pleaded with Lexi. "Please. My boy is eight years old, but his body is ninety. His bones are brittle with arthritis, and every day he gets closer to death. The wish would save his life."

She wiped her hand over her mouth.

"You have every right to the wish," he went on. "I know you were here first. But I would do anything to save my son's life. If you want money, I'll give you everything I have. Please."

She clenched her jaw and looked at Eddie. The meteor's light reflected in his eyes, which looked liquid with emotions.

She swallowed down her own feelings. "You can have the meteor."

"Lexi," Eddie said softly. "Are you sure?"

She was out of words. She just nodded and turned away. All that magic. Hers. And she'd just given it away. But what was she supposed to do? Let a little boy die because she didn't want to be human?

Eddie took her hand. She turned back in time to see the two young women disappear back into the trees.

"Thank you." The father was weeping. "Thank you." He put his hands on the meteor and closed his eyes. The swirling, glittering magic traveled up his arms, then funneled off him in an eddy of light and power and took off as though it was on a mission.

The hum that had been dancing over her skin went with it. The meteor lay cold and dark.

The father got to his feet. "Whatever you want, just tell me. I'm Joel Campbell, by the way. My son is Logan."

Once again, Lexi felt the hollowness inside her where her magic had once resided. "I don't want anything. Wait. Actually, I do. If your boy is so sick, why come to Shadowvale? There have to be other places in the world better equipped to cure him."

The father nodded. "There are. But my wife has enough werewolf blood in her that she's powerless to control the change when there's a full moon. Logan's too young to change yet, and we don't even know if he will. But we heard about Shadowvale and thought this would be a safe place for both of them. But mostly, we've been hoping to find the book that's somewhere in these woods. Maybe fix both of them."

Lexi frowned. "What book?"

"Legend says somewhere in these woods there is a grove of magical trees and within that grove is a book. If you can find it and write your name in it, your curse will be lifted." He looked out at the trees around them. "We've been here two years and haven't found it yet, but now, thanks to you, we won't need to look anymore. Thank you."

"You're welcome," she said softly. She knew she'd done the right thing, but it was too soon for her to feel any joy in that. Could the book help her? She doubted it. Being human wasn't really a curse. And she'd lost her magic because of her own choices.

Not only that, but she doubted such a book even existed. That kind of magic was rare and unusual. And had only ever truly existed once on this planet. How on earth would it have ended up in Shadowvale?

"What's your name? I'd like to know who to thank for saving my son. I'm sure my wife will want to know too."

"Lexi."

"Gardner," Eddie added. He put his arm around her.

"Thank you, Lexi Gardner." Joel was smiling. "If you ever need anything, all you have to do is ask." He took off through the woods, breaking into a run. He let out a whoop of joy as he vanished into the darkness.

"I needed that magic," Lexi said. She sighed. "But I'm sure he needed that wish more."

Eddie hugged her closer. "You did a very good thing. A selfless, amazing thing. You should be proud of yourself. I know you probably don't feel that way right now, but you should. I'm very proud of you."

"Thanks." He was right that she didn't feel that way. She just felt like her big chance had slipped through her fingers.

"The beacon looks like it's still working."

She shook her head. "It's not. That's just the last of the spell. It'll fade soon. The magic is used up. I'd sense if it wasn't."

"Oh. What do you want to do now? Try a different spot?"

She thought hard. What did she want to do? Truth was, she felt resigned to her fate. "I'd just like to go home."

"Really? There could still be another meteor out there for us to get. Or we could look for that book. That sounded interesting."

She took both his hands and stared up at him. "I'm not cursed, Eddie. That book isn't going to help me. Besides that, it's probably just a myth. I doubt that book really exists." She sighed. "I think I've had as many meteors as I'm going to get. I'm done. I'm tired in a way I can't really explain, but I don't want to be here anymore."

Concern filled his eyes. "You mean the woods? Or Shadowvale?"

"The woods. It's time for me to stop hoping for something that's not going to happen and start concentrating on how to make this new life work. Which I will do tomorrow. Right now, I just want to go home and go to bed."

Maybe she'd wake up and it would have all been a dream. She knew that wouldn't happen, but it was hard to stop herself from fantasizing about a way out of this.

"Okay," he said. "Whatever you want. Do you want me to call Thomas to come get us?"

"No." The idea of having to pretend she was all right didn't appeal. She had a lot of thinking to do. She hoisted her bag straps over her shoulder. "I'd rather walk."

He nodded, grabbed his shirt off the ground, and pulled it on. Then he took her hand. "We should get going. It's a long walk."

"If you'd rather call Thomas—"

"I will walk as long and as far as you want to go. But we should text Henry and tell him we're done for the night."

"You're right. We should." Eddie was such a good man. And he was the only thing keeping her sane. "Give me your phone, and I'll send the message."

He handed it over, a little smile bending his mouth as they started to walk. She sent the text, then handed the phone back to him. For a while, he didn't say anything. She was all right with that. She had so much on her mind. How to move forward. How to find peace with this new existence. How to live without magic, something she'd relied on for as long as she'd been on this planet. The last one felt impossible.

Her thoughts began to overwhelm her.

And just then, as if sensing the chaos in her head, Eddie spoke up. "What do you think about the name Charlie?"

She blinked, trying to figure out what he was asking her. "I'm not sure I understand the question."

"For a cat. If we get one. Charlie could be a boy or a girl. It would have to fit the animal's personality, of course, but it's a nice name. Unless you hate it."

She smiled. "I think Charlie's a great name. You really want a cat, don't you?"

He shrugged. "Yes, I do. I can't stop thinking about having one, actually. I've never had anything to look after or take care of. It scares me a little, but I think I'd be good at it. I could learn."

"You don't need to learn. You already know how."

He shook his head. "I don't think I do."

"Eddie, you've been taking care of me in one way or another since we met. I think a cat will be a piece of cake."

He glanced at her. "I hadn't thought about it that way."

"Why don't we see if there's a place in town where we can adopt one? We can go look tomorrow."

"Really? That soon?"

"Yes." Another living creature to look after might be just the distraction she needed. Anything would be better than spending another day inside her head, worried about how she was going to cope.

It was time to just get on with life. She had Eddie. And they might soon have a cat. She would eventually learn to live without magic.

She'd have to if she was going to survive.

CHAPTER THIRTY-THREE

Eddie didn't mind that Lexi fell asleep not long after they got home. He was tired but not enough to sleep. Not yet. He sat on the couch for a long time, just staring at nothing and thinking.

It bothered him that Lexi had given up, but he also understood how disappointed she was. Just because giving Joel the meteor for his son was a good thing to do didn't mean Lexi couldn't also feel bad about losing out on the magic she needed.

She was allowed to be upset. It would take time for her to figure out her new life.

In the meantime, maybe there was something he could do to help. He wasn't sure what. They'd need money to live on, that was for sure. Whatever rent she got from the pub would help, but what portion of that would have to go to things like keeping up the building, the cost of utilities, and insurance?

He needed to find a job. He wasn't sure what he was capable of doing, but he was reasonably smart, and he was very strong. Henry might have some ideas, but Henry was probably asleep by now.

Thomas would be up, though.

Eddie took his phone and went outside onto the steps so he wouldn't wake Lexi up. He used his knuckle to tap the button to dial Thomas.

"Edgar. Good evening. Did she get a meteor?"

"Hi, Thomas. She did, but she ended up giving it away to someone else with a sick child. He needed the wish to save his life."

"You don't say."

"Yes. A man named Joel Campbell."

"He's got a boy named Logan. Not that old but looks like a senior citizen. I know the family."

"That's them."

"How about that. Quite a sacrifice on her part. She doing okay?"

"Not yet, but she will be. Just needs some time."

"Gotta be hard for her. Doing something courageous doesn't always leave you feeling that way."

Eddie nodded. He knew Thomas would understand.

Thomas spoke again. "How are you doing?"

"I'm fine. Proud of her. But wishing I could help, too."

"Sure, only natural to feel that way about the person you care about. Anything I can do to help?"

"Maybe. What do you know about the book in the forest that's supposed to take away your curse if you write your name in it?"

"What I know is it's hard to find. Kacy and I looked a few times. Never found anything. But it's real, I can tell you that much."

"Do you think it would help Lexi? She doesn't think the book exists, by the way."

"The book is real all right. Hard to find as hen's teeth, but it's out there. What would you say Lexi's curse is?"

"That's just it." Eddie sighed. "I don't think she has one, technically. Being human isn't really a curse, even if you think it is."

"Is that what's happened to her?"

"Yes. She used the last of her magic to draw in that meteor."

"Which she gave away. That poor girl. Did the right thing for someone else even though it was the wrong thing for her. Worst part is, I don't think that book would help her one bit since she doesn't actually have a curse."

Eddie heaved out another breath. "I was afraid of that. I have another question."

"Go ahead. Maybe I can give you a better answer this time."

"Do you know anyone who'd want to hire me? I need a job."

"Hmm. You're big and strong, and you've got a good head on your shoulders. What kind of work do you want to do?"

"I don't care. If it pays a decent wage, I'll do it."

"I'll ask around. See what I can find."

Another thought popped into Eddie's head. "One more thing. That idea you said you had. Have you gotten anywhere with it?"

"Not quite yet, but I'm still working on it."

When he didn't say more, Eddie let it be. "Well, you have a good night. Thank you for talking to me."

"Anytime, son. We'll speak again real soon, I promise."

"Thank you. Good night."

"Good night." Thomas hung up.

Eddie set the phone on the step next to him and leaned back, elbows on the step behind him. He stared up at the sky. A streak of light cut between two stars. The meteors were still coming.

It bothered him to think Lexi had missed her opportunity, but what could he do? Could he find a meteor on his own and wish for her to get her magic back?

He stood up. If there was a chance that would work, he had to take it. He went back inside and wrote her a note. *Gone back to the forest. Don't worry. Home by dawn.*

He stuck a granola bar in his back pocket, grabbed the key to the apartment, and headed out. He had no real plan. He just walked in the direction the meteor had been headed, which was back toward the forest.

A few yards past the pub, he changed his mind. The forest hadn't brought them any joy. Was it really the only place he could find a meteor? Maybe it would be better to keep to the streets and watch the skies and when a meteor appeared, track it from there.

He was fast. Could he follow a meteor fast enough to get there first? There was only one way to find out.

The streets took him throughout the town. Some areas looked oddly familiar, giving him a real sense that he'd been there before. Some streets he knew he'd been on. He recognized them from his memories.

Had he terrorized the people in the houses along the way? Had he scared them? He couldn't remember those kinds of details, but he hoped not. He hoped if he had, they would forgive him.

If he knew their names, he would have apologized in person. If they'd be willing to see him in person.

Maybe the way he looked now was enough to keep those memories at bay. Enough to keep them from being scared of him again.

As he walked, he watched the skies as much as he was able. He saw a few more slashes of light cut across the sky, but nothing close enough to bother with. None that looked like they were headed for the forest either.

Every meteor he saw seemed to burn out in the heavens.

Finally, he turned toward home, only to realize he wasn't sure which direction that was. He got his bearings by looking at house numbers and following them in descending order until the street he was on joined another street, then he'd do the same thing.

The sky was turning light when the pub came into view. He'd walked all night with nothing to show for it except a tired body and aching feet.

Still worth it for Lexi, though.

He climbed the stairs to the apartment, let himself in, then took a quick shower before he changed into his pajamas. Lexi was still asleep, spread across the bed, covers tangled around her, but she bore a worried expression.

Bad dreams, maybe? He hoped not. She had enough to deal with. Peaceful rest was what she needed.

He drank a bottle of water, then stretched out on the couch as much as he was able. He didn't mind the couch. It was an easy sacrifice and not one he gave much thought to.

What stayed on his mind as the light coming through the blinds increased was that today was a new day. A day she would face once again without magic.

Would she be all right? He'd do whatever she needed him to do. He owed her. He was the reason she was without magic.

There had to be a way to get her more. Maybe not as much as she needed, but enough that she could feel like her old self again.

He wracked his brain trying to solve that problem, feeling like the answer was so close, but was unable to grasp it before sleep took him.

Chapter Thirty-Four

Lexi woke to the sound of Eddie's soft snores. She sat up. He was once again crammed onto the couch. She shook her head. That was so silly. There was more than enough room for him on the bed. And after everything he'd done for her, he deserved a good night's rest.

They needed to talk about that. Work out a few things. Especially if they were going to be sharing this space for a while.

She stretched and yawned.

She must have fallen asleep right after they'd gotten home. She didn't remember much. Just changing out of her clothes and climbing into bed. She'd had a few unpleasant dreams, but for the most part she'd slept well.

Amazing how a decent night's sleep could give you a new outlook on things. So she didn't have magic. It wasn't what she'd have chosen for herself, but that was where she was. She was going to make the best of it.

There was no other option. Feeling sorry for herself would accomplish nothing. And if the day came that she was able to get her magic back, well, she'd probably appreciate it more. But she was alive and she had a path forward, even if parts of it weren't entirely clear, and even better, she had Eddie.

She'd never placed much value on having a relationship with anyone before. Humans seemed so different from her. And supernaturals had a lot of quirks. But now that she was human ... not being alone mattered.

Being with someone made life easier to bear when you couldn't wave your hand and make your desires come true.

Not only that, but Eddie was special. He understood what it meant to be different from everyone else. And somehow, despite everything he'd been through, he still had a kind heart and a gentle soul.

It was as if all the bad in him had been excised with the monster he once was. She smiled at him, snoring softly on the too-small couch. All she wanted was for him to be happy. For them to have a good life together.

If he wanted a cat, then they were getting a cat. Whichever one he wanted.

She leaned against the headboard and stared at the windows across from her. The day looked bright, but the light had an afternoon quality about it, making her wonder how late it was. Her stomach rumbled. Late enough for her to be hungry.

Eddie must be too. She could do something about that.

Quietly so that he could sleep as long as possible, she slipped out of bed and went to the kitchen. All the ingredients for breakfast were there. Eggs and bacon in the refrigerator. Bread for toast. Butter. Jam.

But breakfast was something she typically prepared by assembling those ingredients, then adding magic to them.

Now she was going to have to cook them herself. Could she do that without ruining the food? Or setting fire to the kitchen?

Making pasta was easier, but that didn't seem much like breakfast.

Well, there was nothing she could do but try. She got out the frying pan and opened the package of bacon, laying strips down while the pan warmed up. Medium heat only, just as a precaution against turning the meat to cinders.

The bacon didn't seem to be doing much in the pan, however. She turned the heat up one notch and promised herself she'd keep an eye on it.

She cracked seven eggs into a bowl and whipped them up. Eddie would get the lion's share of those. He definitely needed more food than she did.

The bacon started to sizzle gently. That was a good sign, but she definitely needed to watch it now.

She stuck bread into the toaster. How long did toast take? If they were each having two pieces, she'd need to toast another batch. She adjusted the knob for doneness so that it was a little less than in the middle, which seemed a safe bet, then pushed the lever down.

The butter was already out. She got the blackberry

jam out of the cabinet. It hadn't been opened yet. The bacon was sizzling harder now. Should she turn it over? That seemed reasonable. She got a fork and did that. It popped, sending a hot droplet of grease onto her arm.

"Ow." Cooking was harder than she imagined. She hadn't realized the bacon would fight back.

The toast popped up. It looked exactly the same as when she'd put it in. So much for that experiment. Could you retoast bread? She'd soon find out. She turned the knob just past the middle and pushed the bread down again.

"Something smells good." Eddie sat up.

"Sorry. Didn't mean to wake you, but I figured I'd see if I could make breakfast without burning the place down."

"I don't see any fire."

"Yet." She smiled at him. "If you're still tired, go lay on the bed. You can't sleep on that couch anymore. It's too small for you."

He shook his head. "The bed is yours."

"We could share it."

"Wouldn't be right. You hardly know me. And this is your place. I'm fine on the couch."

Handsome and chivalrous. She was right that every trace of the monster he'd once been was gone. "You're not fine on the couch, Eddie. It's too small. How about I take the couch and you take the bed then."

The toast popped up again, a much more acceptable shade of brown this time. Progress was being made.

He got up and rolled his shoulders. "Couch doesn't bother me at all. How's breakfast coming? Can I help?"

"You can butter the toast." She went back to the bacon. Apparently, the bed versus couch conversation was over. She had an easy solution to that. She'd go to sleep on the couch tonight while he was in the bathroom changing. Then he couldn't say anything about it.

She flipped the bacon over. It was looking pretty good. "I want to get a paper today and see if there are any help wanted ads in it. That's still a thing, isn't it?"

"I would think so. But then again, I haven't exactly been in the job market for a while. Or ever, really."

She smiled. "That makes two of us. At least we're in this together. Have you asked Henry? I bet he knows a lot of people in town. He might have an idea of who's hiring."

"Good idea. I'll call him. I already told Thomas to let me know if he hears of anything."

"He probably knows more people than Henry."

"I bet he does." Eddie brought a piece of toast over. "Is that enough butter?"

He'd slathered it on like icing a cake.

She snorted. "I think that's enough butter for at least two pieces."

"Too much, huh? Sorry. I'll scrape some off and use it on the other piece."

"Nothing to be sorry for. We're both figuring this cooking thing out."

"I'm glad for that. I don't know if I could do this on my own."

She took the bacon out of the pan and put it on a plate. "I was just thinking that earlier. Life really is easier when you have someone to do it with."

A knock at the door interrupted the cooking.

"I'll get it," Eddie said.

He went to the door and opened it. "Hello."

"Hello," a man's voice answered. "I hope I'm not disturbing you."

Lexi looked over. The man's voice sounded familiar. It was the butler from Amelia Marchand's house. She went to see for herself. "You work for Amelia, don't you?"

"Something like that," the man replied.

"Beckett," Lexi suddenly remembered.

"That's right. Ms. Marchand would like to see both of you in an hour. Is that convenient for you?"

Eddie looked at Lexi. She shrugged. "I think we can make that."

"Excellent. The driver will be here to pick you up then."

Lexi crossed her arms. "What's this about?"

"I'm only the messenger, miss." He touched his forehead with two fingers. "Have a good day."

He jogged down the steps.

Eddie shut the door. "What do you think she wants?"

Lexi chewed her bottom lip. "I have no idea." She held up her hands. "I haven't touched another meridian line, I swear."

"I know you haven't. Otherwise, you wouldn't have attempted to *cook* breakfast." He exhaled with his teeth clenched. "Maybe this is about me."

Lexi frowned, almost amused that he'd think such a thing. "Why would it be about you?"

He looked away. "After you fell asleep last night, I went out again. Looking for another meteor. I was hoping I could get one and bring it back to you. I didn't, obviously. But I walked through a lot of neighborhoods. It's possible someone saw me and ..." He shrugged.

"You think someone recognized you? Eddie, I never saw you as the monster, but there's no way you resemble him now. You look completely human. A very large, very muscular human, but still not a monster. Not by any stretch of the imagination."

He nodded but looked unconvinced. "I guess we'll find out in an hour."

CHAPTER THIRTY-FIVE

The ride to Amelia Marchand's had just begun, and it already seemed too long and too short.

Eddie's nerves were getting the better of him. His mind, all too good at coming up with worst-case scenarios, had already imagined he was about to be banned from Shadowvale. Cast out for the safety of its citizens. Exiled in the name of peace.

Would Lexi come with him? He had no right to ask that of her. In fact, if she was smart, she'd break all ties with him and protect herself. He wouldn't blame her. She really didn't know the kind of terror he'd caused once upon a time.

He stared out the window and sighed. In short, he was miserable. He'd had very little appetite, which had only made him feel worse since Lexi had gone to so much trouble to make them breakfast. She'd done a good job, too.

Her small hand covered his, causing him to look at her.

She smiled. "I really don't think this is about you. And if it is, she probably just wants to see you again. Maybe get to know you. She told me herself she likes to meet all the newcomers to town whenever she can."

"Really?"

Lexi nodded. "Her tiger will probably be there too, just so you know."

"The tiger seems all right." Eddie sat back and tried to relax. Could that really be all this was? An introduction? Seemed too simple an answer to him.

The car pulled up the drive. The Marchand estate was impressive, which did nothing to quell his anxiety. Amelia was clearly a woman of means and power. If he really was being kicked out, would that affect Henry in any way? Eddie hoped not. He'd given Henry enough grief over the years.

The driver stopped in front of a pair of large double doors, mostly blue glass but mottled so they were hard to see through.

The doors opened, and the same man who'd come to the house that morning stepped out, walked to the car and went around to the other side to open Lexi's door. "Welcome back to Indigo House."

"Hello, Beckett," Lexi said.

Eddie opened his own door. He'd never been in a house like this. He stood in the driveway staring at it. He hoped he didn't accidentally break anything.

Beckett accompanied Lexi to the front doors. "If you'll follow me, I'll take you in to the sitting room."

Eddie went after Lexi. She paused so he could catch up and walk beside her. "Some house, isn't it?"

He nodded. "I've never seen anything like it before."

"I have." She winked at him like this was no big deal to her.

For some reason, that calmed him a bit. Maybe because if she could be at ease in a place like this, then why couldn't he?

Except she wasn't about to be sent packing.

If that was his fate, he resolved right then and there to go with dignity. To prove Amelia Marchand's assumptions about him wrong as much as he possibly could.

Beckett ushered them into another incredible room. "Your guests, Ms. Marchand."

Amelia was sitting by the fireplace, which crackled with small flames. The French doors were open to let in fresh air, bringing in the scent of flowers and earth. On the patio beyond sprawled her tiger, who appeared to be sleeping. She closed the book she'd been reading and set it on the side table, which also held a cup of tea. "Thank you for coming on such short notice."

Lexi nodded. "How could we not? We're very curious as to why you asked us, as I'm sure you can imagine."

"I'm sure. Please sit." Amelia gestured toward the seating area, which held two big couches that paralleled each other and another chair that matched hers. "It's nothing bad, I assure you."

Eddie had his doubts. He took the couch across from her, which allowed him a view of the garden. Lexi sat next to him. Beckett, he noticed, remained by the door.

"Would you like something to drink?" Amelia asked.

Eddie shook his head. He didn't want to take anything from her. "No, thank you."

"Nothing for me either," Lexi said.

"If you change your mind, let me know." Amelia gave a little nod to Beckett, who then left. She returned her attention to Eddie, studying him with blatant curiosity. "Nice to see you again. My, you are a large fellow. You used to be Dr. Henry Jekyll's monster, is that right?"

His pulse increased. This was it. He braced himself and nodded. Lying would serve no purpose. "I was. Yes."

"Until Lexi used her magic to free you from the tree."

"That's right. Then she used more magic to save me from a lightning bug attack in the Dark Acres. That magic completed my transformation." He hoped she understood what that meant. That he was no longer that monster.

Amelia nodded. "Quite an impressive feat. Using magic that way, I mean." Her gaze shifted to Lexi. "There aren't many who can control magic that easily or direct it with such finesse. And using it to transform one being into another..."

Her brows lifted as she continued. "But it wasn't hard for someone with your extraordinary abilities. You are a very powerful creature. Possibly more powerful than even I am."

"I was," Lexi corrected her. "No longer."

"I beg to differ. Your magic may be depleted, but you are still that creature. If your magic was restored today, your abilities would return full force, would they not?"

Lexi nodded. "They would."

Eddie no longer understood where this was going.

"Then to me," Amelia said, "you remain that creature. But that isn't relative to why I asked you to come here today. The reason for that is I would like you to teach me to cast the beacon spell you used last night."

Lexi looked confused. "I'm flattered you'd ask me, but that's sylph magic. Only a sylph can create one."

Amelia sighed. "I thought as much. Nothing I could find in any of my books or my years of experience has shown me anything like what I saw last night. It was remarkable."

Eddie sat back, satisfied at last that this really wasn't about him.

Amelia sipped her tea. "I suppose I have a favor to ask of you then."

Lexi seemed a little surprised by that. "I'm not sure what I could do for you, but please, ask."

"Cast a beacon spell for me tonight."

Lexi's eyes narrowed. "I would be happy to, but I don't have the magic to do that."

"What if I give you the magic?"

Lexi's brows lifted. "Then I could do it. But can I ask why?"

"So you agree that if I give you the necessary magic, you will cast a beacon spell for me this evening?"

"Yes, I will. But again, can I ask why?"

Eddie was pretty curious himself. The meteor shower

was over. What could Amelia think she was going to catch?

Amelia held her teacup with both hands, looking over its rim at them. "You must both swear secrecy upon your own lives and your life here in Shadowvale. Do you so swear?"

Interesting turn, Eddie thought. He nodded. "I swear."

"So do I," Lexi said.

Amelia set her cup down. "The Aerarii meteor shower didn't end last night. Tonight is actually the last night."

Eddie glanced at Lexi, who looked as puzzled as he felt. "But the paper said three days and last night was the third."

"Because," Amelia said, "that's all the information I gave the paper. I did that as a safeguard so that I would have one more chance, without competition, to get the magic I need. If I wasn't able to capture a meteor, which I wasn't."

She fussed with the strand of pale blue faceted beads around her neck, making them sparkle in the light. "I realize it was a bit disingenuous, but you saw how many went into that forest to get a meteor."

"I did," Lexi said, her tone a little strident. "I wasn't able to get one myself."

"Well, you did," Amelia corrected her. "But you very generously gave it to Mr. Campbell."

"We found one in the Dark Acres, too," Eddie said.

"But she had to use that magic to save me from a lightning bug attack.

Amelia's brows arched. "Both truly selfless and wonderful acts. But it was the first that gave me the idea to approach you about this. The truth is, I need you to do more than just set up that beacon."

"Oh?"

Amelia nodded. "Once the meteor is captured, I would like you to use that magic to transform Thoreau the same way you transformed Edgar."

Amelia looked out at the tiger, who hadn't moved since they'd arrived. "There is more to him than just a great cat, but you touched him. I'm sure you felt that. If you could sense it in a tree, you could sense it in him."

"I did," Lexi answered.

Eddie watched Lexi closely. She dropped her gaze to stare at her hands. Was she upset? It was hard to say. She seemed to be working hard to control herself.

"One more night," Lexi said softly. She took a breath, then looked up. "You're asking a lot of me."

"I know," Amelia said. "But you may be Thoreau's only hope. Please. It would mean a great deal to me. I will be in your debt, and I always pay my debts."

Eddie wasn't sure what that meant, but this wasn't his choice to make. This was for Lexi to decide.

For a few long seconds, Lexi said nothing. Finally, she nodded. "I'll cast the spell for you, but I need a few things in return."

Amelia leaned back and smiled. "I'd expect nothing

less. I'll give you whatever you want, but you cannot ask for a meridian line. I've already told you they're vital to the town. You must also *promise* to use this magic as we've discussed."

"I promise."

"Good. What do you want?"

"Edgar and I need jobs. Decent paying jobs that will allow us to make a life for ourselves. We could also use some cash."

"I'm sure the jobs can be arranged, and I can give you ten thousand in cash. Will that do?"

Eddie did his best not to react. Ten thousand would help out a lot, especially if they were also guaranteed jobs. It had been a smart thing to ask for.

"That will do," Lexi said. "Thank you."

"All right. What else?"

"I want a little more magic than what the spell requires. Enough so that I have a small reserve just in case I need it to protect Edgar or myself. And I want it now, before we leave. Not right before I have to cast the spell."

Amelia smirked. "What assurances do I have that you won't take that magic and run?"

"What you're offering me is still a drop in the ocean compared to what I actually need. I won't go anywhere. Not without Edgar." She looked at him, taking his hand. "We've already decided to make our life here, haven't we?"

He nodded. "We have."

Lexi looked at Amelia again and gave her a slight smile. "In fact, we're adopting a cat. We wouldn't adopt a cat if we were planning on leaving."

"I should hope not." Amelia raised her finger and gestured to someone.

Beckett joined them with a large envelope, which he set on the table in front of them, then left again.

"Your cash," Amelia said. She inched to the edge of her seat. "But I'll need you to come closer to give you the magic."

Chapter Thirty-Six

Lexi vibrated with power. Amelia had been generous, understanding that a strong beacon required a significant amount. The feeling was wonderful, even if it was temporary and she couldn't use any. That part wasn't so wonderful, but at least she knew she'd be left with a small reserve when the night was over.

That would make it all worthwhile. Mostly.

"I wasn't expecting any of that to happen," Lexi said as she and Eddie walked into the Shadowvale Pet Rescue. Amelia's driver had brought them here. That was also something Lexi hadn't been expecting, but she'd given up trying to guess what was going to happen next.

A whole extra night of meteors. What were the odds that they might actually get one? Still slim, but it was something.

"Well," Eddie said. "You know what I was expecting. And that didn't happen."

"There's no way she'd get rid of you. She knows I'd go with you."

"But what about after she has her meteor? She won't need you anymore."

"No, but like she said, she'll be in my debt. We'll be

safe then. I promise." She put her hand on his arm. "You have nothing to worry about. Now, let's see about a cat."

They had nothing to worry about so long as Amelia got her meteor and Thoreau got transformed. But Lexi would do everything she could to make sure that happened.

Eddie smiled as they went up to the counter. Lexi greeted the young man working the reception desk. His name tag said Tim. "Hi. We're interested in adopting a cat."

"Welcome to the rescue. That's great. Are you Lexi Gardner and Edgar Hyde by any chance?"

"We are," Lexi said. "How did you know?"

"Amelia Marchand said you'd be stopping by. She's already taken care of the adoption fees, if you find a cat you like."

Lexi smiled. "That was nice of her."

"Very." Eddie leaned in. "Maybe we could see the cat you've had the longest. Or the one no one else seems to want. If you have one like that."

The young man nodded. "We do have one. He's a senior, nine years old. Still has a lot of life left in him, loves to play, naps a lot too, so he's not over-the-top active, but you know how it is. People want kittens. Anyway, he's been here about ten months. Sweet guy. Total lovebug. Name's Rambo. I can bring him into Adoption Room Number One if you'd like to go in there and wait." He nodded at the door across the small reception area.

"Sounds good," Lexi said. They were really doing this.

Getting a cat. This was going to be interesting. She really hoped the animal liked Eddie. That was all that mattered to her. That he found the right animal for him.

They went into the adoption room. There was a bench against one wall and cat toys scattered on the floor. Posters on the walls touted the benefits of pets. She and Eddie sat.

"I can't wait," Eddie said softly, his eyes on the door.

She grinned. It was sweet how excited he was.

The door opened, and Tim came in with a lanky orange tabby in his arms. "This is Rambo. He has all his shots, and he's neutered. He's really good with people but not so great with dogs. He seems to like the other cats he's housed with just fine." He set Rambo down on the floor. "I'll let you guys get acquainted. If he's not right for you, we have a few other, younger cats."

"Thanks," Eddie said, but his eyes were on Rambo.

"Good luck." Tim shut the door.

"He's very handsome, isn't he?" Lexi said.

"Very handsome," Eddie agreed. "His eyes look a little sad though. I bet he's tired of being here and not having a home."

Lexi was starting to understand Eddie's desire to adopt a pet. She smiled at the ginger boy. "Hello, Rambo. How are you?"

Rambo looked up at them, then jumped onto the bench into the space between them and leaned up to rub himself against Eddie.

"Hi there." Eddie laughed and scratched the cat's back. "He's not shy."

"No, he's not." Lexi petted the cat's head. He gave off happy vibes, for the most part. She cupped his face in her hands. "What's going on with you, old man?"

The cat peered into her eyes. She shook her head. "His name isn't Rambo. He doesn't mind it, but he prefers Reggie."

"How do you know that?"

Lexi shrugged. "He told me."

"You heard his voice in your head?"

"Sort of. I didn't really hear a voice so much as his thoughts entered my thoughts. It's hard to explain."

"Is that one of your sylph abilities?"

She nodded. "Yes. I've always been able to sense what animals were thinking or feeling."

"That's really special." Eddie ran his hand down the cat's back. "Reggie it is. Can you find out if he'd like to live with us?"

She scratched Reggie under the chin. "What do you think, Reggie? Would you like to get out of here? Live with us? We don't have the biggest place, but there's room for you to run around. And you can be the only animal in the house, if you want."

"And we have windows for him to look out of," Eddie said. "Make sure he knows that. We could get him one of those cat towers so he could sit in it and see out the windows."

Reggie turned around and head-butted Eddie's arm, making a little chirping noise.

Lexi laughed. "He loves all of that. He would definitely like to come home with us. Being here is lonely for him, although he does like other cats, but all his friends have gotten homes. Also, he likes tuna."

Eddie picked the cat up and put him on his shoulder. "Then he'll get tuna. Do we have any?"

"I think we do."

Reggie rubbed his head against Eddie's face, making him smile. "Don't worry, buddy. You're coming with us." Eddie glanced at her. "Lexi, I already love him."

"So do I. Come on. Let's make it official and get him home."

Since everything was paid for, it only took a couple of minutes to fill out the paperwork. They used Eddie's cell phone number as the contact information. Then Tim gave them a cardboard carrier to take Reggie home in, along with a starter kit that included a catnip mouse and a few food samples.

Eddie carried Reggie while Lexi took the starter kit and Reggie's medical file. Amelia's driver hopped out to open the car door for them. "Ms. Marchand will be pleased you found a companion."

Eddie put the carrier in, then slid in after it. Lexi hesitated. "How long do we have you for?"

The driver shrugged. "There was no time limit. Is there somewhere else you need to go?"

"We need some things for the cat. Do you know a place?"

He smiled. "I do. I'd be happy to take you there."

By the time they arrived home, they had a supply of cat food, wet and dry; litter; a litter box; a cat tower, which Eddie would have to put together; some cat toys; a cat bed; little clippers especially designed for trimming cat nails; and a pet brush. The pet store in town was well stocked. Although not as much now as before they'd gone in.

They thanked Amelia's driver, then Eddie gathered into his arms all the bags and the big box that contained the cat tower, while Lexi carried Reggie and his file. The cash from Amelia was tucked into her purse. They'd spent a little of it getting the cat supplies, but those had all been necessary.

The rest of the money they'd be very careful with. She'd get rent from the pub every month, too, but a lot of that would have to go toward expenses, so she didn't want to rely on it. She hoped the promised jobs came soon.

She unlocked the door and stepped out of the way so Eddie could get everything in.

He set the big box down, then closed the door. "Did we buy too much stuff for him?"

Lexi shook her head. "No. He needs all of that."

Eddie smiled. "I think so too. I'll get the tower put together right away."

She crouched down next to the carrier. "Thanks." She

opened the top of the cardboard carrier. "All right, Reggie, you're home. Have a look around."

His orange head popped out, and he cautiously took a look.

"I hope he likes it here," Eddie said.

Reggie let out a little meow and hopped out of the box.

Lexi stood. "I think he does. I'll make us some sandwiches for lunch. We only have a few hours before we have to meet Amelia again."

He set the rest of the bags down. "Are you going to be okay with all of this? Having all that magic just to give it away again?"

"It will be hard. But hard things are often the ones most worth doing, right?" She smiled at him.

"Right."

She'd been trying not to think about giving the magic up. "And anyway, I have to be okay with it because I don't have a choice. But it's what's best. Doing this will help us both out. It means we have no worries about staying here and we'll have jobs."

They might have boring, unmagical lives, but at least they'd be together.

"If you're not happy about it, it's okay to complain to me. I know it's going to be hard for you. You don't have to pretend otherwise."

She went into the kitchen while Eddie got to work constructing the cat tower and Reggie, after a good snoop around, decided to oversee the work on his new headquarters.

Sandwiches were pretty easy, but they couldn't live on those alone. Or could they? She was getting the hang of breakfast. And pasta was now learned. Were those plus sandwiches enough? Maybe it was to begin with.

Eddie stood the tower up, but before he could move it, Reggie jumped onto the middle shelf. He laughed. "He likes the tower."

"That's great."

With Reggie still on it, Eddie slid the carpet-covered edifice over to the windows. "There you go, Reggie. Now you can survey your kingdom, inside and out."

Lexi added chips to the plates, then took the sandwiches to the table. Eddie joined her, but as they were about to eat, his phone buzzed.

He looked at the screen. "Text from Henry. He and Izzy want us to come over tonight for dinner." He glanced at Lexi. "What should I tell him? We swore to Amelia not to say anything about what was happening tonight. But I don't want to not give him a reason either."

Lexi thought for a second. "Could we just say we're tired and ask if tomorrow night is all right instead?"

"I hate lying."

"So do I. But we can't tell him the truth. We promised. And this isn't something we can screw up."

He held out the phone to her. "Can you answer his text for me?"

She nodded. *Can we do tomorrow night instead? We're tired and looking forward to a night in.*

She showed it to him before she hit send. "Is that okay?"

He nodded and picked up his sandwich.

She hit send, then put the phone down on the table between them. She took a bite of her sandwich.

Then the phone rang.

Chapter Thirty-Seven

Eddie looked at the screen to see Henry was now calling him. "I should take this."

Lexi nodded. "It's okay."

He picked up the phone and answered it. "Hello, Henry."

"Hey, Edgar. I know we were texting, but I thought it might be easier just to talk to you."

"It is. Texting is hard for me. My fingers are too large for the screen. Lexi had to send that for me." He left the table and walked over to the cat tower. Reggie was lying on one of the carpeted shelves, peering down at the street.

"I hadn't thought about that. You should get a stylus."

"A stylus?"

"It's like a pen but with a rubber tip that you can use in place of your finger. I've got a few lying around. I'll give you one when you come over."

Eddie petted Reggie's back. He was so soft. "Thank you. So tomorrow night is all right then?"

"It's great. I should have known you'd be tired. Three nights of being up until dawn can do that to you."

Eddie was glad he hadn't been forced to tell an elaborate lie to Henry. "Aren't you and Izzy tired also?"

"We are, but we took today off to do nothing but sleep." Henry laughed. "It was nice, actually. We haven't had a day like that in a long time. Maybe not ever. The cats were thrilled to have us home with them all day."

"You have cats?"

"Yes," Henry said. "Two Flame Point Siamese. Saffron and Clementine. You'll meet them when you come over. You're all right with cats, aren't you?"

It was Eddie's turn to laugh. "Very okay. Lexi and I adopted one today. He's a handsome orange boy named Reggie."

"Outstanding. Did you get him from the Shadowvale Pet Rescue?"

"We did."

"Great place. That's where I got the kittens for Izzy. But besides dinner, I wanted to talk to you about something else."

"Oh?" Henry's voice had taken on a more serious tone. Eddie wasn't worried, but he was instantly curious.

"Do you have any of my memories? I ask only because I have some memories of when you were ... in control. For lack of a better term. So I was wondering if the opposite were true."

"I don't think so," Eddie said. "Although I do seem to know some things that must have come from you. Random scientific things. Like all of the periodic table of elements."

"As it happens, that's exactly what I wanted to know. I've already mentioned that I would like to do some brain scans on you to compare to the ones I did previously, but I am in need of a research assistant. Now that we're no longer a part of each other, I've been able to shift the focus of my research significantly. Izzy helped me for a while, but she's busy with her own business, and having someone who generally understands what I'm doing would be invaluable. What do you say? Are you interested? It pays well and comes with full benefits since your employment would actually be through the hospital."

Eddie didn't know what to say at first. Was this Amelia's doing? "Are you sure you want someone like me in your lab? I'm a large person, Henry. I might be too big for the space."

Henry laughed. "Edgar, I'm not a small man myself. I think you'd be fine. You could start right away if that helps make the decision."

He needed to know more. "Have you been looking for a research assistant for a while?"

"I've wanted one for a while and put the request in a few months back, but it just got approved today. I was going to tell you at dinner tonight. Couldn't wait."

Maybe it was Amelia's doing then. "Are you sure I'm the right person for this job? There must be better-qualified candidates."

"I don't know how anyone could be better qualified than someone I used to share a brain with. Anything you don't know, I'm willing to teach you. What do you say, Edgar? Will you at least think about it?"

"I will. It's a generous offer, and I could use a job. One thing, I go by Eddie now. Trying to distance myself from who I used to be."

"I get that. Eddie it is. And if you have any questions about the job, just ask. You know how to reach me. Or we can talk tomorrow night. Seven p.m., okay? I'll text you the address."

"Sounds good." He walked back to the table. "Thanks." He hung up and sat down.

Lexi was almost done with her sandwich. She looked up. "Did I hear right? He offered you a job?"

He ate a chip. "He did. Said the hiring request just got approved today. I don't know if that was Amelia or not, but the timing sure is interesting."

"What kind of a job is it?"

"Research assistant. Working with him, obviously."

"Are you going to take it?"

Eddie took a bite of his sandwich and thought about that as he chewed. "I don't get the sense that he's offering it to me out of pity. And he said it paid well and had good benefits. Those are probably important, right?"

"Sure. That would cover things like medical expenses. Maybe even dental too."

He thought some more. "How would I get there? The hospital isn't that close."

"We could get a car."

"Do you have a license? I don't."

"No. Never needed one." She ate the last chip on her plate. "What about a bike?"

He slanted his eyes at her and tried not to laugh. "I don't know if they make a bike that can hold someone my size. And even if they did, I don't know how to ride one."

"I'm sure they make bikes for bigger people. And it's not that hard. Even I know how to ride a bike. It's fun. I'll teach you. In fact, we could both get bikes. Then we could go places together. We have the money. Bikes would be a good investment."

He liked the sound of them going places together. "That could be a solution. I need to think about the job. I never pictured myself in that kind of work. I always thought it would be something physical. Hauling stuff. Or digging ditches."

"Well, Henry wants you for your intelligence. That's a pretty nice compliment."

Eddie nodded. "It is. I just need to get comfortable with it, I guess."

Reggie hopped down and trotted over to see them. He jumped up onto one of the other chairs at the table and meowed, making them both laugh.

"What's the matter, Reggie?" Eddie asked. "You want a sandwich too?"

Lexi let out a little gasp as she flattened her palm on the table. "We never put out food or water for him. Or his litter box. Poor cat must think we're terrible parents. Hang on, Reggie. We'll get you fixed up."

"You want help?" Eddie asked.

"No, I've got it. You eat." She got up and went into the kitchen to get bowls.

While she took care of Reggie's needs, Eddie ate and thought. Lexi had called them parents, which made him smile. Terrible parents, but she was making everything right.

How could he turn down a good-paying job when he had two mouths to feed? Two beings to take care of?

He'd call Henry back and take the job. And pray Henry didn't decide he'd made a mistake.

CHAPTER THIRTY-EIGHT

As Lexi and Eddie walked through the forest, she worked through her mixed feelings about this evening. She wanted the magic. That wasn't something she'd ever turn down. It felt fantastic to have that within her again. But she didn't like that it was just temporary.

She also didn't like that she was about to get another huge influx of magic, only to give it away again. It wasn't because she resented where it was going. She'd be happy to make things right with Thoreau, whatever that meant. She always loved helping animals. Her displeasure came from what a torment it would be to hold that magic so briefly.

She would mourn the loss of it. She knew that. It would take her a day to get over it. Not because she was petty or small-minded. Her body would react to having it and losing it so rapidly. She would need to sleep and recover.

And then somehow pull herself together enough to be sociable at dinner the next night with Henry and Izzy.

Being a human was hard on so many levels. She'd never understood that until now. Maybe that was her lesson to learn from all of this. A deeper understanding of the species she shared the planet with.

She found a feather on the forest floor and added it to her bag with the others. She and Eddie had left early to meet Amelia so that Lexi could collect everything she needed to cast another beacon spell. It took time to do it right, and she could not afford for anything to go wrong with the spell.

"How about this?" Eddie said. He held up a smooth white rock. "Looks like a good one to me."

Lexi nodded. "That will do nicely. If there are more, grab them."

He bent to pick up another one, then brought them over and put them in her bag. "What else do you need?"

She looked at everything that had been collected. "A few more feathers wouldn't hurt. I still need cobwebs and ferns, but I'll collect those last. The ferns work best when they're fresh. How far are we from where we're supposed to meet her?"

They were near the stream again. His gaze followed it. "We're maybe a ten-minute walk. As long as we're by the stream, you should have no trouble finding ferns."

"Let's head toward the meeting site, then. It's going to take me a while to set this up."

When they were just about there, she found the ferns and cobwebs she needed and added them to her bag. The sky was almost completely dark. Stars had already begun to gleam in the purpling sky, but the phosphorescent moss provided an adequate amount of light.

Time to start constructing the beacon.

A sense of sadness came over Lexi. She didn't try to fight it. Her spirit knew that the magic within her was about to be gone. Again.

Better just to feel what she needed to feel and deal with it than to pretend she was all right. She wasn't. But she would be. Being around Eddie, and now Reggie, made being sad nearly impossible.

Eddie moved closer, watching as she carefully set each piece into place as she created the patterns that would fortify the beacon's magic pull. "Those look like Fibonacci sequences."

She looked up. "What does?"

"The patterns you're making. They're beautiful."

She smiled. "They're a form of cosmic magic. Or they will be when I charge the spell with the magic Amelia gave me. Like calls to like."

As she was fixing the candle in the center, Amelia arrived with Thoreau and Beckett. Amelia greeted them with a nod. "You were prompt. I'm glad to see that."

Lexi straightened to look at her. "Did you think I wasn't coming?"

Amelia arched one eyebrow but didn't answer the question. Beckett had some kind of contraption slung over one shoulder on a strap. He pulled it off and opened it up. A chair made of canvas stretched on a metal frame.

He put it down, and Amelia sat in it. Thoreau settled beside her. Beckett leaned against a tree.

With the magic in her, Lexi could sense death about

him again. What a curious thing. But she didn't have time to ponder that. She had to prepare. She put the finishing touches on the beacon. Adjusted a rock so the smoother side was up. Turned a feather another centimeter left. Small but important corrections. Once that was done, she stepped back. All the beacon needed now was to be charged.

She walked over to Amelia. "It would help if I could get a read on Thoreau. Get a sense of what's going on in him. Anything you can tell me about him would be helpful, too."

Amelia pursed her lips, and for a moment, Lexi didn't think she was going to say anything. Then she spoke.

"I have long believed that Thoreau has been bespelled so that he carries the soul and spirit of my beloved Pasqual. My magic was never able to confirm this. The magic that surrounds him is far too complicated. You've felt it."

Lexi nodded. "I have. It's strong and layered. That much I picked up on." It was a little dark, too, something Lexi had no explanation for.

"As have I. I've never been able to crack it, and to be honest, I was afraid to be too aggressive. Recently, however, an empath was able to read Thoreau and said it was as if two voices were trying to speak to her. To me, that confirms my suspicions. Pasqual has been imprisoned inside Thoreau."

Lexi narrowed her eyes. "Why would someone do that to Pasqual?"

"Revenge? Jealousy? To hurt me? Why does anyone do anything?"

That wasn't the kind of precise answer Lexi had been hoping for, but if Amelia didn't know, she couldn't say. Lexi stared down at the beautiful creature. "What if it's not Pasqual?"

Amelia frowned as if she refused to consider that. "It has to be. Why else would Thoreau come to me?"

Lexi could think of all kinds of reasons for that, but she kept quiet. "Just so you're prepared for a different outcome than what you want. If there's someone or something in Thoreau, I can bring it out and transform it to its true form again. But I can't guarantee that someone or something is going to be what you're hoping for."

Amelia lifted her chin, her mouth set in a firm line. "I will deal with whatever happens."

Lexi nodded and turned her attention to Thoreau. "Hello, handsome tiger. I'm going to touch you and send a little magic into you, all right? It won't hurt. But you might not like the way it feels either. I promise to be as gentle as I can be."

She put her hands on the big cat's face. His fur was impossibly soft. It made her think of Reggie, her own little house tiger. Animals were so pure and guileless. They didn't deserve to have bad things happen to them.

She sent a microscopic thread of magic into Thoreau, as small as she could manage. She didn't need an angry, snarling beast on her hands.

He whuffed softly, his eyes coming open to thin slits.

"I'm a friend. I promise. I'm here to help. You sense that, don't you?"

He whuffed again, and his eyes closed.

She widened the thread bit by bit, careful to do it with patience and fluidity. No sudden changes. It took some doing, but at last the stream was wide enough to read the animal. He was unsettled with his state.

Because he wasn't alone. The dark magic she'd felt belonged to another creature entirely. That creature had no real voice. It was so entwined in the tiger's own spirit that it merely existed. The tiger was the creature's prison.

She pulled the magic back until every bit of it had returned to her, then she let go of Thoreau and stood. She looked at Amelia. "What kind of being is Pasqual?"

"Vampire."

Lexi nodded. That could explain the dark magic she'd felt. Vampires didn't exactly give off warm, fuzzy vibes.

But there could also be something much more dangerous inside Thoreau.

"Well?" Amelia said. "What did you find?"

Lexi hesitated, but the sky was dark and full of stars. There was no time to do things delicately. "Thoreau is full of dark magic. That might be Pasqual. It jibes with the sort of magical signature vampires put off. It could also be the magic that was used to imprison Pasqual, or whatever being that is, inside Thoreau."

Beckett peeled off the tree and came forward, suddenly interested. "But?"

Lexi shot him a quick look. "But it might not be either of those. Dark magic could be all sorts of things."

"Speak in plain English," Amelia commanded.

This wasn't going to be well received, but it needed to be said. "Thoreau might be a Trojan horse. He may have been sent to do you harm. Not him specifically but what's inside him, because whoever sent him to you knew you'd sense the magic he's holding. Knew you'd dig until you found a way to release it. And that thing in him could be something very bad."

Fear and anger filled Amelia's sharp gaze. She stood up. "Pasqual has been trapped inside this animal. I know it. I can feel it. There's *nothing* bad in him or Thoreau. What you're picking up on is the dark magic used to bespell Pasqual. That's all."

Lexi understood. Amelia wanted the man she loved returned to her. Lexi just couldn't be sure that's who—or what—was trapped within Thoreau.

Beckett cleared his throat. "How bad is very bad?"

Lexi sighed and shook her head. "I don't know."

"Worst-case scenario."

Lexi answered plainly, hoping she was wrong. "A demon."

Beckett looked at Amelia. "If she's right—"

"She's not," Amelia snapped back.

Eddie came to stand beside Lexi. "Are you going to be in danger?"

"I don't think so. If the thing I release from Thoreau is out for blood, it won't be mine." She tipped her head at

Amelia. "It'll be yours. Although what it does after it gets your blood, I can't say. And I won't be able to stop it without magic."

Amelia sat back down, looking a little less sure of herself. "Then that's on me. If it's a demon, I'll deal with it." She steeled her face and glared at Beckett. "And if it gets the best of me, then you'll finally get what you came here for."

He nodded slowly. "I guess I will." He glanced at Lexi. "I've fought demons before. Not my favorite thing to do, but needs must."

"I'll help, too," Eddie said.

Lexi did not want him hurt. He might have some supernatural abilities like strength and speed, but she wasn't so sure how he'd fare against such an evil entity.

A shaft of light cracked the darkness above them, making all of them lift their eyes skyward.

Amelia spoke first. "Charge the beacon. The shower's beginning."

"Amelia," Beckett started. "I don't think this is a good idea."

"I don't care," Amelia said. She steadied her gaze on Lexi. "Whatever happens is on me. I'll make sure you're taken care of."

Lexi didn't know what that meant, but she'd already promised to capture a meteor for this woman. She wasn't one to go back on her word.

And she wasn't about to start now.

CHAPTER THIRTY-NINE

Every protective instinct in Eddie had stood up and taken notice at the word demon. If that was what Lexi was going to release from Thoreau, he would be ready. He would fight with Beckett to protect both women, but Lexi was his first concern.

He loved her. He would die for her, if it came to that. Without hesitation.

But he doubted the situation would deteriorate to that point. All he'd need to do was get hold of the demon long enough to snap it in half. That felt like a good plan. One he was very capable of carrying out. Possibly more violent than necessary, but he wasn't going to take chances when it came to Lexi's safety.

He stood nearby as she kneeled beside the beacon and charged it with magic. Once that happened, there was no going back.

Just like the night before, the elaborate creation she'd made of bones, sticks, feathers, ferns, rocks, and cobwebs came to life with an undulating blue-green light. It pulsed and swirled and twisted over the objects she'd used, gathering speed and strength until it culminated around the candle, joined with the flame, and sent a narrow jet of light straight up into the stars.

Lexi rocked back on her heels, hands flat on her thighs. She looked tired. Drained. "It's done."

Amelia got out of her chair and walked over to inspect the beacon. She studied it a while before saying anything, peering with keen interest at what Lexi had created. Amelia clasped her hands behind her back and looked slightly disappointed. "Sylph magic, through and through."

Lexi, still kneeling, glanced at her. "Hoping to figure it out for yourself?"

"Hoping to at least learn a few things about it." Amelia shook her head and sighed. "But it's too complex for me. It's truly beautiful, though. Your magic is more than impressive. It's humbling."

Lexi took a deep breath, making Eddie think she was either trying not to say what she was thinking or looking for the right words. "Thank you. Perhaps now you can see why it's so hard to lose it."

"I never doubted that." Amelia's gaze followed the line of magic into the heavens. "How long will it take to draw a meteor in?"

Eddie went over to Lexi and offered her a hand. She took it and allowed him to help her up. "I don't know. You gave me a significant amount of magic, so this is a stronger beacon than what I set up last night. I'm hoping the meteor comes quickly after that."

He knew what she really wanted was a chance at a

meteor for herself, if possible. He hoped so. But he expected she'd be tired after this was all said and done.

"I'm hoping that, too," Amelia said. She looked over her shoulder at Thoreau, who appeared to be sleeping. "It won't hurt him, will it?"

"It won't be comfortable. And there's nothing I can do about that. Magic like this is intense," Lexi answered. "Ask Eddie."

Amelia made eye contact with Eddie.

He nodded. "It was rough. But worth it."

"Try explaining that to a tiger," Beckett muttered.

"The good news," Lexi said, "is that if I do pull a demon out of Thoreau, he won't be in great shape. Not initially anyway. It's a little like a butterfly coming out of a chrysalis. There's an adjustment period. That will give us an advantage."

Amelia frowned. "There is *no* demon in Thoreau."

For once, Eddie hoped Lexi was wrong about that. He wanted Amelia to be happy. He wanted her to be pleased with what Lexi had done. It was their best chance at getting to stay here. He also didn't want any of them to get hurt.

Beckett strolled over, hands in his pockets. "I think you're going to get a chance to find out very soon." He tipped his head back. "Look."

High up, so high it seemed beyond the stars, a pinpoint of light was making its way toward them.

As they watched, it got bigger and streaked closer to the beckoning thread of magic. Right before their eyes, the magic latched onto the point of light and began to pull the meteor toward them.

"It's like a tractor beam," Beckett said.

"It is," Lexi agreed. "Amelia, get ahold of Thoreau. We don't need him running off right now if he gets spooked by the meteor."

"He won't go anywhere." But Eddie saw that Amelia crouched beside the tiger and took a firm grip on the scruff of his neck.

Eddie touched Lexi's arm and whispered, "Are you ready for this?"

She shrugged, then nodded. "As much as I can be."

Light filled the sky, growing brighter and brighter as the meteor drew closer.

Beckett shook his head. "There's no way people in town aren't going to notice this."

Amelia frowned. "I realize that. But by the time anyone ventures out this way, hopefully we'll be done." She raised her brows and tipped her head in Lexi's direction. "You will work fast, won't you?"

"I'll try. But magic can't always be rushed. You know that."

Amelia sighed and returned to watching the meteor, but she squinted immediately. It was too brilliant to look at, and a second later, it completed its trip to earth, landing dead center in the beacon.

"This is it." Lexi rubbed her hands together as she gazed at the source of so much magic. "Bring Thoreau closer if you can."

Eddie ignored Amelia and the tiger. He only had eyes for Lexi at the moment. She spread her fingers as she approached the meteor. It washed her in red and purple arcs of light, casting its glow on the surrounding woods.

The sharp scent of ozone permeated the air. This was the biggest meteor he'd seen so far. Was that because the beacon had been more powerful?

Lexi kneeled down and flattened her hands over the meteor's surface, sucking in a breath the moment she made contact. The light traveled up her arms. Her head lolled back, eyes closed in a rapturous expression. Inch by inch, her body absorbed the power that the meteor had gathered.

Finally, the meteor was depleted. It went dark. But Lexi radiated power. Slowly, she opened her eyes and got to her feet, a halo of soft light surrounding her from head to toe. She turned toward the tiger.

Eddie stayed a few steps behind her. He wanted to be as close as possible in case she did release a demon, but also because she might need him.

Amelia stared in wonder. Her eyes reflected the pulsating magic. "No human could hold that much power and live."

The tiger picked up its massive head and squinted at Lexi. Thankfully, it didn't seem frightened or wary.

Lexi smiled at the tiger. "Hello, my handsome friend. I'm going to help you now. Stay strong. Everything I'm about to do is for your good." She reached toward Thoreau but spoke to Amelia, keeping her tone just as light and even as it had been when talking to him. "Amelia, you need to let go of him and get a safe distance away. Now."

Amelia released Thoreau's scruff and pushed to her feet. Beckett came to her assistance and helped her move back.

Then Lexi took a breath. And laid her hands on the great beast.

The radiance that enveloped her traveled down her arms, through her hands, and onto Thoreau until they were both swathed in it.

The tiger lifted his head and flexed his paws so that his giant talons dug into the earth. He let out a low growl, teeth bared.

"It's all right," Eddie said in a soft, firm voice. "I know what it feels like. It's not nice. But I went through it too."

Thoreau snarled and tried to pull away from Lexi. She grabbed his fur and held on.

Concerned for Lexi, but also wanting this to go right for Thoreau and Amelia, Eddie went closer. "You can do this, Thoreau. Don't fight it. Just give in and let it happen. The sensation isn't going to last forever."

Another low growl was followed by an uncertain whuff, then Thoreau's eyes rolled back in his head, and he collapsed onto his side.

A sharp crackle of power shot out of Lexi and rippled through the forest in a wave of brilliant, electric green. After that, a deep, sudden blackness fell. Eddie could feel it on his skin, heavy and clammy, like fog.

The darkness clung with an uncomfortable stickiness, but after a second or two, it lifted. Eddie's eyes adjusted to the return of the ambient light from the stars and moon and the phosphorescent moss.

The first thing he saw was the tiger, still on his side, still out cold. Then next to him, a pale, naked man slumped prone on the forest floor.

Chapter Forty

Amelia took a hesitant step forward to see better, but her heart understood what was happening even if her brain was undecided. Then her brain caught up.

"Pasqual!" She ran to him, falling to her knees at his side. She cradled his head in her lap, brushing the leaves from his hair and skin as she rained kisses on his brow. "My darling, my beloved. Speak to me. Are you all right?"

His cheeks were hollow, his body angular with visible bones, and his skin was as pale as fresh snow, but she'd know his darkly handsome face anywhere. This was Pasqual. The man she'd created this town for. The only man she'd ever loved. "Please, my love. I need to know you're all right. Can you hear me? Just give me a sign."

When he didn't respond, she kissed him again, brushing his hair off his forehead even as her tears covered his face. His eyes moved behind his lids, proof of life, even if he was unconscious. She hugged him closer, trying to warm him. Her beloved had returned. She'd been right about Thoreau.

Thoreau. She looked up.

Only a few feet away, Thoreau lay motionless. Amelia couldn't bear the thought that her precious tiger had paid the price for Pasqual's release. "Beckett, please," she cried out. "See to Thoreau."

Beyond Thoreau, Edgar held the sylph tenderly in his arms like a small child. Concern furrowed his brow and clouded his eyes.

Amelia frowned. Lexi couldn't be hurt. She couldn't. Amelia owed her everything. She managed to catch Edgar's gaze. "Is she all right?"

His expression didn't change, and he never once took his eyes off of Lexi when he answered. "She will be. She's strong. But not having magic makes her weak."

Amelia nodded. "I understand."

Finally, he looked up. "You owe her. What she did for you did this to her." Then he bent his head to Lexi again and began whispering softly to her.

Edgar was right. Amelia owed the sylph. Far more than she'd paid. Amelia would do something to make it right. Thomas had already given her an idea. She just had to determine how it might work. And then bring it to fruition.

Movement on her lap. Pasqual stirred. His lids fluttered open. "A-Amelia?"

She nodded, her throat constricted with emotion. "Yes," she managed. She swallowed. "Yes, my love. I'm here." More tears fell.

He shivered.

She eased him to the ground again and ripped off the woven silk duster she'd thrown on over her caftan. She draped it over him, tucking it around his body. "I should have brought a blanket. How are you feeling?"

"Unwell." He grimaced, bearing the small points of his razor-sharp fangs. "What ... happened?"

She shook her head. There was too much to explain now. "You were taken from me, but now you're back. I'll tell you more later. You need blood, don't you?"

He sighed and made a small movement that she interpreted as a nod.

"As soon as I can get you home." Although she wasn't sure how that was going to happen. Would he be able to walk? She had no idea.

The crunch of leaves snagged her attention away. She glanced toward the sound. Thoreau's head was up, and he was trying to sit. Beckett was petting his head and speaking soft, soothing words to him.

Lexi was moving now too. Edgar was helping her to stand. She kept a tight grip on his arm and gestured toward Amelia. Edgar nodded, and together they made their way over. Lexi looked down at Pasqual. "That's him?"

Amelia nodded.

"I'm glad I was wrong."

"I am, too," Amelia said. "Thank you. Thank you for bringing him back to me. I will never forget this. What you did."

"He needs blood," Lexi said. "I don't know much about vampires, but I know that. Give him your wrist. If he tries to take too much, Eddie will stop him."

Amelia nodded. She should have thought of that. She was too overcome by emotion to think straight. "Pasqual, did you hear? Take my wrist." She pulled the sleeve of her caftan back. "Drink what you need so we can get you home."

She pressed her skin to his mouth. With weak hands, he took hold of her arm. The pinch of pain that followed felt like bliss to Amelia.

Her beloved had returned. Nothing else mattered.

He drank, but there was none of the desperation she expected. He seemed too weak, but slowly his color improved. It would be a while before he was himself again, she imagined, but that was fine. They had time. She would do whatever necessary to make him well again.

She kept watch over Pasqual. "Beckett?"

"Yes?"

"How's Thoreau?"

Finally, Pasqual released her arm and lay back, eyes closed. The puncture wounds on her wrist sealed over and disappeared. She looked up as Beckett answered.

"He seems to be all right. Animals are resilient." He rubbed the tiger's head. Thoreau was sitting upright but looked tired. She understood completely. She was exhausted. Filled with more joy than she thought she could hold, but exhausted.

She exhaled, trying to find her second wind. "I'm so glad to hear that. We should get home. Can you get the car any closer?"

They'd brought the Mercedes G Wagon, a beast of a vehicle capable of going off-road. And with enough space to hold a tiger in the back so long as the last row of seats were down, which they were since that was how Thoreau had traveled here.

Beckett nodded. "I'll do my best." He grabbed the folding chair, then looked at the tiger. "Come on, Thoreau. We'll get you settled in the back."

He and Thoreau left, leaving her and Pasqual with Edgar and Lexi. "Would you two like a ride? It might be tight, but I'm sure we can manage."

Lexi shook her head. "We're staying. I'm not missing my last chance to get the magic I need." She glanced at the sky. "Thank you, though."

"All right. I wish you luck. We'll talk soon, I'm sure. Thank you again. I really can't say that enough." She put her hands on the ground to push herself up.

Edgar appeared at her side, hand out.

She took it and let him pull her up. He assisted Pasqual to his feet next. Pasqual pulled the duster on, wrapping it around himself.

Edgar took a look in the direction Beckett had gone. "Do you need help to the car?"

"No, we'll be fine. Beckett will be along shortly. Thank you," Amelia said. Beckett would drive in as much as he could, then come get them. She smiled at Edgar. "Very kind of you to offer. Have a good night."

"You too," he said.

She turned her smile to Pasqual. "I already am."

CHAPTER FORTY-ONE

Lexi had no real game plan other than watching the sky and hoping they got lucky. She couldn't be bothered to come up with anything more than that. She was out of magic, save the smallest reserve, nearly out of energy, and once again feeling like she'd lost everything.

She hadn't. She knew that. She still had Eddie by her side, and that was huge, but in the moment, it wasn't enough to shake the grief of having held all the magic she'd needed only to give it away. Again.

"Which direction do you want to go?" he asked.

"Doesn't matter. I just think the odds of another one coming here are zero."

"Agreed. Should we just walk until we find a good spot?"

She nodded, trying to pretend like everything was fine. "I liked when we sat by the tree. Something like that again would be good."

It didn't take them long to locate such a spot. It was on a small rise, too, which gave them a nice clear view of a large section of sky.

Eddie settled down first, then she sat next to him,

leaning on him. She let out a soft sigh, happy to be resting.

"I know you're tired," he said. "You've already had a big night."

"That's for sure."

"What you did for Amelia ... that was a *lot*."

"It was." It had been so hard. But it had been the right thing. Thoreau and Pasqual were now free of the spell they'd been under.

"But it was worth it," Eddie added.

He was right. She took a breath and made herself acknowledge that. "Yes. Means our future here is secure. And with you working for Henry and whatever job I end up getting, we should be in good shape." She clung to that belief, because she needed it to be true.

Having all that magic, being temporarily whole, only to lose it again, had gutted her. She hated that she felt like this again. Like life as she knew it was over. Even if that was true and she was on the path of a new life, being okay with that again was going to take some doing.

She'd anticipated these feelings, but knowing they were coming and actually experiencing them were very different things.

She tipped her head back, eyes on the sky.

The next thing she knew, Eddie was gently shaking her. "It's going to be morning soon."

She came wide awake instantly, a sense of panic like a dousing of cold water. She looked up. Clouds were already rolling across the gray sky, and there wasn't a star to be seen. "What? I slept? Why did you let me sleep?"

"It's okay. You didn't miss anything. If I'd seen a meteor, I would have woken you up sooner, but I didn't. Just one that looked like it wasn't going to land anywhere around here. I just thought we should go home. Reggie's been all by himself for a while now."

She slumped back down and nodded. She felt like crying. She'd slept through her last chance. Even if Eddie had been watching, what if she'd seen something he hadn't? She inhaled, the air shuddering into her lungs. There was nothing she could do about it now. "Right," she whispered. "Home."

He helped her up. She collected her bag, and they started walking. When they breached the line of trees just before the road, a familiar sedan sat parked on the shoulder.

Thomas got out and opened the rear passenger door. "Thought you two might be headed out about now. Can I interest you in a ride home?"

That act of kindness nearly did Lexi in. She couldn't speak or the tears would come. She just nodded and climbed in.

"Thank you," Eddie said.

"Anytime, son." Thomas got behind the wheel and drove them to the apartment without saying another word.

They arrived home under full cloud cover, the gloom brightening a little more with each passing minute.

Lexi opened the door to get out but then reached through to the front seat and squeezed Thomas's shoulder. "Thanks."

"You're welcome."

She dug into her pocket and pulled out the little carved tortoise he'd lent her. She handed it back. "It worked. Just not for me."

"Sorry about that, Miss Lexi."

"It's okay." He was such a good man. So thoughtful. And that thoughtfulness had made her feel a small bit better. She put her hand back on his shoulder for a moment longer, then slid out and started up the steps, Eddie behind her.

She opened the apartment door, and Reggie came running, meowing as he ran. She laughed. Any other response was impossible. She scooped the cat up and hugged him, burying her face in his fur. "Hi, baby. I'm so glad you're here."

Eddie closed the door before putting his arms around both of them. "Today, we'll just rest." His stomach rumbled. "And eat."

She smiled. Something about being home and Reggie's welcome had soothed another part of her soul. She looked up at Eddie. "I'm hungry too."

Eddie's brows lifted. "You are?"

"Pretty sure Reggie would like something to eat also."

"You take care of him, and I'll see what we can make for breakfast."

"Deal." She kissed Reggie's face, then set him down

and went into the kitchen after Eddie. "Don't you have to meet Henry at the hospital?"

"Yes, but I'll call him and let him know it won't be until later."

She got Reggie a dish of tuna cat food. He must have smelled it, because he got excited as soon as she opened the can. He was bobbling back and forth, shifting his weight from side to side. She laughed again at his antics. "It looks like he's dancing."

Eddie glanced over. "Maybe he is."

She put the dish down, and Reggie went straight at it.

"Eggs and bacon again? With toast?" Eddie offered.

"Sure. Might as well learn how to do that well before we branch out."

"Maybe for our next thing we can learn to do pancakes."

"That sounds good. But complicated."

He smiled as he put a pan on the burner. "We're smart. We should be able to figure it out."

She loved his confidence and optimism. "You mind if I take a quick shower?"

"Go ahead. I can handle breakfast."

"Thanks." She grabbed her pajamas and went into the bathroom. She turned on the water and waited for it to get hot, then she stripped down and climbed in. She stood under the spray, eyes closed, and let it beat on her.

She willed the hot water to take away all the sad feelings that still remained. Her life was going to be fine.

Different. But fine. She would adjust and adapt. And she wouldn't have to do it alone.

She could have stayed under the water for a long time, but she knew Eddie wouldn't eat without her. Reluctantly, she soaped up, rinsed off, and got out. Once she was dry, she put her pajamas on and wrapped her damp hair in a towel.

The bacon smelled good. She went out to find the table set and the plates ready. Eddie was in his seat, and Reggie was in another of the chairs.

Eddie shook his head at the cat. "You had your breakfast."

She smiled. "Maybe he wants bacon."

"Is that all right to give to cats?"

"I think it would be. It's just meat." She took her seat. "Thanks for doing this."

He broke a little piece of bacon off and gave it to Reggie. "You're welcome. I called Henry. Told him we had a long night that we'd explain over dinner and asked if I could come to the hospital tomorrow instead. He said that was fine."

"But we're still on for dinner?"

"Right."

She picked up a slice of toast. "Then after this, we're sleeping. And you are *not* going to be on the couch."

He looked like he wanted to argue that, then thought better of it.

Satisfied, she ate her breakfast. Reggie got two more little pieces of bacon before it was over.

They cleaned up the kitchen. She brushed her teeth, then turned the bathroom over to Eddie so he could shower. Reggie went back to his cat tower.

She collapsed into bed, her eyes closing instantly. She dreamed of magical forests and Reggie, who'd become the size of a tiger. Eddie was at her side, and in the dream, everything was perfect and happy, and tiny, magical meteors drifted into her hands like snowflakes.

Movement woke her briefly. Eddie had closed the blinds, but there was enough light to see him passed out on the other side of the bed.

The movement came from Reggie, who was on his back between them, stretched out as long as he could be, eyes closed, and looking very much like he was grinning.

Maybe he was having the same dream.

She closed her eyes and went back to sleep, a smile on her face, too.

CHAPTER FORTY-TWO

Despite her fatigue, Amelia sat at Pasqual's bedside. She'd put him in the room that adjoined hers. The two master bedrooms had been designed with the intent that they'd be shared exactly like this.

Perhaps not exactly like this. She'd never imagined he'd be taken from her only to be returned frail and nearly decimated. Never imagined she'd have to nurse him back to health. She would, of course, and she'd do it to the best her abilities and pocketbook would allow. Thankfully, her funds were in no danger of depletion.

Once they'd gotten home, she had Beckett bring him here. She washed him as best she could with a basin and a washcloth, then dressed him in silk pajamas and tucked him under the covers. He was skin and bones. A shell of his former self.

She'd wept the entire time she ministered to him, her heart broken over what had been done to him. What he'd been made to endure.

She studied his face, still handsome even in his condition, and wondered how this would shape things going forward. The horror of it all was behind them, but she had not yet overcome the feelings it had left her with. She doubted he'd be rid of them easily either.

Whoever had done this to him must be made to pay. Death might be too kind. She was angry in a way that only marginally paralleled what she'd felt when she'd first realized Pasqual was gone.

That anger had dissipated quickly, however, because she'd known in her soul that he would never leave her voluntarily. She'd been right about that.

Beckett came in through the small sitting room, silver tray in hand. On top of it was a single bag of red liquid. "The blood you ordered arrived. I thought you'd want it brought up right away."

"Yes, thank you."

"How's he doing?"

"About the same." He'd been asleep since before they returned home. "I hate to wake him, but the blood will help. He needs it."

Beckett nodded and held the tray out to her. She took the blood. He tucked the empty tray behind his back. "If you want me to contact the Thibodeauxes …"

"No. Not yet. He won't want anyone seeing him like this." She held the blood in her hands. Body temperature. It had either been delivered warm or Beckett had seen to that. Probably Beckett's doing. For all his purpose and prickliness, he was also a kind and caring man. When he wanted to be.

"They are his family. Distant, I know, but relations all the same."

"I realize that, but not yet. Maybe in a day or two." Pasqual had always been a proud man. Most vampires shared that characteristic. He would want to see his family at some point, she knew that, but she also knew he'd be horrified to have anyone see him in his current state. "Make sure word of Pasqual's return doesn't get out yet, would you? Send a note to Edgar and Lexi, too. He doesn't need visitors until he's better."

"I'll take care of it. Do you need anything else?"

She shook her head and held up the bag. "No. Thank you for this. How's Thoreau?"

"Sleeping on the rug in the great room."

That rug was silk, an antique from Northern India worth more than her Rolls-Royce. She smiled to think of it as Thoreau's bed. Good for him. He should be comfortable. "Did you light a fire in the fireplace for him?"

"I did."

"Make sure he gets steak for dinner."

"Cook is carving up a standing rib roast for him."

"Perfect. That will be all."

Beckett gave a little bow, then left.

Amelia set the bag on her lap, then took Pasqual's hand. "Pasqual, my darling, wake up. You need to feed again." She shook him, gently. Startling a vampire awake, especially one in such delicate condition, was a risky move.

His eyes slowly came open. The deep brown irises flecked with amber honey had no vibrancy.

She smiled in spite of how his appearance made her

heart hurt and held up the bag. "I have what you need. And there's more downstairs."

He reached out for it. "Thank you, my love."

"Do you need help?"

"I believe I can manage."

She gave him the bag. "I will do everything in my power to see you right again." That included making sure nothing like this ever happened again.

He maneuvered the bag to his mouth and drank directly from it, draining it in a short amount of time. When he was done, she took it from him and carried it to the bathroom trash. He was still awake when she got back, so she sat on the bed again.

"Did that help?"

He nodded. "Yes. But I'll need a lot more."

"You want another? I'll have it brought up."

He put his hand over the covers on his stomach. "No. Something tells me to go slowly. But maybe in another hour or so."

"All right."

His lids were heavy, but he fought it. "Have you slept?"

"Just a little. I'm fine." She'd napped in the chair near the bed but only for about half an hour. She couldn't bear not to watch him. To be sure he was all right. She'd dreamed while she'd slept, and it had been about him. It hadn't been a happy dream.

He managed a little smirk. "You're still a bad liar, I see."

She pursed her lips. He was definitely feeling a little better. "Don't worry about me. You should try to sleep some more."

"I will. But first, tell me what happened."

She didn't want to. Not yet. She feared it might anger him into action, and he was in no condition to do anything but stay in this bed and heal. "Soon. We both need to rest. That must come first."

He took her hand. "I missed you so much. I knew I was imprisoned, but I had no idea how or why or when it would be over. It was like ... a very long, very bad dream. And I am thrilled to be awake again."

"I missed you more than I have words to express. Having you here with me is everything I've been hoping for." She lifted his hand to her mouth and kissed it. "We have a lot to talk about. And we will, soon. But you have to get better first."

"I will. I can already feel my strength returning. Tell me. How long have I been gone?"

She hesitated. "Years, my love."

His mouth went slack and fell open as his expression changed to one of shock and dismay. *"Years?"*

She nodded. The time they'd lost hurt. He might be immortal, but she was not. He had to know by looking at her that she'd aged.

"Have you been here all this time? Waiting for me? Did you know what happened to me? Where I was?" He tried to sit up.

She pushed him down, and it was easy enough that

she knew he still had a ways to go before he was himself again. "Pasqual, please don't get upset. You don't have the strength or stamina to be agitated right now. Forget the past until you're better. We have all the time in the world to talk about it, all right?"

With a frustrated sigh, he fell back to his pillow. "Who did this to me? Tell me that much."

She wished she could. She shook her head. "I don't know. I was hoping you'd be able to tell me that."

He shook his head. "My memories are all a dark, muddled mass. I know we both have enemies, but for one of them to do this ..."

She forced her anger down so it wouldn't show. She made herself smile. "You're home now. And you're safe. Shadowvale is my town. Nothing happens here that I don't know about and cannot control. All you need to worry about is healing. I love you, sweetheart."

"I love you, too."

She sat with him a while longer, until his eyes closed, and she sensed he was sleeping again. She straightened the covers around him, then thought about returning to the chair and sleeping a bit herself.

She stood, about to move, then changed her mind. She lay down next to him, her head beside his on the pillow, her hand holding his, and closed her eyes.

She would never be without him again. And anyone who attempted to take him away from her would sorely regret it.

Chapter Forty-Three

Eddie woke up before Lexi. He did his best to be quiet so she could sleep longer. Reggie was next to her on his side, one leg stretched out over her arm. It was very cute.

With a smile on his face, he slipped out of bed and went to look at his clothing options. He wasn't sure what to wear to dinner at Henry's.

A quick double knock at the door put an end to the quiet. Lexi stirred. Eddie hurried to the door before whoever was out there knocked again.

He opened it and found a teenage boy holding an enormous bouquet of flowers in a vase and wearing a T-shirt imprinted with the name and logo of Best Blooms, a florist in town. He swallowed as he looked up at Eddie. "Delivery, sir."

"Thank you." Eddie took the flowers.

The kid took off down the steps.

He shut the door and turned to put them on the kitchen counter.

"Who sent those?"

Lexi was awake. He twisted back around. "I don't know."

She was sitting up in bed, holding Reggie like a baby. Reggie was pawing at her hair. "Is there a card? There is. I can see it. The flowers are beautiful."

Eddie brought the bouquet to her so she could pluck the card out. "I was trying to let you sleep."

"It's okay. We have to get ready for dinner soon." She kissed Reggie on the head, then let him go so she could open the card. She read it out loud. "A thousand thanks for bringing Pasqual back to me. Please don't let anyone know he's here yet. He needs time to recover. I'm sure you understand. We'll speak soon. Until then, my eternal gratitude, Amelia."

She looked at Eddie and shrugged. "I wasn't planning on telling anyone."

He lifted one shoulder. "I kind of figured we'd tell Henry and his wife. That would be okay, don't you think?"

"Sure. Unless they want to rush over there and see him, which they probably won't. She just doesn't want him bothered until he's feeling better. I get that. Although Henry is a doctor. But whatever."

Reggie jumped down and went to his food bowls. The one with dry food in it was mostly full, but the one with wet food was empty. Eddie picked that one up. "This cat eats a lot."

"He probably didn't get much wet food at the rescue. He's just making up for what he missed out on. Plus he's kind of skinny. He can eat all he wants."

Eddie looked at the cat. "Is that right, Reggie? You didn't get much wet food before?"

Reggie sat in front of his dining area and let out a sad little meow.

Eddie laughed. "Okay, you don't have to ask twice." He went to get a can. "Lexi, what should I wear tonight?"

Lexi got out of bed. "I'll pick something out for you. We're going to need to do laundry soon. Good thing I bought detergent." She gave him a curious look. "Any chance you know how to do laundry?"

He shook his head. "I take it you don't either."

She laughed. "Not a clue. You think we could get Thomas to show us?"

"Probably. Or maybe Henry can show us tonight."

"You're assuming he knows how. If that's true, shouldn't you remember?"

"Good point. I don't really understand why I know some things and why I don't know others. Mostly I seem to share his scientific knowledge. Which is why he thinks the job as his research assistant will work for me."

She blinked. "The job. Did you go?"

"No, I called him and said tomorrow would be better. He was good with that."

She nodded and looked relieved. "Smart move."

They got dressed for dinner. Eddie in tan pants and a navy sweater. Lexi in a black skirt and pale gray top and mossy green cardigan. She made sure Reggie had plenty of food, water, and a clean litter box, while Eddie called Thomas for a ride.

He gave them a big smile when he arrived. "How you two doing?"

"Good," Eddie answered. "How are you?"

"I'm fine, just fine. You're all dressed up. Where you going?"

"To Dr. Henry Jekyll's house for dinner."

Thomas nodded. "What are you bringing?"

Lexi looked at Eddie, and he looked at her. He returned his attention to Thomas. "Are we supposed to bring something?"

"Someone invites you to dinner, it's not polite to show up empty-handed."

Lexi grimaced. "We didn't know that."

"It's all right. Just get in," Thomas said. "We'll make a quick stop and you'll be all fixed up."

He took them in the opposite direction to a place on Main Street called Black Horse Bakery and parked alongside. "Just as I suspected."

"What's that, Thomas?" Lexi asked.

"Usually by now, the bakery's closed. But they aren't." He shook his head, chuckling softly. "Gotta love this town. Now listen, everything in there is free. Not sure what they'll have left this late in the day, but I'm sure they'll have something you can take. Maybe not a cake but cookies at least."

Eddie nodded at Lexi. "You pick it. You have better taste than me."

She smiled. "That's not true. But I'll go get something." She hopped out and went in.

Eddie leaned forward. "Thanks for the help, Thomas."

"That's what friends do."

"Any chance you could show us how to do laundry?"

He chuckled. "That's really my daughter's department. But I can ask her."

"I don't want to bother her. Just writing the instructions down would be good enough."

"I'll see what I can do."

"Do you know where in town I could buy a bike? Something sturdy enough to hold me?"

Thomas frowned at him through the rearview mirror. "What do you want a bike for?"

"I got a job. Working for Henry at the hospital. Research assistant."

Thomas smiled. "Well, how about that. What time do you have to be there?"

"Nine a.m. I start tomorrow."

"I'll be by at eight thirty."

"I wasn't asking for a —"

"You don't need to."

Lexi got in with two boxes. The smaller one she handed to Thomas. "This is for you. Chocolate pecan pie. The woman behind the counter said it was your favorite."

He nodded. "She's right about that. Did you get one too?"

"No, I got a seven-layer raspberry dream cake."

"That sounds pretty good too." He put the pie box on the seat next to him and pulled back onto Main. "Nice selection in there for so late in the day. When they'd normally be closed. Funny how that works out."

They chatted while he drove them to Henry's.

It was a big white brick house with black shutters and a red door. Lots of yard around it, too. Not as big as Amelia's mansion, but hers was probably the biggest one in town. The house next to Henry's was a little smaller but just as pretty. It had a For Sale sign in front of it.

"Nice place," Thomas said as he pulled into the drive. "They can't have lived here long. This used to be the Shoenfelds' house, but I'd heard they moved. Guess Dr. Jekyll bought it."

"I guess so," Eddie said. "Thanks for the ride."

"You bet. Call me when you're ready to come home."

"Thanks." Lexi hoisted the cake box. "We will. Have a good night."

"You too."

They got out of the car and went to the front door, but a pretty brunette opened it before they could knock. Delicious, savory aromas wafted out, garlic and spices and the tang of tomatoes.

"Izzy," Eddie whispered.

She smiled. "That's right. Do you remember me?"

"I ... I think I do." The memories were hazy, but small snippets seemed to get clearer as he looked at her. "Are you all right with me being here?"

She laughed. "Yes, of course. I'm thrilled you're here. I'm thrilled at how all of this has turned out. Come in. You must be Lexi."

"I am," Lexi said. "This is for you." She handed Izzy the box. "Raspberry dream cake."

"Oh," Izzy cooed. "Black Horse Bakery is amazing. Thank you. We will definitely have this for dessert. I attempted a chocolate cake, but between us, it looks a little dry, so this is perfect. I'll stick this in the fridge in a second. Henry's in the living room. I'll show you."

Izzy led them in. "We just moved in about six months ago, so the decorating is a work in progress, but we're getting there."

"Looks wonderful to me," Lexi said.

Izzy led them to a blue and white room with big, oversize furniture and a large screen television. Henry stood there, looking genuinely glad to see them. "Welcome. I'm so glad you came. I hope you're hungry. And also that you like Italian. Izzy made lasagna."

"Sounds great," Lexi said. "Eddie and I have a long way to go when it comes to cooking, so a homemade meal of any kind is a treat."

Henry nodded. "I'm not that great in the kitchen either." He winked at Izzy. "Thankfully, Izzy's got it handled."

Izzy smiled. "I do my best. I'll go put this cake in the fridge and be right back." She headed out.

"Henry, I know you can't cook," Eddie said. He added a smile. "Because I can't cook either. I seem to be lacking in a lot of basic skills. Like how to do laundry and how to pick out what to wear. Lexi does that for me."

Henry snorted. "So does Izzy for me if we're going

anywhere important. As for laundry, Izzy can give you the basics, if you want. Can I get you something to drink?" He went over to a bar cart loaded with options. "Water, plain or sparkling; soda; red wine; beer; coffee; tea ..."

"Water," Lexi said. "Sparkling, please."

Eddie nodded. "Plain water for me."

Just then, two beautiful cats came running through, one chasing the other. Izzy came in after them, shaking her head and smiling. "Those two hooligans are so naughty. They're just showing off because we have company."

"They know exactly what they're doing," Henry said as he filled two glasses with ice, then water. "Those are our cats I told you about, Eddie. Saffy and Clemmy."

"We love cats," Lexi said.

Henry's brows rose in question. "Eddie mentioned you adopted one. How's that going?"

"Great," Eddie said. "We adopted an older cat. He'd been at the rescue the longest. An orange one named Reggie. Well, the rescue called him Rambo, but he told Lexi that wasn't his real name and he preferred Reggie. So that's what we call him."

Henry and Izzy both looked at each other, then at Lexi, but Izzy spoke first. "You adopted a talking cat?"

"Not exactly," Lexi said. "I can sort of communicate with animals."

"She can read their thoughts," Eddie said proudly.

"In that case," Izzy said, "Lexi and I need to talk."

CHAPTER FORTY-FOUR

Lexi carried her sparkling water in as she followed Izzy to the kitchen. It was a beautiful space done in dark wood floors, light granite counters, and cobalt blue cabinets. The rectangular island in the center held a big bowl of artfully layered salad. Next to it was a basket lined with a white linen towel. The smell of the food made her mouth water. "What can I help with?"

Izzy shook her head. "I just have to take the lasagna out and stick the garlic bread in for a few minutes to warm up." She put oven mitts on. "What I really want help with is Saffy and Clemmy."

"What's the problem?" Lexi sipped her water. The fizz was refreshing.

"Nothing yet, and that's how I'd like to keep it." She opened the oven and got the lasagna out, then put in a foil-wrapped loaf of bread. She closed the oven door before turning to Lexi. "Henry and I want to start a family, but we're wondering how the cats will take it. They're spoiled rotten and basically treated like our kids. We think they might get jealous if our attention suddenly shifts."

Lexi nodded. "And you want me to see what they think about it?"

"Yes. Could you? Is that a weird thing to ask?"

Lexi set her glass down on the counter. "No, not at all. I think it's nice that you care about the cats' feelings. Animals are more sensitive than most people realize."

"Yes, they are. You're absolutely right." Izzy leaned near the sink. "I can't understand their thoughts, but I'm an empath, so I can usually sense what they're feeling."

Lexi laughed. "You're an empath?"

"I am." Izzy got a strange look on her face. "Is that funny?"

Lexi quickly shook her head. "No, not at all. I only laughed because there's a chance we're related. Somewhere way back in the annals of time. I'm a sylph, which is a very old and, these days, rare being. But being an empath means there's sylph blood in your lineage somewhere. That's where your gift comes from."

Izzy's mouth came open. "Seriously? That's kind of amazing. So your kind is responsible for my powers? I've always wondered."

Lexi nodded. "Yep."

"That means," Izzy went on, "we're probably cousins of some sort? Many times removed."

"There's a strong possibility."

"That is so cool. I don't have a lot of family." Izzy made an odd face. Like family gave her bad memories. "Anyway, maybe we could get together sometime. Just you and me for lunch or something. I'd love to get to know you better."

"Sure," Lexi said. "I'd like that, too." Having friends was never something she'd cared about, but now that she was essentially human, she did. She felt the need for friends. And being part of the community would make life easier for her and Eddie. Not only that, Izzy was a sweet person. "How about after dinner I have a chat with the cats and see what they think about having a baby brother or sister?"

"I'd love that." The aroma of garlic and butter filled the kitchen. Izzy looked at the time. "That bread should be about done. I just need to put it in that basket, then we're ready to eat. Want to help me carry a few things to the table?"

"I'd be happy to."

Together they took the lasagna, garlic bread, and a large bowl of salad out to the table in the dining room. An arched opening adjoined the living room where Henry and Eddie were deep in conversation about something scientific. They looked very serious.

Izzy stood under the arch. "Okay, boys, get your drinks and come in. It's time to eat."

Henry and Eddie came into the dining room, glasses in hand. Henry kissed his wife on the cheek. "Smells great."

"It does," Eddie said. "I can't wait to dig in."

Lexi put her hand on Eddie's arm as she spoke to Izzy.

"Fair warning. He has a large appetite, so if you were hoping for leftovers, you might not get them."

Eddie nodded. "She's right. I eat a lot. But I'm not that hungry."

Izzy laughed. "I'm fine with no leftovers. And Eddie, I expect you to eat all you want. I made a big pan of lasagna so no worries there, all right?"

Henry nudged Eddie. "I had a feeling you'd want at least seconds, so we're good."

They all took seats, Henry and Izzy on one side, Eddie and Lexi on the other. Izzy helped herself to salad, filling the small bowl next to her plate, then she passed the big bowl to Lexi.

The cats zipped through the room but going the opposite direction this time, making them all laugh.

"Those two," Izzy said.

Henry cut the lasagna into squares and served it. He put two pieces on Eddie's plate. "How's that to start with?"

Eddie nodded. "That's great. Thank you."

Henry put a piece on Lexi's plate next while he continued to talk to Eddie. "Excited about starting work tomorrow?"

Eddie spread his napkin on his lap the same way Lexi was doing. "I am. Nervous too. I hope I live up to your expectations."

Henry slid a square of lasagna onto Izzy's plate, then put one on his own. "Based on our conversation in the living room, I'm not worried about that at all."

Izzy passed the garlic bread around next. "Lexi, are you looking for a job too?"

"Yes." She hesitated, having almost said that Amelia was supposed to be finding her one, but that would lead into why, and that might mean telling too much. "Do you know of anyone who's hiring?"

Izzy shook her head. "Not that I know of, but I was thinking about your ability with animals. That seems like a pretty valuable and useful skill. I'm sure there are people who'd pay for your assistance with their pets. I get hired to read pets all the time. Your ability would be even better." She drizzled Italian dressing on her salad. "You know, I once helped Amelia Marchand with her tiger. Do you know who she is?"

Lexi glanced at Eddie. He'd stopped eating and was looking back at her. So Izzy was the empath Amelia had hired.

Henry reached for his drink. "I take it you know Amelia then. Doesn't surprise me. She tries to get to know anyone new to town, and I'm pretty sure that applies to both of you. Technically."

"We've met," Lexi said as she forked up a bite of lasagna. "But we can't say more than that. Yet." She sighed. "Sorry. I don't want to keep anything from you, but we were made to swear."

Clearly amused, Henry went back to his salad, spearing a hunk of tomato. "That sounds exactly like Amelia. Did it have something to do with the meteor shower? Never mind, I'm sure you can't answer that."

"I can't," Lexi said. She ate the lasagna. It was delicious and cheesy and quite possibly one of the best things she'd eaten. Could she ever learn to make something like this? She gestured at Henry. "But I will say this. You're a good guesser."

Henry chuckled.

Izzy leaned forward. "Did you get to meet Thoreau?"

Henry cut his eyes at her. "Iz, they swore not to talk about it."

Lexi smiled. "He's really something, isn't he?"

Eddie frowned. "Lexi."

Lexi held her grin as she looked at Izzy, who just smiled right back. "I'll have you know that sylphs and empaths are related, so Izzy and I are probably cousins, and family doesn't keep secrets. However, we did swear not to speak about it, but as soon as we can, we will."

Henry looked back and forth between the two women. "Could you really be related?"

"Yes," Lexi said. "Izzy being an empath means she has a sylph relative somewhere in her family history."

He seemed fascinated. "I could run a comparative DNA test. See if you are related and if so, how closely." He looked at Eddie. "This might be a good thing to get you started on. This is exciting."

Eddie nodded. "It is."

"I'm game," Izzy said.

Eddie glanced at Lexi. "What do you think? Do you want to see if you and Izzy really are related?"

Lexi took a breath and thought about it. Family. *Actual*

family. It was an exhilarating proposition. "What would I have to do?"

Eddie shrugged. "Just a cheek swab." He looked at Henry. "Right?"

"Right," he answered. "That's it. We can do it in the lab. Won't take a minute."

That seemed easy enough. Lexi smiled at Eddie. "I guess I'm coming in to work with you tomorrow."

CHAPTER FORTY-FIVE

After dinner, Eddie and Henry were sent back to the living room. Eddie felt like he should help clean up, but Izzy had shooed him and Henry off good-naturedly, making it plain they weren't needed. Lexi had stayed, already laughing with Izzy like they had a private joke between them. Izzy promised to show Lexi how to operate the washer and dryer, too.

The women seemed to be getting along very well. He was happy about that. Lexi could use a friend.

Henry took a seat in the big leather recliner. Eddie opted for the couch. Henry rested his hand on his stomach. "That was good. I ate too much, but it was hard to stop."

"It was very good." Eddie'd eaten four pieces in total, plus two bowls of salad and three slices of garlic bread. He could have had a fifth piece of lasagna, but he knew there was dessert. "Is that lasagna hard to make? Do you think Izzy would teach us?"

Henry smiled. "I'm sure she would. As for how hard it is, I have no idea. Seems complicated to me, but then again, what do I know? Hey, how are you getting to work tomorrow? You got a ride here, didn't you?"

Eddie nodded. "That was Thomas. Sunshine Cab. He's bringing me to work too."

"Does that mean neither you nor Lexi have a car?"

"We don't. No licenses either." He shrugged. "I don't know how to drive. I'm not sure if Lexi does. I'm going to get a bike. We both are. Lexi says they make them with heavy-duty frames for people like me."

Henry laughed. "I'm not sure there are any other people like you. But listen, if you want a vehicle, it's not hard to learn to drive, and as long as you didn't take it outside of Shadowvale, I don't think you'd really need a license. We don't have any police. Just peacekeepers. And they aren't going to be concerned about something like that. So long as you aren't racing through the streets."

Eddie thought about that. Having a car would be good. For both of them. Walking was fine, but not when it rained. And they couldn't rely on Thomas forever. That wasn't fair to his business. "Is there a vehicle I would fit in? Comfortably, I mean."

"You're a big guy, but absolutely. You might like a pickup truck. Those tend to be a bit roomier than the average car. Or maybe an SUV. That would give you some room too."

"Thomas could probably teach me."

Henry shrugged one shoulder. "Or I could. I'm sure you'd fit into my Land Rover."

"You'd teach me to drive?"

Henry nodded. "Yes. If you want me to. I'd be happy to do it."

"You would?"

"Yes." Henry's eyes lit with a glint of emotion Eddie couldn't quite read. He leaned forward, elbows on his knees, and knit his fingers together. "I don't know how else to say this except to put it in plain language, but I've sort of started to think of you like a ... brother. I hope that doesn't put you off, but that's how I feel. Like I have a responsibility toward you."

Eddie didn't know how to respond. He'd never imagined Henry would look at him that way.

Henry seemed to take Eddie's silence as uncertainty. "I guess that's weird, right? Look, just forget I said anything."

"No." Eddie shook his head. "It's not weird. It's nice. And unexpected. But you really don't owe me anything."

"But I do. You wouldn't be here if not for what Izzy and I did to pull you out of me. Because of that, I survived and you ... you had to start over."

Eddie was eternally grateful for that restart. It had led Lexi to him. It had changed the path of his life. He cleared his throat softly. "You realize it could have gone the other way. I could have been the one that survived, and you wouldn't have gotten any kind of second chance."

"But that's not what happened. And now you're here and you've been reborn as this new person, and I have a lot of reasons to want to help you. I guess what I'm asking is ... will you let me?"

Eddie nodded, momentarily unable to speak. Then he found his words. "You're a good man, Henry. You didn't deserve the curse of me."

"You didn't deserve to be in that position in the first place. Didn't ask for it either. It's just the hand you were dealt."

Eddie couldn't argue that. He nodded in agreement.

Henry sat back. "The only thing we can do is move forward and make the best of it. That's what I'm trying to do."

"Me, too," Eddie said. "I'm happy for this new chance. I thought people would be afraid of me, knowing my past, but so far, it doesn't seem that's the case. At least not that I've heard about."

"Good." Henry smiled. "I never imagined we'd be here, but I'm glad we are. And I'm thrilled we're going to work together. My sense is our collaboration will move the research forward in unexpected ways. Tell you what. After work, I'll drive you home and we can take some back roads so you can try your hand at driving."

"All right."

Izzy and Lexi came in, each carrying two plates with a slice of raspberry dream cake and a fork on it. "Dessert," Izzy announced, "is served."

Lexi brought Eddie his plate and sat next to him. "I can't wait to try this. It smells great."

Izzy handed a plate to Henry before taking a seat in

the recliner opposite his. "And then afterwards, you're going to see what the cats think about a new addition to the family. Right, Lexi?"

Lexi nodded as she picked up her fork. "Yep."

A little twinge of worry pricked at Eddie. "I guess I should have asked this when you were talking with Reggie, but won't that mean using magic?"

She smiled at him. "No. Communing with animals is a basic sylph skill. Now if I were doing something to the animal like healing them, that would take magic. Talk, as they say, is cheap."

Henry laughed. "I guess that's truer than we realized. But let me get this right. Your magic doesn't automatically regenerate itself?"

"It does, but it's a very slow process and requires us to be in an area where magic already exists. It's never been a problem for me before because sylphs are born with so much magic, most never run out before they transition. By the time the magic starts to wane, most of us are already headed to our next plane of existence."

Eddie looked at her. "Did you change your mind? Are you leaving?"

"I was then," she answered. She smiled as she gazed into his eyes. "I'm not now."

Because she couldn't. She was out of magic. So what would happen when she got enough magic back? Would she leave him then?

"Hey," she said quietly. "Don't look so worried. I'm not going anywhere."

Henry made a happy noise. "Great choice on the cake, Lexi. This is really good."

"I've never had a bad thing from Black Horse," Izzy added. "But this might be a new favorite."

Eddie took a bite of his and nodded his approval, but he couldn't stop thinking about what Lexi had said. Of course, she wasn't going anywhere. She couldn't. But Shadowvale was a strange town. There was no telling what might happen tomorrow. Lexi might end up with more magic than she could use.

Would she change her mind about leaving if that happened? He didn't want to talk about it in front of Henry and Izzy, so he did his best to keep his mood light. But inside, he was worried.

What if she'd been so enthusiastic about adopting Reggie so that Eddie wouldn't be alone when she left? Did she think Reggie would make up for her leaving?

He started feeling sick to his stomach. He didn't want to be without her. He loved her. He'd already come to think of his life in terms of her.

He choked down his cake, nodded in response to the conversation, and made himself laugh when a joke was told.

Izzy stood to collect the empty plates. "I'll see if I can round those cats up and bring them in."

Henry got to his feet. "I can help."

In a matter of seconds, Eddie and Lexi were alone. He turned to her. "Are you going to leave me when you get your magic back? Tell me the truth. I need to know."

She smiled, cupped his face in her hands, and kissed him. "No, I'm not. I swear it on Reggie's sweet little soul. I love you. And him. Me leaving isn't something you need to worry about. Even if I do get some magic back. That will just make our lives better."

Eddie exhaled and bent forward to touch his forehead to hers. "I love you too. I was worried. I wouldn't blame you if you wanted more from your life than ... this."

She laughed and kissed him again. "This life is exactly what I want. I just never knew it until I met you."

CHAPTER FORTY-SIX

Lexi would have kissed Eddie some more, but Izzy and Henry returned, each with a cat in their arms. She would do her best later to further reassure him that she was exactly where she wanted to be. Right now, she had cats to talk to.

She held her hands out. "I have to touch them."

Izzy brought her a cat. "This is Clementine. Clemmy for short. She's probably the bossier of the two. Definitely the one in charge."

Henry rolled his eyes. "I'll say. She's the Amelia Marchand of cats."

They all laughed, Eddie included. He seemed to be doing better since she'd explained things to him.

Lexi petted the sweet little animal. "Hello, Clementine. You're very beautiful. Do you know that?"

Lexi smirked and looked at Henry and Izzy. "She knows that."

"That's Clemmy," Henry said.

Lexi went back to the cat. "Your people want to have a baby. It doesn't mean they would love you any less, of course, but a human baby needs a lot more attention than a cat. They're hoping you understand that and that you and your sister would love and protect the baby."

Lexi listened to the thoughts filling her head. Clementine's thoughts. She nodded a few times. "Mm-hmm. Yes, that's right. Okay. I'll tell them."

She gave Clementine a good scratch under the chin. "Clementine understands. She's a little worried something will change and you won't love her and Saffron as much. But she also said they would love the baby so long as the baby loves them."

Izzy put her hand to her mouth. "Oh, Clemmy. Nothing will ever change. Mama loves you and Saffy both. You were my first babies."

Henry looked a little misty-eyed as he petted Saffron, who was still on his lap. "We would absolutely raise our child to treat the cats with love and respect. All animals."

Lexi let Clemmy go and held out her hands for Saffron. "If I may?"

Henry brought the cat to her. "There you go."

Lexi repeated the same conversation with Saffy. Her thoughts were slightly different than her sister's. Lexi laughed. "Saffron is just fine with a baby so long as the child doesn't pull her tail. She also said more treats would help her adjust. More treats for her, fewer treats for Clemmy."

Izzy clicked her tongue and laughed. "Saffy!"

Eddie shook his head, grinning. "No playdates with Reggie for these two. They might give him naughty ideas."

"Speaking of Reggie, we should probably get home," Lexi said. She looked at Eddie. "You have a big first day of work tomorrow."

He nodded. "That I do. I'll call Thomas."

"That reminds me," Henry said. "I want to give you that stylus. I think it'll help you with texting on your phone. Hang on." He disappeared for a moment, returning with something that looked like a pen in his hand. "Here you go. Just use the rubber tip instead of your finger."

Eddie gave it a try and smiled. "That works very well. Thank you. I should be able to text now. I'll try it out by sending a message to Thomas to pick us up." He worked on his phone with the stylus. "There. Done. That was much easier. Thank you. And thanks again for dinner."

Lexi put Saffron on the floor and stood. "Yes, dinner was delicious. Some night you'll have to join us at the pub. We might not be able to cook, but we can still host."

"Hang on," Izzy said. "There's cake left."

"Please," Lexi said. "Keep a few slices for yourself. We can't eat all of that."

Eddie cleared his throat and raised his brows, making Henry chuckle. "You might want to ask him about that."

She smiled. "Okay, maybe he can eat all of it, but keep a few slices anyway."

"Yeah," Eddie said. "Definitely take some for yourselves."

Izzy soon brought the box out to them from the

kitchen. "Thank you so much. There were four pieces left, so I took two for us, okay?"

"Perfect," Lexi said.

"Thank you so much for checking in with our cats for us." Izzy glanced at Henry. "I feel like we can get serious about trying for a baby now."

He looked pretty pleased with that. "You won't hear me complain." He shook Eddie's hand. "See you tomorrow in the lab."

Eddie nodded. "Nine a.m. I can't wait."

He got the door for Lexi, and they went outside, still saying goodbye to Izzy and Henry.

Thomas pulled into the driveway as they were finishing up. He got out and opened the car door for them. He waved at Henry. "Evening, Dr. Jekyll."

Henry waved back. "Nice to see you, Thomas."

With a final goodbye, Lexi got into the car, carefully balancing the cake box. Eddie followed after her.

Thomas returned to his spot behind the wheel, and they were off. After a few minutes, he asked, "How was your night?"

"It was great," Lexi answered. She looked at Eddie for confirmation.

He nodded. "It was a very good night. Henry is a good man. And I like his wife very much. Henry's going to teach me to drive."

Lexi looked at him. This was the first she'd heard of it, but then she and Izzy had discussed some things she'd yet to share with Eddie. "He is?"

"Yes. He said if we get a car and only drive it in town, we don't really need licenses." He raised his gaze to Thomas. "Does that sound right to you?"

Thomas chuckled as he turned down the alley beside the pub. "I let my license expire almost fifteen years ago. No need for one in Shadowvale, unless you plan on leaving. Which I don't."

He parked by the steps leading up to the apartment. "See you in the morning, Eddie. You have a good night, both of you."

"Thank you and good night to you," Lexi said. She held the cake box in one hand and climbed out. She waited for Eddie to get out and then headed up the steps.

He pulled the apartment key from his pocket and unlocked the door. "That was a nice night, wasn't it?"

"It was. Our first big outing as a couple."

He grinned as he pushed the door open. "We're a couple. I like that."

"I like it too." She went in.

Reggie came running to greet them, meowing in his funny little way.

"Hi, baby." She put the cake on the kitchen counter.

Eddie picked Reggie up. "We met two other cats tonight. Girl cats. Very pretty."

Reggie was purring away and kneading his paws on Eddie's shoulder. He rubbed his face on Eddie's chin.

Lexi watched, amused. "I don't think he cares about girl cats. Just that his people are home."

"It's good to be home with both of you." Eddie looked at her. "You promise you're not going to leave?"

"I swear it." She came over to him and wrapped her arms around him. "No matter what happens. I'm here to stay."

He leaned down like he was going to kiss her when someone knocked on the door.

CHAPTER FORTY-SEVEN

Eddie frowned at the interruption but kissed Lexi anyway. "I'll see who it is. You take Reggie."

"Gladly." She scooped the cat out of his arms. "Are you hungry, baby? Let's go see what's in your dish."

He went to the door and opened it.

Beckett stood on the other side. "Sorry to come at such a late hour, but Amelia would like to see Lexi as soon as possible."

Eddie made no move to get Lexi. Instead, he leaned forward enough to see down to the street. A Rolls-Royce was parked there. "About what?"

"I'm not at liberty to say."

Lexi appeared at Eddie's side. "Amelia wants to see me?"

Beckett nodded. "She's asked that you come to her home immediately. I'm here to drive you."

Lexi crossed her arms. "I'm out of magic. There's nothing more I can do to help her or Pasqual. Or Thoreau. Not only that, but it's late and Eddie starts his new job tomorrow."

"The request was not for Edgar, only you."

She narrowed her eyes slightly. "I'm not going anywhere without him."

Eddie grinned.

Beckett sighed. "He is welcome to come, too, then. She thought you might feel that way."

Lexi shook her head. "Great, but I still can't help her. The whole out-of-magic thing, remember?"

Beckett momentarily clenched his jaw. "She doesn't need your help. Well, not exactly. She'd like to help you."

Eddie wondered if this was about a job. "Maybe we should go and at least see what she wants."

Lexi seemed to consider that, then she refocused on Beckett. "We'll come on one condition."

"And that is?" Beckett asked.

Lexi adjusted her arms, still crossed over her chest. "Tell me why you have the aura of death around you."

Beckett's mouth came open and he exhaled loudly, glancing toward the alleyway. "The things I do ..." He looked at her again. "I'm a reaper. Can we go now?"

She nodded. "Just as soon as I give Reggie fresh water. We'll be down in five minutes."

"Very good." Beckett headed back to the car.

Reggie didn't need fresh water, as far as Eddie knew. He shut the door. "Do you think it's about a job?"

"I have no idea, but if she wants my help again, I'm asking for more money and more magic. I don't mind helping, but if we're buying a car, the money we have isn't going to go very far."

"Good point. Also, you deserve something in return.

You're the one doing the work, after all." He looked at Reggie's water bowl. It was full.

"He doesn't need water," Lexi said. "I was just stalling. You think we should go and hear her out, right?"

"I do. Upsetting her is probably not a good idea."

"I agree with that." She stroked Reggie's back. He was sitting on the kitchen counter, but since Lexi was making no move to shoo him, Eddie didn't say anything either. "I guess we should go."

The ride to Amelia's didn't take long, and before he knew it, they were walking through the big house again and being ushered into the same sitting room. A fire crackled in the hearth. Thoreau was nowhere to be found.

Amelia was standing by the French doors looking out onto the garden. She turned when they entered. "Thank you for coming. I know it's late. I apologize for that, but the hour couldn't be helped. Please, have a seat. Something to drink?"

Eddie shook his head. "No, thank you."

"Not for me, either," Lexi answered as she sat on the couch. "We just came from dinner. We were about to get ready for bed. How's Pasqual?"

"He is doing much better. Thank you for asking." Amelia smiled briefly. "Again, I apologize, but I've been ... researching something, and the timetable for all of this has sped up unexpectedly."

Eddie sat next to Lexi. "The timetable for what?"

Amelia left her spot by the doors and sat in her chair

near the fire. She took a deep breath. "It's not often I don't know where to start, but there's a lot to tell you. I suppose I should just begin. I know you'd like to get your magic back. Or at least a portion of it."

Lexi nodded. "I would."

"I would very much like to make that happen for you in light of all you did for me." Amelia seemed to be searching for her next words. "You're aware that I know what you did for Thomas's daughter. Have you done anything like that before?"

"If you mean taking magic from another person, then yes. But it's not my preference. It can be hard on the person losing the magic, and the quality of the magic is often diminished. Pure magic, like what was in the meteors or what comes through the meridian lines, is always better."

"I can understand that." Amelia sat back and didn't say anything, again seeming to search for what to say next.

Eddie held his tongue. He was merely a spectator.

Lexi shifted, moving a little closer to him. "Is there someone you want me to help?"

Amelia looked frustrated. "Not *someone*, no. Rather, it's the town that needs help. After a fashion." She sighed. "Thomas gave me the idea. He thought that you might be able to help some of the more desperate cases in town by taking on their curses."

Lexi's brows bent. "I could. Curses are a form of magic. Dark magic." She gave a little shake of her head.

"Again, neither of those things would be my first choice. The dark magic or taking the magic from someone. But if there's someone in grave need, I could consider it."

Eddie had to say something. "But you said it was the town that needs help?"

Amelia nodded. "Do you know about the book in the forest?"

"We heard about it," Eddie said. "If you write your name in it, your curse goes away."

"That's right," Amelia said.

"Are you saying that's true? That such a thing exists?" Lexi asked.

"Yes to both of those questions."

"That's nearly impossible." Lexi frowned. "For that to be true, it would require some kind of magic receptacle to hold all of those curses. There's only a handful of containers I know of which are capable of doing that. Are you telling me you once had enough magic to create such a thing?"

Amelia laughed. "No. I never had that kind of magic. But I had enough to be put in charge of such a thing."

Lexi glanced at Eddie. He wasn't sure what they were talking about, but it seemed like something important was about to be revealed.

Lexi didn't speak for a few seconds. "I'm not sure what you're trying to tell me. Or ask me. How does this magic receptacle have anything to do with the town needing help?"

"It's been a while since anyone's found the secret

grove that holds the book. That's because the receptacle is nearly full. That's why the Aerarii came here. They were drawn by that surplus of magic."

"Like draws like," Lexi said softly. Then, with more conviction in her voice, "But that receptacle is holding curses. Dark magic. What the Aerarii brought was neither good nor bad. It was pure, unadulterated cosmic power. Magic in its purest form. That's why it could grant wishes. Magic like that can be used for anything."

"All true. But that receptacle still represents a large quantity of very strong magic. It called the Aerarii here."

"So what's the problem?" Eddie asked.

"The problem is that receptacle can't hold much more. It needs to be emptied." Amelia picked up a small glass from the side table and sipped whatever was in it. "If it's not, that dark magic will seep out. It will taint the meridian lines."

She blew out a slow breath. "It will destroy the town."

"How do I fit into all of this?" Lexi asked. "Because I want to be sure I understand."

Amelia looked at her. "You're capable of utilizing dark magic."

"I am," Lexi said. She frowned. Then she shook her head. "Are you asking me what I think you are?"

"Yes," Amelia answered. "I'm asking you to empty that receptacle. In exchange, you'll have as much magic as you want."

Eddie wasn't sure he was following. Magic for Lexi

was good. But dark magic? "What exactly is this receptacle?"

Lexi nodded. "I'd like to know too."

Amelia lifted her chin defiantly, but there was worry in her eyes. "Pandora's box."

CHAPTER FORTY-EIGHT

"Pandora's box," Lexi repeated. She needed to say it for herself, to make it seem real. How much magic did Amelia possess to be put in charge of such a thing? "That was destroyed ages ago."

"The *story* of its destruction was created ages ago," Amelia corrected. "The belief was that such a story would protect the box from those who wished to loose the evil within. And so far, that story has done its job."

Eddie lurched forward. "You want Lexi to absorb *evil*?"

"When you put it that way," Amelia began, "I understand how it sounds, but you heard her. Sylphs are able to convert magic. Of any kind."

"That's true," Lexi said. "But what you need is a different kind of sylph. One who specializes in dark magic. A sin-eater."

Amelia arched her brows. "Do you know one?"

Lexi frowned. "Not anymore." Sin-eaters had an expiration date. At some point, the dark magic won. For that reason, most sylphs avoided dark magic altogether.

Amelia persisted. "There is a tremendous amount of

magic to be had. As much as you want, and you've made it clear you want your magic back. Isn't that true?"

"It is," Lexi said. The idea was tempting. She would have as much magic as she wanted. It would make their lives much easier. But at what potential cost? Was she willing to ruin their lives for this chance? "But I couldn't take all of it. I'm sure it holds more than anyone could handle. But some would be doable."

"I don't like this," Eddie said.

"Neither do I," Amelia said. "But difficult situations often require difficult solutions. If there were any other way, I wouldn't ask. I haven't been able to find another way. I can't let the town be ruined. Especially not now that Pasqual has returned. I know there are risks. I am willing to compensate you in whatever manner you desire."

Eddie looked at Lexi. "What kind of risks?"

She met his gaze but didn't answer. She didn't want to because she knew he wouldn't like what she had to say. Why should he? She didn't like the answer herself.

"I deserve to know, Lexi."

She nodded. "You do." She inhaled. "Taking in that much dark magic is tricky. It has to be done slowly. And once it's absorbed, my system has to process it. There's no telling how long that will take." She swallowed. "Or if it will be successful."

Eddie looked stricken. "Are you telling me you could die?"

"No," Lexi said quickly. "But it could change me into something ... different." She cut her eyes at Amelia.

The older woman muttered, "A sin eater."

"Is she right?" Eddie asked.

"Yes." Lexi exhaled. "Or worse."

"Worse?" He shook his head. "I don't understand."

"It's dark magic. It's very persuasive. It could turn me into something else."

Eddie frowned. "A monster?"

She had to be honest with him. "Maybe."

"Lexi, this sounds too dangerous."

"It might be. I've never done anything like this before. I've taken in small quantities of dark magic. More than what I took from Kacy but never in the amounts we're talking about." She lifted her head and stared briefly at the ceiling, trying to weigh it all out. Saving the entire town and possibly getting her magic back or letting the town be destroyed and remaining essentially human?

Didn't seem like much to weigh when she considered it that way.

"This sounds too dangerous," Eddie repeated, the anger and fear in his voice obvious.

"I would do it carefully. And I wouldn't take more than I needed. But that doesn't mean I've decided, either." She took his hand, twining her fingers with his before speaking to Amelia. "I need time to think about this."

"Of course," Amelia said. "Please understand that when I say I will compensate you, I mean it. Whatever you want that's within my power, I will make it happen.

Money, possessions, travel, a new house, land, anything you want."

Lexi squeezed Eddie's hand. "Would you mind letting me talk to Amelia alone for a bit? I won't be long. Then we can go home and talk about it."

He didn't want to leave her. She could see that in his hesitation. Then he nodded. "I'll be outside."

Amelia wiggled her finger at Beckett, who was standing near the door. "Bring the car around, would you?"

"It's never left," he responded. Then he bowed and gestured toward the open door. "Right this way, Mr. Hyde."

Reluctantly, Eddie got to his feet. Lexi stood up, too. "Just a few minutes."

He nodded and kissed her cheek. "You don't have to do this, you know. We're fine just the way we are."

"You're right. We are. But the town ..."

He sighed. "I know." He shot a glance at Amelia, then walked out.

For a moment, neither woman said anything. Then Amelia broke the silence. "He loves you very much. No surprise, seeing as how you gave him his life back. You could do that very same thing for the town."

Lexi narrowed her eyes. "I understand what's at stake here. I'm not sure you do."

"You might not recover. I comprehend that. I wish that wasn't a possibility, but my first concern is this town and the people in it. Those people need this place. It keeps them safe. It gives them shelter from a world where they'd have no life at all."

Amelia sipped her drink again. "Even if the magic changes you, removing it from the box buys Shadowvale many more years."

"So you get what you want regardless of what happens to me."

"In black and white, yes. Perhaps that's cold of me, but you must see things from my point of view. I have to consider thousands. Not just one."

"I do. But I'm not thinking only of myself. I'm also thinking about Eddie." And Reggie, if she was being honest, but she wasn't sure Amelia would think a cat was important. He was no tiger, after all.

"You don't think Edgar would survive without you?"

"I think he would survive. I just don't know what it would do to him. If the monster in him could reemerge. I can't let that happen to him."

"The monster no longer exists in him. You know that," Amelia said. "But I understand your concern all the same. I will promise you this. If you do this for the town and it doesn't go well for you, he will be protected. Taken care of, in whatever way is best."

Lexi let out a soft snort. "That sounds to me like you covering all your bases. If Eddie goes rogue, you just basically told me you'd take him out."

Amelia blinked, her eyes holding a look of utter revulsion. "I've told you nothing of the sort. I would never—"

"But you can see how your words might be interpreted." Lexi sat back. "If I do this, I want your promise in writing. A firm commitment to watch over him and protect him and provide for him if something happens to me. That's the only way I'll say yes."

Amelia nodded. "I understand. I will have that done and sent to you as soon as possible. Then we have an agreement?"

Lexi got up. "Not yet we don't. I still need time to think about this and talk it over with Eddie. I know what's at stake for the town. But I also know what's at stake for me. And him. I'll give you my answer as soon as I can."

"Don't wait too long. I don't know how much longer the box will last."

CHAPTER FORTY-NINE

Eddie changed into his pajamas and now stood by the windows that looked onto Main Street, his thoughts weighed down by the decision in front of Lexi. Perhaps what weighed on him the most was that it wasn't his decision.

If it had been, he would have said no and been done with it. But he wasn't the one who'd lost his magic, and he knew he couldn't comprehend what that must feel like. He'd seen how that loss had affected Lexi. How hard she'd taken it.

But taking on the curses inside Pandora's box seemed too risky. He'd been a monster. He knew what that was like. He wouldn't wish it on his worst enemy. He glanced over his shoulder at the sound of something skittering across the hardwood floor.

Reggie was chasing a ball of crinkled Mylar, swatting it and having a big time going after it.

Eddie smiled. Lexi was soaking in the tub, trying to weigh everything out.

Was the town really in danger? Or was that Amelia's

way of getting Lexi to do her bidding? He didn't know enough about magic or Amelia to know the answers.

Amelia certainly had a lot to protect. Not just the town but Pasqual. Was this tied to him in some way? Again, he didn't know. Would Henry? Or Izzy?

He hated to bother them, but other than Thomas, he had no one else to ask. And Amelia hadn't said anything about keeping the information secret. He got his phone out and called Henry.

"Eddie?"

"Yes. Sorry to call so late, but I need to know something, and you're the only person I could ask. You or Izzy, that is."

"Sure, no problem. We were just watching some TV. What's going on?"

He explained about Lexi's situation and the offer Amelia had made to her as best he could, trying not to forget any details that might be important. "So what do you think? Would Amelia be making any of that up?"

Henry took a breath before answering. "I don't see why she would. The only gain for her in this situation is keeping the town safe. And giving magic back to Lexi. Although it's a gift that comes with potentially high cost."

"I agree."

"You don't want her to do it, do you?"

"Would you want Izzy to?"

"No, but I would recognize that it's her decision. And Lexi clearly has a gift for helping. She wants to, doesn't she? Izzy's like that too."

"She hasn't come out and said it yet, but I think so. I understand. She wants her magic back, and like you said, she has a gift for helping."

"She helped you."

Eddie sighed. "At great cost to herself."

"And this time it's not just one person. It's a whole town full of people."

"She's going to say yes. I know she is."

"And you're worried," Henry said. "I very much understand."

"I *was* a creature of dark magic. I know what she's taking on. I don't want it to change her." Eddie turned to stare at the bathroom door. "I love her."

"I know you do." Henry went quiet a moment. "Maybe there's some way we can tip the odds in her favor."

"Meaning?"

"I don't know yet. I need to talk to Izzy. Maybe I'll have an answer for you tomorrow morning."

"Okay." Eddie couldn't ask for more than that. "Thank you."

"Anytime. And listen, if she was strong enough to transform you, she should be able to handle this. You might be worrying for nothing."

"And I might not be."

"Also true. Sorry I don't have more to offer."

"No, talking helped. I'll see you in the morning."

"Great. See you then."

Eddie hung up. Reggie jumped into the cat tower, sat

on one of the perches, then kicked his leg over his head and started grooming himself. Eddie gave him a few pets.

The bathroom door opened, and Lexi emerged, wrapped in a robe, her pajamas peeking out underneath. Wisps of steam escaped out the door.

Eddie tried to read her body language. As much as he didn't want to know her decision, he also did. "Did you decide?"

She nodded, her expression solemn. "I'm going to do it. I have to. I know you're worried. I am too. But we've already decided to make this place our home. We can't very well decide that, then watch it be destroyed knowing we could have done something to prevent that destruction."

He almost couldn't put his next thought into words. "But what if you get hurt? What if the dark magic wins?"

She tugged the robe's belt tighter and smiled as she walked over to pet Reggie too. "I won't let it. I'm determined not to."

"I talked to Henry about it. I hope that was all right. I needed to know if he thought Amelia might not be telling the truth about any of this."

Lexi's smile disappeared. "And?"

"He thinks she's on the up-and-up. He also said he'd talk to Izzy and see if there was any way they might be able to help you. Give you some kind of advantage against the dark magic."

"Really? Because if they could, that would be great."

"Do you know of anything that might help?"

"More magic. But if I had more magic, I wouldn't need to do this in the first place." She came to him, wrapping her arms around him. "I won't pretend not to be scared. I am. But it's the right thing to do."

He held her, wishing he could do something to keep her safe. "If the dark magic wins—"

"It won't."

"But if it does, I won't leave you. I promise you that. I won't let you be alone."

She shook her head, still pressed against him. "Eddie, you can't make that promise. You have no idea what I might become."

"Yes, I do." He kissed the top of her head. "No matter what happens, I'll be by your side. I want you to know that."

She gazed up at him, eyes damp with unshed tears. "I can't ask you to do that."

"You're not asking. I'm telling you." He owed her his life. Staying with her regardless of what happened was the least he could do. "I am not going anywhere."

"You really mean that, don't you?"

He nodded. "With all my heart."

She let go of him and stepped back, twisting her hands together. "In that case, I think there's something we should do before I tell Amelia yes."

"What's that?"

She took another step back. "If you don't want to, I

completely understand, but it would make things easier as far as this building goes and—"

He grabbed her hands and pulled her back to him. "Lexi, what is it?"

Worry bracketed her eyes as she looked at him. "We should get married."

Chapter Fifty

Lexi knew it was a ridiculous thing to ask of him, but if they were legally married and something happened to her, he'd be able to do whatever needed to be done. Like have her committed. And the rent from the pub would be his without any issues.

Eddie nodded. "Yes."

"Are you sure?"

He laughed. "I am very sure." He hugged her. "We'll ask Henry tomorrow if he knows someone who can marry us."

Relief swept through her. "Okay, good."

"I'll shut the blinds. We should try to get some sleep. Tomorrow is going to be a very busy day."

"Yes, it is." And a long one for her if Amelia took her to the grove.

As they headed for the bed, Reggie jumped down from his cat tower and dashed straight ahead, beating them to it. After jumping onto the bed, he flopped down, then rolled over and showed his tummy, looking at them upside down. His antics made them both laugh.

Lexi needed that. Laughing helped lighten the weight

of what was coming. Helped her forget that this new life she was just getting used to might be about to disappear. "He really likes being in bed, doesn't he?"

"He does. I'm so glad we adopted him. I don't understand how no one wanted him. I think he's perfect."

She nodded. "So do I." She glanced at Eddie. "I think you're perfect, too. I'm sorry for making you worry about me. I wish there was another way, but I can't let the town be destroyed. Not when I can stop it."

"I know. I don't like the risk, but I love you for being willing to sacrifice yourself. I love who you are. I'd do anything to take that risk away from you, but I can't, and that's what bothers me. But that's my problem to deal with." He gave her a quick kiss. "Come on. Let's get some sleep."

She nodded, although she wasn't sure sleep would come. Her mind was too busy. She took off her robe and climbed into bed all the same.

Eddie got in on his side. Reggie stood up and moved closer between them, then fell over again, curling up into a loose ball. Purring, he kneaded Eddie's side through the covers.

Before long, Eddie's soft snores joined the purring.

Lexi stared at the ceiling, her mind whirling with thoughts of what was to come. There was no one she knew to ask for advice. No one who knew anything about the process of converting dark magic, anyway.

She'd done it in small doses. How much different could it be in large doses? She'd do it slowly. However slowly she needed to. There was no hurry once she began. She would be very careful not to let it overwhelm her.

What was that old saying? The way to eat an elephant was one bite at a time. Well, that was what she was going to do. Eat this elephant one bite at a time.

She wouldn't let Amelia rush her. No matter what urgency the woman thought there was, Lexi would set the pace.

A new idea came to her. Maybe she could do it over the course of a few days. If she could take a small amount the first time, then convert that into pure magic before taking any more, that would give her an edge.

The stronger a sylph was, the more powerful and capable they were. Right now, she was neither.

She nodded at the idea. It was solid. In fact, if she could stretch out the process over a week, there would be almost no risk. The key was small doses and building up her energy reserves. If she could do that, she'd considerably lessen the risk of the dark magic overpowering her.

She turned to look at Eddie. She kind of wanted to wake him up and tell him she'd figured out how to do it, but he was sleeping so peacefully. He needed sleep as much as she did. And now she might be able to get some.

When she next opened her eyes, light was coming through the blinds, although it was partially blocked by Reggie. He was sitting next to her and staring at her.

When he realized she was awake, he pawed at her face and meowed. Loudly.

"Okay, I get it. You're hungry." She poked Eddie. "Your cat wants breakfast."

He laughed sleepily. "I heard him."

"How could you not? He needs a volume button." She got up, yawned, and headed for the kitchen. She grabbed him a can of food and put it in a clean dish as quickly as she could.

Eddie staggered in behind her. "It's a good thing he woke us up. We need to leave in less than an hour."

"We do?"

He looked at his phone. "Actually, more like forty-five minutes. Thomas said he'd be here at eight thirty."

"Okay, I'll get ready. I think breakfast is going to have to be something that's already prepared."

"Like what?"

She opened the cabinet and took out a box. "How about these toaster pops? They're blueberry, and they have frosting."

He gave her a skeptical look. "I could eat that whole box."

She shrugged one shoulder. "Then do it. We can get more."

He took the box from her, examining it. "They don't look very nutritious."

"They aren't. They're junk food. But sylphs don't have the same issues with junk food that humans do. Our metabolisms can handle all the excess sugar and carbs."

His brows lifted. "Does that still apply now that you're more human than sylph?"

She grimaced. "Good point. Maybe I'll just have an apple."

As they got ready to head to the hospital, she told him about her idea of syphoning off the dark magic in stages so that she could process it in small batches and not have to worry about it getting the best of her.

He nodded as he ate his fourth toaster pop. "I like that idea a lot better."

"Me, too. And now we don't really need to get married."

His eyes narrowed. "I think we do."

She smiled. "Okay. Then we will."

Thomas showed up at exactly eight thirty. They got in the car and told him the news about their decision to make things legal.

"Congratulations. You two make a good couple. Smart, handsome, and fearless. You're going to have some good-looking babies. If you decide to go that route."

Lexi laughed. "We haven't talked about that yet, but who knows? Do you have any idea who might be able to perform the ceremony for us?"

"Sure do. Deacon Evermore. He's the main peacekeeper in town. He can do it. I'll give you his number before I drop you off."

"Much appreciated," Eddie said.

Once at the hospital's main entrance, Thomas programmed Deacon's number into Eddie's phone, congratulated them again, and said goodbye.

Lexi looked around as they went inside. "Do you know if his lab is in the same place as his office?"

"No, but I'm sure the information desk can tell us. We still need to get visitor passes, anyway."

They did that and were directed to Henry's office. They took the elevator up.

He came out as soon as they were in the waiting room. "Good morning." He looked at Lexi. "Izzy came in with me, so I've already done her DNA swab. We can get you done in just a few minutes. Also, she thinks that she might be able to help you once you've absorbed the dark magic from the box. She believes she can use her empath abilities to pull some of that dark magic out."

Lexi shook her head. "It's a great idea, but it's counterproductive. I need that magic to stay inside me so it can be processed. Pulling it out just means I'll have less magic. And it'll have to go somewhere." She glanced at Eddie. "That's what you did with Edgar, right?"

Henry made a face. "Right. We weren't thinking. Of course, it won't work. My apologies."

"It's okay," Eddie said. "We appreciate that you wanted to help. Thankfully, Lexi has it all worked out."

"You do?" Henry asked.

She nodded. "I'm going to do it in small batches over the course of several days. A week would be ideal, but I'll have to see what works for Amelia. Doing it that way means I won't get overwhelmed."

"That's a fantastic idea. Well done."

Lexi smiled and took Eddie's hand. "We have some other news too. And a question."

"You do?" Henry smiled too. "Must be good. What is it?"

Eddie's chest puffed up slightly, which tickled Lexi. For a man of his size, he somehow also managed to be pretty cute. "We're getting married. We'd like you and Izzy to be our witnesses."

Chapter Fifty-One

Izzy showed up twenty minutes after Henry called her. She gave Eddie and Lexi big hugs. "I'm so happy for you guys. I think it's just fantastic."

Then she took Lexi's hand. "You and I are going shopping for a wedding dress. Unless you already have something?"

Lexi blinked. "To be honest, I hadn't thought about that."

"Well, you should have something nice to get married in, don't you think?"

"I guess?"

"You should," Izzy assured her. She looked at her husband. "Did you do the DNA swab already?"

"I did," he answered.

"Great. Then I'm taking her shopping. You boys have a good day at work. See you later."

Lexi went along with Izzy because there didn't seem to be an option not to. "I don't really have a lot of extra money to spend on a dress at the moment."

"You won't need much. The place I'm taking you has *the best* buys. They're like magic. Literally."

Lexi smiled. "Stella's Bargain Bin?"

"You've been there?"

Lexi nodded as they headed down in the elevator. "I have. Amazing deals." She gestured to her jeans and top. "These are from there. All of Eddie's stuff is from there. He didn't have anything, so I had to get him some clothes."

Izzy nodded. "I imagine when you're a tree, clothes aren't a big deal." Her eyes held genuine regret. "I felt a little bad that Henry and I did that to him, but at the time it seemed like a good solution for someone who couldn't be set free otherwise. It was that or ... nothing. I'm so glad you came along and fixed him up."

"Me, too. He's changed my life in a way I didn't know it needed changing."

Izzy smiled. "A good man can do that. Henry was that way for me."

Stella greeted them as soon as they walked into the Bargain Bin. "Hello, ladies. Looking for something special?"

"A wedding dress or something suitable to get married in," Izzy said. "For my friend."

Stella nodded. "You're the one who bought most of that big and tall lot I had come in."

"That was me," Lexi said.

"If you need any more of that, you're in luck. They dropped off another box. It's sitting by the dressing rooms waiting for me to get to, but you can poke around in there if you want. Wedding dresses and evening wear are on the rack against the back wall."

Izzy glanced toward the dressing rooms. "You want to look through that box first? Then we can focus on you."

Lexi nodded. "Sure." She smiled at Stella. "Thanks for the heads-up."

"Anytime." Stella went back to her sudoku.

Lexi went straight to the large box and opened it. There was a garment bag inside, folded in half. Under it were a few other things, including a shoe box. She pulled out the garment bag. It was thick and weighty with the clothing inside. She hung it on a nearby rack and unzipped it.

"Of course," she said softly. Then she laughed. Inside was a charcoal suit with a crisp white shirt and blue patterned silk tie.

"Hey," Izzy said. "That would be perfect for Eddie to get married in. Unless he has a suit already."

Lexi shook her head. "Nope. How much you want to bet the shoes that go with this are in that box?"

Izzy smiled. "That is sort of how Stella's works."

"So I'm finding out."

The box did indeed have dress shoes. Also in the big box were a couple more dress shirts, still in the packages; three pairs of dress socks; a dark red ball cap; a pair of black track pants with a matching jacket; and two T-shirts. One was from the Creamatorium, and the other was from a place called Club 42.

"I know that place. It's pretty cool," Izzy said. "It's a

jazz club over on Fiddler Street. We should double date there some night."

"Sounds good." Lexi put everything back in the box and carried the whole thing to the counter. "I'll take it all."

"Thought you might," Stella said without looking up.

The wedding dresses and formal wear were next.

"What's your style?" Izzy asked.

"Nothing that's trying too hard," Lexi answered. "I like pretty. Easy. Natural."

"Like this?" Izzy pulled out a white lace maxi dress that looked like it might have been from the '70s.

Lexi smiled. "That's not bad, actually."

Izzy thrust it at her. "Try it on. Probably needs a little alteration, but let's see how it looks on you."

Lexi took it to the dressing room and tried it on. She checked herself out in the mirror. The gown was a little large. If she'd had her magic, she could have fixed that with a wave of her hand. The gown was still very pretty. The sections of lace that made up the body of the dress and the sleeves were all connected by wide sheer ribbon. Underneath it all was a simple white cotton slip the same length as the gown.

It was a very romantic dress. With a little flower crown, she'd be set. She inhaled. She was actually going to marry Eddie. Smiling, she stepped out of the dressing room. "What do you think?"

Izzy grinned and bit her bottom lip. "It's super romantic in a flower child earth mother kind of way. I think it suits you. You've got that sort of vibe, which I mean as a compliment. But what do you think?"

Lexi stared at herself in the mirror. "It needs to be taken in a little, but I like it." She looked at Izzy. "I could definitely marry Eddie in this dress."

Izzy pressed her hands together and looked like she might cry. "This is so exciting. Stella? We need a seamstress."

"I don't know," Lexi said. "How much is that going to cost? And how long will it take? We need to get married before ... everything else."

Izzy nodded. "I know." She went to the counter. "What do think, Stella? Can we get this done by this afternoon?"

Stella pushed her bright green reading glasses onto the top of her head. "Let me get my pins and see how much needs to be done."

Before Lexi knew it, Stella had the dress taken in at the waist with pins and was standing back, assessing it. "That's nothing. I can do that myself with needle and thread. Give me an hour."

"An hour?" Lexi couldn't believe it.

Stella's artfully penciled brows rose. "Too long?"

"No, it's fast," Lexi reassured her. "Very fast."

Stella put her hands on her hips, stretching her fuzzy lime-green sweater across her ample bosom. "You two go get a coffee or something. Give me that hour."

Lexi nodded. "Okay. Um, how much will that be? For the alterations?"

"In house? For something this easy? Don't worry about it." Stella winked at her. "My wedding present to you."

"That is very kind. Thank you. We'll be back in an hour."

Lexi grabbed Izzy's elbow and propelled her outside so that Stella could get to work. "That's amazing."

Izzy shrugged like that was a foregone conclusion. "Stella's kind of a legend."

"I can see why," Lexi said. "Is there somewhere around here we can get a coffee or tea? My treat for you doing this."

"There's Deja Brew not far away." Izzy put her hand on Lexi's arm. "But you don't owe me anything. That's just what family does, right?"

"You don't know that we're related yet."

"Yes, I do. In here." Izzy touched her chest. "I can feel it. It's what I do, you know. I'm an empath. I feel things. And I feel this."

Lexi didn't know how to respond at first. She'd never had family. Not in the immediate sense of the word. There were other sylphs out in the world, she knew that, but it was rare to come across one. Now she had Izzy, who seemed so sure that they were related, and Eddie, who was about to become her husband.

For someone who didn't have any magic to spare, today seemed like a pretty magical day.

Chapter Fifty-Two

Eddie wasn't sure how it had all happened, but here he was, wearing a suit, standing in Henry's backyard, in front of a man named Deacon Evermore, waiting for Lexi to come out of the house and marry him.

Even dreams weren't usually this good.

Henry was at his side, acting as his best man and witness. Kacy was nearby. She started to play Pachelbel's Canon in D on her flute.

The French door at the back of the house opened, and Izzy came out in a pretty blue dress. She had a sparkly clip in her hair and a big smile on her face. She walked toward them and took her spot across from Henry, smiling at them before looking back at the house.

Then a vision in white appeared in the doorway.

Lexi, swathed in white lace, carried a bouquet of wildflowers with more woven into her hair like a crown. Thomas was at her side, escorting her. He was in a dark suit and looked as proud as could be.

Eddie's mouth came open as his heart thumped faster in his chest. She looked so beautiful. Too beautiful for a guy like him and yet, there she was, walking toward him with a smile on her face that seemed only for him.

Maybe he was dreaming.

"Hi," she whispered as she joined him.

"Hi," he whispered back. Not a dream.

Thomas touched both their arms. "Blessings on both of you." Then he went to stand by his daughter, who ended her solo as he did.

Deacon led them through some simple vows to which they both answered, "I do." He looked at Eddie. "Do you have the rings?"

Lexi frowned. "We don't—"

With a smile, Eddie reached into his pocket and took out a thin gold band and a larger, wider one. He handed that one to Lexi. "Henry knew a place."

Henry had also loaned him the money, telling him whenever he got around to paying it back was fine with him.

Eddie planned to do that when he got his first paycheck.

Lexi looked at Henry and mouthed the words, "Thank you."

Deacon made them repeat some more words about the rings and what they meant, then directed them one at a time to place the rings on each other's finger.

Once that was done, he smiled. "By the power vested in me by the town of Shadowvale, I now pronounce you husband and wife. You may kiss the bride."

Eddie leaned down and kissed Lexi, who kissed him back.

When they came apart, everyone was clapping for them.

Lexi just smiled up at him. "We did it."

Eddie nodded. "We did."

Deacon clapped him on the back. "Congratulations. I hope you have many happy years. You need anything, either of you, just call me. See you all later."

"Thank you," Eddie said. Deacon made his way out. Eddie felt like he was in a whirlwind. In a good way.

Izzy hugged him. "Congratulations. Henry and I are pleased for you both."

"Thanks. And thank you for letting us use your backyard."

"Our pleasure," Henry said.

Thomas and Kacy offered their congratulations next, wishing them well and promising to see them soon. Thomas had to drive someone somewhere, so they said their goodbyes and left.

Then Eddie felt Lexi's hand in his. He wanted to say a million different things to her, but the words wouldn't come. He was lost in the moment. Happy beyond belief. Trying to take it all in and acknowledge that this was truly his life. He owed the woman beside him the world.

"Look this way," Henry said.

Eddie did and saw Henry snapping pictures with his phone. He put his arm around Lexi. "You look beautiful, by the way. You look like a goddess of the forest." He glanced at himself. "And I look like ..."

He wasn't sure. But he probably looked ridiculous.

"You look more handsome than any man has a right to look," Lexi said. "That suit fits you like it was made for you." She smiled straight ahead since Henry was still taking pictures. "Too bad I'll probably never get to see you in it again."

Eddie looked at her. "Why not?"

She shrugged. "I just can't imagine when you'd need to wear a suit again."

If she liked him in it, he definitely wanted to wear it again. "How about we come up with a reason? Like dinner out? Or is this too fancy?"

She smiled. "No, I like that idea. At the right restaurant, it would be perfect. Dinner out. When everything's ... settled."

He nodded. "Let's do that."

His phone rang. He'd forgotten it was in his pocket. He pulled it out. The number wasn't familiar. He answered anyway. "Hello?"

"This is Beckett. Amelia needs Lexi's answer now. Things are getting precarious. Her word. If Lexi's going to do this, it has to be *now*."

The reminder of what was yet to come dampened Eddie's mood.

Lexi was watching him. She frowned. "What's wrong? Who is it?"

Eddie knew she'd read his face. He moved the phone

away from his mouth. "Beckett. Amelia needs to know your answer."

"Tell her I'm going to do it."

He moved the phone back up. "Beckett?"

"I heard. Where are you? I can pick you up."

"We need to go home and change. Twenty minutes?"

"I'll tell her. See you then."

Eddie hung up. "We have to go. Amelia wants to get things started. Beckett's coming to pick us up at our place in twenty minutes."

Henry rubbed his chin. "Let Izzy and I change, and we'll drive you."

"Are you coming with us?" Lexi asked.

"I ..." Henry looked at Izzy, then back at Lexi. "Do you want us to?"

She nodded. "Amelia can't tell me no. I'm the one who's taking all the risk. I should have whoever I want with me."

"Good plan," Eddie said. Henry was a doctor. If anything went wrong, he might be able to help. Not that anything would go wrong. Lexi had figured out how to do this without risk. But still. Just in case.

Henry and Izzy changed quickly, both of them reappearing within minutes in jeans, T-shirts, and pullovers. They had sneakers on, too.

Henry dangled his keys. "Let's go."

They all piled into his Land Rover, and he drove them to their apartment. Beckett was already there, waiting in the Rolls.

He got out as Henry parked. Lexi and Eddie jumped out and made for the steps. Beckett stared at their clothes. "Did you two do what I think you did?"

"We got married," Eddie said. "So if that's what you're thinking—"

"It is." His eyes rounded in surprise. "Best wishes to you both."

"Thanks," Lexi said. "Henry and Izzy are coming with us."

Beckett nodded. "Amelia won't like that, but you don't care, do you?"

"Nope." Lexi stood at the door. Eddie got the key out. "I'm not doing this without them, so she'll just have to adjust."

Beckett smiled wryly and leaned against the car without saying another word.

Eddie got them inside. "Should we just wear what Henry and Izzy are?"

Lexi nodded. "Jeans and boots or sneakers and something halfway warm on top."

Reggie woke up from where he was sleeping in his cat tower. He meowed at them, which sounded very much like a scolding for waking him up, then curled into a tighter ball and went back to sleep.

Eddie knew he wanted attention, but they didn't have much time. He gave Reggie a few scratches on the head. "When we get back, I'll play with you, okay, buddy?"

He changed into jeans, a T-shirt, and the fleece pullover Lexi had gotten him. He put on a pair of work boots with the outfit. She ended up in jeans, a long-sleeved T-shirt, and a V-neck sweater. She gave Reggie a kiss on the head before tying her sneakers, then she and Eddie headed for the door.

A thought came to Eddie. "I did it wrong."

She stopped, hand on the knob, and looked at him. "You did what wrong?"

"I was supposed to carry you over the threshold. That's what grooms do. Don't ask me how I know. I just do."

She smiled. "When we get back, you can do it then."

"Okay." This was all happening so fast. Too fast. Why was Amelia so insistent they come now? He didn't like it, but it was too late to say anything. Lexi had already given her word.

They hustled down the steps.

Beckett opened the passenger door for them.

Eddie let Lexi go ahead of him. He made eye contact with Beckett, trying to see the reaper in him. Wondering if the power to take souls was something that could be seen. "Are you coming with us to the forest?"

Beckett nodded.

Eddie gave the man a defiant stare. "It had better be as Amelia's companion and nothing else."

CHAPTER FIFTY-THREE

Amelia took the front passenger seat next to Beckett and stayed silent as they drove toward the Enchanted Forest. There was too much on her mind to make small talk. The future of Shadowvale hung in the balance.

There was no conversation from the back seat either. Eddie and Lexi seemed to be lost in their own thoughts. She doubted it was Shadowvale's future that was keeping them quiet, however.

She glanced into the side mirror at the Land Rover following them. She didn't like that Henry and Isadora had been invited, but she didn't have the time or energy to argue the subject. Lexi didn't seem like someone who was going to back down easily, either. So Amelia let it be and hoped that Henry and Isadora had the good sense to keep the location of the grove to themselves.

Maybe they wouldn't be able to remember it once they left. Most didn't. But Isadora was a skilled empath. Her mind worked better than most.

Amelia stared out the window as they entered the Enchanted Forest. Dusk was approaching, but there was still a good deal of light left to see by. It wouldn't last long, though. Especially not when they were submerged in the forest. They'd have the sprite moss and a little light from the stars and moon.

After all of this was over, she and Pasqual were going to have a quiet supper in the dining room. Just the two of them. Like the old days. She smiled and closed her eyes for a moment, relishing the knowledge that he was home again. It still hadn't truly sunk in.

His strength grew every day, and he was looking more and more like his old self. Maybe she'd throw a party in his honor when he was ready. Properly announce his return. It was something for them to discuss, surely.

Thinking of him softened her mood. She opened her eyes. She had Lexi to thank for his return. She shouldn't be too hard on the woman for wanting her friends with her as she took on this very challenging task.

"Just up ahead is fine," she said to Beckett, motioning to the side of the road.

"Very good." He pulled over and parked.

Henry parked behind them.

They all filtered out of the vehicles and stood on the shoulder.

Amelia addressed them. "Follow me. Don't deviate. The grove is protected, and with the current state of things, the forest will do everything possible to distract us and prevent us from arriving."

Lexi narrowed her gaze. "Why is there such a rush all of a sudden? I know you said the magic is nearly overflowing, but if no one can find the grove, what's the hurry?"

The taste in Amelia's mouth turned sour. "Because against all odds, someone did find it last night and wrote their name in the book. The box may have already begun to spill its contents, for all I know. The meridian lines may have even begun to pick up the taint of darkness. I can only hope we're not too late."

Lexi cast a quick glance at Eddie, her expression holding new concern. She faced Amelia again. "Before we head in, I need to tell you that I was hoping to do this in stages. Small bites, if you know what I mean. Maybe over several days. A week would be ideal. That would give me time to process the dark magic and greatly reduce the risk of me being affected by it."

Amelia frowned. "That won't work. Once the container is opened, it'll be impossible to close again until it's at least half emptied. It would be like standing in front of a fire hose and saying you're only going to take a drink."

Eddie growled softly. "I don't like this. Lexi does it her way or—"

Amelia stepped toward him. "No. Her way won't work. I'm sorry, but no one can control what's inside that jar. There are only two options. It can either be absorbed or set free, and the latter is absolutely unacceptable."

Lexi put her hand on his arm and spoke in a calm voice. "It's all right. I can do this." She lifted her chin and smiled at him. "It wasn't what I planned, but I'll manage it."

Eddie's frown stayed fixed.

"It's settled then." Amelia didn't have time to wait for further discussion. Neither did Shadowvale. She started walking into the forest and headed down a narrow, barely noticeable footpath.

She was dreading what she might find when she reached the grove. If the jar had already begun to spill its contents, this attempt to right things would go from rescue to recovery. And recovery would be much, *much* harder.

After a while, the path disappeared, but she knew the way. The forest, already dim, darkened further, but some light filtered through the canopy. Here and there, sprite moss flecked the trees at nearly regular intervals. Green fireflies, the safe ones, began to appear in the distance.

As they grew closer to the grove, larger blue lights appeared. Fairies. She paid close attention to them. To their number and the intensity of the blue light they gave off. At least they were still around. Fairies were often the harbingers of change. If a large quantity of dark magic had already leaked into the forest, she doubted there would be so many of them about.

Their lights were bright and strong, another indication that all was relatively well.

It wasn't enough to relieve the sick feeling in her stomach, but it was at least a sign that things were perhaps not as dire as she imagined. That they still had time to empty the jar.

A fine mist began to cover the ground, making it difficult to see more than a few feet in any direction. Amelia didn't slow. They were nearing the grove. She could feel it. The presence of such concentrated magic raised goosebumps on her skin. Perhaps Lexi felt it too. She glanced back, but the sylph showed no signs of noticing it.

Minutes passed, and the fog thickened, rising higher around them. It stayed that way as she continued on. Then suddenly it fell away.

Someone behind her let out a small gasp.

They were in the grove.

"This is beautiful," Isadora said softly.

Amelia nodded. It was very beautiful and lit with its own glow of magic.

Underfoot was a spongy carpet of blue-green moss. A perfect circle of trees surrounded them, their twelve thick trunks stretching far overhead. The branches made a dome, covering the sky except for a perfect circle in the center that showed a disc of deep gray night sky already sparkling with stars.

But it was what was at the heart of the grove that was most impressive: an open book about the size and thickness of a suitcase. It sat on an intricately carved pedestal, and the pages seemed to shine with an internal light.

Amelia stepped forward and addressed the woman she wished to speak with. "Lylianna? I've brought the one I told you about."

Twelve fierce warrior women stepped out of the trees, bows taut with arrows drawn and pointed at the group behind Amelia. They wore slim breeches of tanned leather and tunics of pale green and ivory silk that emphasized their bark-brown skin. They surrounded Amelia and her companions.

Lylianna was at the front of the group. She took a step toward Amelia, but her gaze was on those with her. "You said one woman. A sylph. Who are all these that accompany you?"

"Beckett you know," Amelia answered. "The rest are the sylph's friends. There was no time to argue. I let them come. They understand."

Lylianna frowned but lowered her bow. The other nymphs followed her lead. "She looks human."

"She's a sylph. I promise." Amelia glanced back at Lexi. "Come forward, please."

Lexi joined her. "You're nymphs. These are your trees, and you guard this grove and the book it holds?"

"We do," Lylianna answered. She tilted her head and appraised Lexi. "You're a sin-eater?"

"No, just a sylph with very little magic left. But I am a sylph. And I will do my best to take as much of the dark magic as I am able."

Lylianna's frown returned as she looked at Amelia. "She won't do."

"She's all we have," Amelia shot back. Desperation twisted her belly. "Her heart is good, her intentions right, and she knows the risk."

Lexi nodded, although she seemed tense. "I do. And I willingly accept it."

"And these with you," Lylianna said. "They know this is a sacred place? Meant to be kept secret?"

Lexi bowed her head in answer. "I promise that they will." She looked at her friends. "Tell her."

"We will," they all said in unison, nodding.

Lylianna stared intensely at Lexi. "This is a hard task you take on."

"I know."

After a few moments, her gaze softened. "I wish you well, sister."

"Thank you," Lexi answered.

Lylianna gave Amelia a nod, then returned to her place with the other nymphs. As a group, the twelve turned and disappeared back into their trees.

Amelia exhaled. She walked over to the book and put her hand on it. The pages were warm with magic. Too warm. The edges had already begun to curl and darken. They hadn't arrived a moment too soon.

Please let this work. She couldn't bear to lose her home. Pasqual needed a safe place to live. They all did.

She put on a calm expression and met Lexi's gaze. "Beneath this book is the source of Shadowvale's magic, both dark and light. That source is protected by the nymphs and my magic. This town was created to provide a safe haven for Pasqual, but doing so required me to make a great sacrifice. Now, Lexi, you must make one too."

Chapter Fifty-Four

Lexi nodded. "I'm ready and willing." That was the truth, although her stomach was rolling and her hands were shaking with nerves. Nothing she could do about that but ignore it.

"Good," Amelia said. "My sacrifice was agreeing to protect a very dangerous object from mankind. To become the guardian of an object that had been failing for ages past. And while Shadowvale was built to contain it as much as possible, there is, as you know, too much magic within it now."

"Yes," Lexi said.

Amelia hesitated as if she knew her next actions would be the point of no return. She gently closed the book and lifted it off the pedestal with such ease that Lexi understood Amelia's power was far greater than she let on. The book must weigh a tremendous amount.

Amelia carefully set the book on the ground, revealing the pedestal to be hollow. Then she reached inside and lifted out a tall, stocky, lidded jar covered in designs that looked as though they belonged in an ancient Greek temple.

"This is it. The object I was made guardian of," Amelia said. A hairline crack ran from where the lid met the mouth of the vessel. Inky tendrils oozed from the crack, reaching out like they were trying to escape. She took a breath, her grip firm on the large jar. "The one and only Pandora's box."

She set it on the ground in front of the pedestal and walked back to Lexi. Amelia stood in front of her. "It doesn't need to be completely emptied. I don't expect that. Just that the pressure of so much dark magic is eased."

"I understand." Lexi stared past her at the jar. Was it Lexi's imagination, or were the tendrils of dark magic getting longer? Grasping in her direction?

"We leave you to it, then," Amelia said. She walked past Lexi, her footfalls swallowed by the moss.

"No," Eddie said. "I'm not leaving her."

Lexi turned to see him. More than anything, she wanted him to stay, but she sensed it wasn't a good idea.

"You must leave," Amelia said firmly. "We all must. It's between her and the magic now. There's nothing more you can do to help her. This is for her and her alone, but if you stay within this grove when the magic is released, there is every chance it will seek you out as its new home. Is that what you want? Your monster back?" She pointed up at his chest. "Because I guarantee you, his equivalent is in that jar."

Panic flashed on Eddie's face. He shook his head, and the panic disappeared. "I want to help her."

"I know you do," Amelia said, her tone softer now. More understanding. "But you can't. Not now. Not here."

Lexi went to him and put her hand on his arm. She wanted him to stay, but she wanted him unharmed even more. "It's okay. You're helping me just by being here. And when I'm done, you'll be at my side again."

He nodded, but he didn't look happy. He took her hand. "Be safe."

She smiled for his benefit. "I will."

"I love you." He kissed her.

"I love you, too." She held her smile as she looked at Henry and Izzy. "Thank you for being here."

Izzy smiled back, but it didn't reach her eyes. Henry touched Eddie's shoulder. "Come on. Let's give her some space."

Eddie held her gaze for a moment longer, a thousand emotions visible, then he went with Henry and Izzy. Amelia followed. Beckett had already gone. As the four of them walked through the trees, the mist returned, erasing them from Lexi's sight.

When the mist cleared, she was alone in the grove, surrounded by the trees. She wondered if the nymphs within would come to her aid if something went wrong. Nymphs and sylphs were related. That probably didn't mean much now.

With a soft sigh, she faced the jar and gave it her full attention. She looked at it from all sides, moving toward it as she did. The black tendrils were definitely longer. Voices echoed in the grove, sinister laughter, and words that were mostly indecipherable. The sounds seemed to swirl around her, heard in one ear first, then the other.

It was unnerving. And a sure sign that the dark magic wanted out. It recognized Lexi was the path.

She swallowed. Why had she agreed to do this? She clenched her fists. Now was not the time for self-doubt.

She went closer to the jar and kneeled in front of it. Once she took the lid off, there was no going back.

There was no reason to put it off, either. She wasn't going to be any more prepared no matter how long she waited.

She put her hands on the jar. Heat seeped through the vessel as it vibrated with hungry, desperate energy. She looked up at the stars. At all that cosmic power. She might not have gotten a meteor, but she was about to have all the magic she wanted.

If she could survive it.

She blew out a breath, then a soft glint caught her eye. The slim band of gold on her ring finger. She smiled. She wasn't doing this for herself alone. She was doing it for her and Eddie. He was out there, waiting on her, supporting her. Her smile grew a little bigger. She was doing it for him and for Reggie, who deserved the best life possible.

That ring took some of her nerves away. Gave her a little boost of courage. Reminded her that she'd found a home and she wanted to keep it. She lifted her chin. She was a sylph. A creature of great power and magic. All she had to do was get some of that magic back.

She used a little of the magic she had left to open herself to the world around her. Immediately, she felt everything. The grove vibrated with power, but so did the jar. The power reminded her of who she'd once been. The power she'd once held. She could do this. She *would* do this.

She clasped the lid and lifted it off the jar.

The dark magic spilled forth with great intensity, hitting her exactly as Amelia had described it. Like the water from a fire hose. Lexi braced herself and leaned into the heady flood of power, holding on to the jar for all she was worth.

What magic remained in her began to encompass the new magic filling her, doing its best to protect her from the darkness. But it was like trying to dam the ocean at its deepest point. Dark magic saturated her.

She tasted the bittersweetness of it, the pain and regret, the anguish, the misery and sorrow. But with that came the seduction of power. The false vow that such darkness paraded about as if it was the only way to make life worth living. The kiss of greed. The caress of envy. The yearning to have more, be more, need more.

More, more, more. It pealed through her, making it hard to think of anything else.

The rich scent of exotic incense drifted into her nostrils as the darkness whispered to her in a language as ancient as she was, telling her everything she wanted to hear. Promising a life that no one could ever attain. Gold and jewels that would cause a sultan envy. Wealth and power that kings could only dream of, if she would just yield herself to those base desires, body and soul.

She knew better, understood that these were lies. But this was the fight. The darkness wanted her to believe its deceptions and let it take hold of her. It wanted to own her. To become her. To obliterate her and turn her into a new creature of shadows and madness.

She couldn't bear much more. Already her thoughts were bombarded with images of all she might have if only she chose what was being offered. If only she stepped into the abyss that had opened up before her.

With the last fragment of energy she had left, she clamped the lid back on the jar. She panted with the effort, her body was as weary as her mind and her spirit. She had no idea how much magic she'd taken, but it would have to be enough.

There was no room inside of her for more. The flow subsided, but she barely noticed. The scent of incense turned rancid. The darkness turned on her, shoving her toward the abyss. There was no grove. No trees. No sky full of stars above her.

Only blackness. And it was calling her name.

CHAPTER FIFTY-FIVE

Eddie paced from tree to tree. He couldn't be still. Not while Lexi was inside that grove, fighting for ... He didn't want to think it was for her life.

He scrubbed a hand over his face. "How much longer? I don't like this."

Izzy came to him. "She's going to be okay. You know that, don't you? You have to believe that. For her."

He nodded and tried to breathe. "It's hard."

"I know," Izzy said. "I don't like waiting either."

Beckett walked over next, digging something out of his jacket pocket. He held out a palmful of colorful cellophane-wrapped hard candies. "Take one. They're green apple. The sugar helps."

Eddie doubted that, but any distraction was a good one. He helped himself to a sweet. "Thank you."

Beckett offered them to Izzy next. She took one with a smile.

Eddie unwrapped the candy and popped it in his mouth. He put the wrapper in the pocket of his jeans. The sour-sweet bite of the candy made his cheeks ache, but it gave him something else to focus on.

The sugar didn't distract him for long, however.

He went back to pacing. How much longer could she be? How long did it take to absorb all that magic? The jar was big, but it wasn't *that* big. But he understood that magic didn't necessarily prescribe to the laws of physics.

There was no telling how much that jar held.

Mist swirled around his feet. He lifted his head to see the nymph, Lylianna, standing at the entrance to the grove. She held Lexi in her arms. Lexi was limp, and for a moment, he wasn't sure she was breathing.

He bit down on the candy, shattering it. "Is she ..."

Lylianna shook her head. "Just overcome. She will need to rest as she deals with the dark magic. You have a safe place to take her?"

Once upon a time, he would have ripped up every tree in that grove by its roots. Now, he just nodded as he walked to her. "I do."

"Will the town be safe now?" Amelia asked.

"Yes," Lylianna answered. "Thanks to her, it will be secure for many years to come."

Then she held Lexi out to Eddie. He took her into his arms. She was heavier than he remembered. Somehow, he knew that was the weight of the dark magic. His heart ached. His soul raged. He was furious at this outcome. And scared to death it would be her end.

But the anger was winning. Maybe the monster wasn't completely gone. If Lexi didn't recover, he'd know for sure. He forced himself to relax, for Lexi's sake. The muscles in his jaw throbbed from clenching his teeth.

Lylianna put her hand on Lexi's head. "Fight hard, my sister." Then she disappeared into the trees.

Eddie turned and glared at Amelia. This was all her fault. "Get us out of here now."

With a quick nod, Amelia began walking. Henry and Izzy went after her, but Beckett hung back, matching his pace with Eddie's. "She's not going to die."

Eddie stared straight ahead, watching the path so no branches scratched at Lexi. "You know that, do you?"

"If it was her time, I'd know it."

Eddie exhaled, trying not to let his anger get the best of him. Beckett was offering encouragement the best way he knew how. He softened his tone. "Thank you."

Beckett dropped back, letting Eddie walk alone again.

It took forever to get to the car. Lexi didn't stir once. Not a twitch or a tremor.

Beckett opened the rear passenger door of the Rolls.

Eddie looked at Henry instead. "Can you take us home?"

Henry nodded. "Sure."

"Edgar," Amelia called out to him, her tone clearly meant to soothe. "I know you're angry, but she agreed to do this. She knew there was a risk."

Eddie ignored Amelia and carried Lexi to the Land Rover, where Izzy was opening the door for him. He paused, then looked at Amelia. A familiar rage seethed inside him. Could she tell what he was feeling? She paled slightly, making him think she could. "Go home and be glad the one you love is healthy and well and there with you."

With Lexi still in his arms, he backed into the vehicle, careful of his every move. Once he was in, Izzy helped get them both situated so she could close the door.

Before she had it shut, Beckett was driving Amelia away.

Henry got behind the wheel. He twisted to look at Lexi, then Eddie. He said nothing, just turned around and started the car. Izzy climbed in, and Henry wheeled the vehicle around and got them headed for town.

A minute later, he spoke. "We should get some vitals on her. It'll give me a baseline. Let me know if there's anything I can do to help. If you want me to."

Eddie nodded. He watched Lexi's face for any chance she might be waking up. "Yes. I want whatever help you can give her. Please."

"Sure," Henry said. "I'll drop you off, then run home and get my bag."

Izzy turned, looking over the edge of her seat. "I'll stay with you, Eddie. I can help too."

"Okay," he said softly. He brushed a little hair out of Lexi's eyes and willed her to wake up.

As soon as they arrived at the apartment, Eddie opened the door, made sure he had Lexi firmly in his arms, then got out. Izzy hopped out too.

"Be right back," Henry yelled before taking off.

Eddie held Lexi with one arm so he could fish the key out of his pocket. He tossed it to Izzy. "Get the door?"

"Right away." She ran up the steps ahead of him.

He paused at the door. This wasn't how he'd intended to carry Lexi over the threshold. He stepped inside. Izzy had the lights on already. Eddie carried Lexi to the bed and laid her down on top of the covers.

"Your place is nice," Izzy said. "It's big."

"It's Lexi's place, really." Reggie slunk around Eddie's legs, rubbing himself on Eddie's jeans.

Izzy came over by him. "Does she have a nightgown or something? I can get her changed if you want." She smiled at Reggie. "Hi, kitty cat. Do you want something?"

Eddie nodded. "Food probably. She has pajamas in one of those drawers." He pointed to the dresser Lexi used.

"I'll take care of it," Izzy said.

Eddie scooped Reggie up and held him close. Lexi looked so small and lifeless just lying there. "She better be all right," he whispered into Reggie's fur.

Izzy came back with a nightgown in her hands.

Eddie carried Reggie into the kitchen and set him down by his bowls. Eddie got a can of food out and put it in a dish, then picked up the water bowl, rinsed it and refilled it. Being occupied was good.

By the time he was done and Reggie was eating, Izzy had Lexi changed and tucked under the covers.

He took a chair from the little sitting area by the windows and brought it to the bedside so he could sit and watch Lexi.

"She's going to be all right," Izzy said.

"I hope so." But no one could know what was going to happen to Lexi. If she was fighting the same kind of dark magic that had created him, what were her chances of actually winning?

"She has to be," Izzy said. She let out a deep sigh. "Do you want me to make some coffee or something?"

"I don't know if we have any." At least Lexi looked peaceful now. Maybe she really was just sleeping. Maybe she'd wake up tomorrow morning and be herself again.

"Do you mind if I look?"

"Go ahead." He kept his eyes on Lexi as Izzy rummaged in the kitchen. She would wake up, wouldn't she? His head got the best of him, imagining all kinds of ways this could play out. None of them were good.

The smell of coffee brewing brought him out of his thoughts. He glanced over. She had three cups out, along with the carton of milk, a bag of sugar, and a plate of cookies.

She shrugged when she saw him looking. "It's too much, isn't it? Sorry. I got a little carried away."

"No, it's fine," he said. "Any distraction is a welcome one. Coffee smells good."

Three rapid knocks rang out from the door.

"Henry," Izzy said. "I'll get it."

Eddie let her.

Henry came in, a large black doctor's bag in his hand. "How is she? Any change?"

"No." Eddie got up from the chair.

"I'll take her vitals, see if it tells us anything."

Eddie went into the kitchen and poured himself a cup of coffee to give Henry some room.

He stood there drinking the coffee and eating a cookie because he didn't know what else to do.

Izzy joined him. "Your cat is a very handsome boy."

Eddie smiled. Reggie was always a reason to smile. "He's the best. Not that your cats aren't. I just meant—"

She laughed. "I know what you meant. All cats are the best. It's just how cats are."

He nodded. She knew.

Henry came into the kitchen, stethoscope in his hand. "Her vitals are all good. Strong and stable. Nothing there to be concerned about. Whatever's going on is between her and the dark magic."

Eddie exhaled as he looked at the woman he loved, still unconscious. "That's what I'm worried about."

CHAPTER FIFTY-SIX

Three days. No change.

Other than the two times she'd sat up, opened her eyes, and let out a stream of words that were either gibberish or some ancient language Eddie didn't recognize. Both times, her eyes had been completely black. And both times, she lay right back down and returned to her comatose state.

The two incidents had bothered him deeply. He now lived in a constant state of worry. Henry had been kind enough to excuse him from work, which was unfair to Henry seeing as how Eddie had only just begun, but he wasn't willing to leave Lexi alone. Henry didn't question him, just told him not to worry about coming in until Lexi was well.

Eddie was grateful. There was nothing he could do for her, but she was too vulnerable to be by herself. If something happened and he wasn't there, Eddie wouldn't be able to forgive himself. He almost couldn't now. He should have argued against her taking on the dark magic more.

But Lexi would have done it anyway. She'd never have

been able to live with herself if the town had been lost because she'd said no.

He understood that. He admired it. And yet, here she was. Lost in a battle and he had no idea how it was going. If she was winning. He couldn't think about the alternative. He twisted his wedding ring around his finger. Touching it had become a comfort to him.

Thomas and Kacy had come by every day. The first day they brought a chicken and noodle casserole, homemade by Kacy. Eddie ate it not because he was hungry but because Lexi needed him to stay strong. It was good. The second day, Thomas brought Eddie a couple of detective novels and a pint of ice cream from the Creamatorium. The third day, they'd brought cookies from Black Horse Bakery.

It was nice to have company, but the sadness in their eyes when they looked at her was hard for him to take. It was one thing to feel that sadness himself. It was another to see it reflected in the eyes of those around him.

Amelia had sent Beckett twice to see how Lexi was and ask if there was anything she needed. Eddie had said no both times. What Lexi needed was to be free of the dark magic. Amelia already knew that.

He slept in the chair. Reggie slept on the bed all of the time now, curled around Lexi's head on the pillow or pressed against her side. Always touching her. He seemed to understand she was fighting something, that she needed help. His constant companionship made Eddie love the little cat even more.

Eddie checked the time. Izzy and Henry would arrive soon. They'd been coming by after Henry left the lab.

Eddie closed his eyes to rest until they knocked.

When they did, he let them in. "Hello."

They stepped inside. Henry's gaze went directly to the bed. "Any change?"

"No. But she hasn't sat up again either."

"I suppose that's something," Henry said.

Izzy had a bouquet of flowers in one hand and a tote bag over her shoulder. "I'm going to find something to put these in."

Eddie just nodded. "Thanks. She'd like those."

Henry was already bedside, checking her pulse. "Still strong. That's a good sign. She's not fading."

Eddie nodded again. He didn't know what else to do. He was sick and tired of not knowing what to do.

Henry rubbed his brow. "If it's okay with you, I thought we could have Izzy try to read her. See if she can get a sense of what's going on with Lexi."

"Yes," Eddie said. "Good." That was something at least.

Izzy brought the flowers over. She'd stuck them in a drinking glass with some water. She set them on the bedside table. "I won't do anything to interrupt whatever's going on in her, I promise."

"I know," Eddie said. Beyond a shadow of a doubt, he trusted these two.

Izzy sat on the edge of the bed and took Lexi's hand. She closed her eyes and went very still.

He and Henry just stood, watching.

Izzy's lids flew open. Her eyes held concern. "She needs help."

Eddie stepped forward, heart racing. "What kind of help? What can I do?"

Izzy stretched out her hand. "I'm going to try something. Go around to the other side and take her hand."

"Anything. Whatever she needs." He clasped Lexi's hand. She was warm. Warmer than what seemed normal.

"I'm going to attempt to take emotion from you and transfer it to her. Think good, strong thoughts. Think about how much you love her. Happy, supportive things. Nothing negative, okay?"

Eddie nodded. "I will."

Izzy had a firm grip on him. She closed her eyes again.

Henry caught Eddie's gaze. "She learned this from another empath. I helped him save Izzy from …" He looked away and scratched the side of his head.

"From what?" Eddie asked.

"From … you." Henry grimaced. "Sorry. I only meant to say that I've seen it work because I helped do it once myself."

"It's okay," Eddie said. "It worked, right?"

"It did."

That was all that mattered.

Lexi groaned softly and tossed her head back and forth.

"Don't let go of her," Izzy said.

Eddie felt a sudden longing, but it wasn't coming from within. It was coming from Lexi. She needed him. He sat on the edge of the bed and held her hand between both of his. He filled his head with good thoughts, all directed at her. *I love you, Lexi. You are strong, and you will win this fight. Don't give up. Show the darkness who you are. What you're made of. How powerful you are. Reggie and I are here. We're with you. We both love you. And we aren't going anywhere.*

Izzy squeezed her eyes tighter and began to breathe with her mouth open. "Stay with her. She's getting stronger."

Eddie held tight to Lexi's hand. He focused on her and her alone and willed his strength and his love into her.

Lexi sat up, eyes open and clear. Her hand tightened around his. She cried out, but it wasn't a sound of pain. It was the sound of a warrior facing down an enemy. Every sinew in her body seemed to tense as she bent her head. A growl erupted from her throat, a feral, furious noise that raised the small hairs on the back of his neck.

Reggie had been sitting near Lexi's feet. He got up on all fours, arching his back, his tail expanding like a bottle brush, but he didn't run.

Lexi took a deep breath, then she coughed, expelling strands of black vapor that disappeared into the air.

Her whole body shuddered, and she collapsed back onto the pillow. Her hand went limp.

Izzy, eyes opened, looked terrified. "I have no idea what just happened."

But Eddie smiled and kissed Lexi's knuckles as joy shot through him. "I do. She won. Look at her."

Just like the first time he'd seen her, Lexi was glowing again.

Chapter Fifty-Seven

Lexi was done being in bed. Four days was long enough. Too long. She was still a little weak, but her strength would return. Probably when she was out of bed and moving again. And maybe after she'd had a proper meal. Soup was fine, but she needed something more substantial. Meat. Potatoes. Bread.

Her stomach growled. She pressed her hand to her belly, trying to squelch the noise. Reggie had heard it, however. He lifted his head from where he was sleeping next to her and looked at her with sleepy eyes like he was trying to be sure she was really awake.

Probably so she could feed him. She laughed softly. She leaned up on her elbows, slightly lightheaded.

Eddie was asleep on the couch. She shook her head at him. At all he'd done for her. She'd never repay him, but she had a very long lifetime to try. She moved carefully so she wouldn't wake him and went into the bathroom.

She wanted to eat, but she also wanted a hot bath. Reggie trotted in behind her, sat on the bathmat and let out a plaintive cry.

"Hush," she whispered. "You're going to wake your daddy." He probably already had. The meow in the bathroom echoed off the tile and seemed as loud as a siren.

The only way to keep Reggie quiet was to feed him. She started the water so the tub could fill, dumped in a significant amount of bubble liquid, then eased out of the bathroom, hoping Eddie hadn't been woken up.

She rolled her eyes. "So much for that."

He smiled at her from the kitchen, where he was fixing Reggie a dish of breakfast. "I'm glad I woke up. It's good to see you on your feet again."

"It's good to be on my feet again."

"How do you feel?"

She tipped her head back and forth. "A little weak. But also starving."

He nodded. "That sounds about right. What about your ... magic?"

She could tell he'd been a little reluctant to ask. She wiggled her fingers, and behind her, the bed made itself. She put on a big smile. "I am fully charged and operational."

He put Reggie's dish on the floor. Reggie fell on it like he hadn't eaten in days instead of what was probably less than six hours ago. "Then it worked?"

"It did. I didn't think ..." She took a breath, about to *not* complete that sentence. But she owed him the truth. "I didn't think I was going to make it. But you and Izzy made the difference. I knew you were there. Despite the dark magic getting its claws in me, I could sense the two of you. It helped tremendously."

She smiled at the orange cat still plowing through his breakfast. "Reggie, too. Him being close to me, touching me, it was like my lifeline."

Eddie frowned. "If I had known—"

"How could you?" She shook her head and went over to him, reaching up to take his handsome, wonderful face in her hands. "Thank you. For everything. I know I owe Henry and Izzy a big thanks as well."

"Thomas and Kacy too. They came to visit you every day."

"We should have them all over for dinner."

"We don't know how to cook."

She laughed. "We'll take them all *out* for dinner. We never had a wedding reception. What's the nicest restaurant in town?"

He shook his head. "I have no idea, but I bet Thomas does. Do you want me to call him?"

"Please. Then call the restaurant and make a reservation for us for tonight."

"I should make sure everyone's free, too."

"Yes. That's important." She kissed him. "I'm going to take a long soak and try to feel more like myself again."

"You want a sandwich? I could make you one."

"I would love one. Thank you."

She was up to her neck in bubbles when he brought in a plate and a glass of milk.

He handed her the plate and put the glass on the little

table next to the tub. "Peanut butter and jelly. Is that okay?"

"It sounds perfect. I can't wait to eat it." She carefully balanced the plate on the rim of the tub and picked up one half of the sandwich. She nearly took half of it in the first bite. It was delicious. Possibly one of the best things she'd ever tasted.

"Seven tonight all right for dinner?"

She took a sip of milk to unstick the peanut butter from the roof of her mouth. "Can everyone make it?"

"They can. I booked the private room at a place called the Table." He smiled. "From Thomas's description, it sounds like the kind of place I could wear my suit."

"Even better." She grinned as she took another bite.

A few minutes before seven, she and Eddie walked into the restaurant with Thomas and Kacy, who'd driven them. Henry and Izzy were waiting in the foyer.

Izzy's smile was ear to ear. "It's so good to see you." She shot Henry a quick glance before continuing. "We have news, but we'll wait until we're seated."

A young woman led them to the private dining room, handed them all menus, and told them Josh, their server, would be with them shortly. Sparkling goblets of ice water waited at each place setting. Soft jazz played in the background, and dark wood walls contrasted nicely with the white tablecloth covering the big, round table. The crystal chandelier overhead glinted off the silver cutlery.

They all took a seat—Thomas and Kacy next to one another, just as Henry and Izzy were, which let Lexi sit beside Eddie. She wouldn't have had it any other way. She wanted him near her all the time. Her brush with dark magic had shown her just how vulnerable she could be. His presence made her feel safe, despite having her magic back. Eddie, in his own way, was better than magic.

Lexi picked up her menu but didn't look at it. "All right, Izzy. What's your news?"

Izzy's big smile returned. "Henry got the results of the DNA tests we took. You and I are definitely related."

Henry nodded. "The tests I did were whole genome sequencing, very complete and the most accurate."

Eddie leaned forward. "Those produce ten thousand times more DNA data than any other kind of testing."

"That's right," Henry said. He looked at Lexi again. "The farther away someone gets from an ancestor, the fewer genes they have in common with that ancestor. But I can say with great sincerity that you and Izzy are something like an aunt and a niece many generations removed."

Lexi blinked in surprise. "That's ... that's amazing." She laughed as she glanced at Izzy. "We're really family." Maybe it was because she wasn't quite herself yet, but she suddenly felt emotional. Family, no matter how far removed, was still family.

Izzy swallowed like she was fighting tears, too. "I know. Isn't it something? I'm so happy about it."

"Me, too," Lexi said softly.

Eddie put his arm around her. "It's great news."

"Aunt Lexi," Izzy said, smiling.

Lexi laughed. "Just Lexi will do fine."

Their server, Josh, came in. "Good evening. Welcome to the Table. Which one of you is Lexi?"

She raised her hand. "I am."

"There's someone here to see you, if that's all right with you? I can bring them in."

Lexi frowned. "Who?"

A familiar face appeared behind Josh.

Beckett. "Forgive me for interrupting, but Amelia sent me with a message."

Lexi nodded at Josh. "It's all right."

Josh acknowledged her with a short bow of his head. "I'll give you a few moments then."

As he left, Lexi cast a curious look around the table. Everyone else seemed as curious as she was. "What's the message, then?"

Beckett stepped all the way into the room. "She's very pleased to hear that you've recovered. She wanted to tell you that she's still deeply indebted to you for all you did for her and the town. As a small token of her appreciation, she wanted me to present you with these."

He dug into his pocket and pulled out two keys. He handed them to her.

She took them, but they didn't make any sense to her. "What are they for?"

"Those keys unlock the front door of the house at 106 Cresthaven Avenue."

Izzy let out a little gasp. "106 Cresthaven Avenue is the house right next to ours."

Beckett nodded. "If the house is not to your liking—"

Lexi laughed and looked at Eddie. "I think it'll be just fine."

Eddie's eyes had gone wide. "A house?"

"Yes," Beckett said. "And in the garage you'll find two new vehicles. One for each of you. The keys for those are in them."

"That's too much," Lexi said.

Eddie shook his head. "No, it's not."

Beckett smiled. "I agree with him. It's not too much. But it's a good start." He reached into a different pocket. "There's one more thing, but you can open it whenever you're ready. I don't want to interrupt your evening any more than I already have."

He set a small velvet pouch near her on the table. "Have a good evening. Oh, and Amelia's picking up the bill for this dinner, so order extravagantly." He gave her a wink and left.

"Wow," Lexi said. She picked up the pouch. It was weighty with what felt like little pebbles.

"That was nice of her," Thomas said. "Guess I'm getting the filet mignon."

They all laughed.

Eddie nudged her. "Open the bag. I want to see what's in there."

Lexi loosened the drawstrings and emptied the contents onto the table.

Gems of all sizes and colors spilled out onto the table, but the one that instantly caught Lexi's eye was a large, round diamond. As everyone else gasped and began talking, Lexi picked the diamond up and held it between her fingers so that Eddie could see it better.

"She knows we got married. Do you think she sent this one on purpose?"

He smiled. "For your ring? Maybe."

"I don't really need a big diamond like this. To be honest, I'm much more drawn to sapphires and emeralds." She smiled at him. Even though she had her magic back and could make whatever money they needed, selling a big diamond wouldn't require any magic at all. These gems would keep them financially stable for a long time.

"Whatever you want," Eddie said.

She picked up the diamond and turned it in her fingers, watching the light play off it. "We'll have a lot more room in that house than we do now."

He nodded. "We will. I don't know what we'll do with it."

She lifted one shoulder. "Well ... we'll have the space to get Reggie a buddy. If that's something you'd be interested in?"

"I'd be very interested in that." He kissed her.

She clenched the diamond in her fist as she kissed him back. Moving into that house would show him that she was serious about staying, too. So would adopting another cat. She didn't ever want Eddie to worry about her leaving.

All thoughts of that were out of her head. She'd never

wanted to be in one place for any length of time, but her life was here now. With her husband, her cat, and her newfound family.

Maybe she was more human than she realized. Turned out it wasn't such a bad thing after all.

PARANORMAL WOMEN'S FICTION

Midlife Fairy Tale Series:

The Accidental Queen

The Summer Palace

First Fangs Club Series:

Sucks To Be Me

Suck It Up Buttercup

Sucker Punch

The Suck Stops Here

Embrace The Suck

Code Name: Mockingbird (A Paranormal Women's Fiction Novella)

COZY MYSTERY:

Jayne Frost Series:

Miss Frost Solves A Cold Case: A Nocturne Falls Mystery

Miss Frost Ices The Imp: A Nocturne Falls Mystery

Miss Frost Saves The Sandman: A Nocturne Falls Mystery

Miss Frost Cracks A Caper: A Nocturne Falls Mystery

When Birdie Babysat Spider: A Jayne Frost Short

Miss Frost Braves The Blizzard: A Nocturne Falls Mystery

Miss Frost Chills The Cheater: A Nocturne Falls Mystery

Miss Frost Says I Do: A Nocturne Falls Mystery

Lost in Las Vegas: A Frost And Crowe Mystery

Wrapped up in Christmas: A Frost And Crowe Mystery

Mystified In Music City: A Frost And Crowe Mystery

HappilyEverlasting Series:

Witchful Thinking

PARANORMAL ROMANCE

Nocturne Falls Series:

The Vampire's Mail Order Bride

The Werewolf Meets His Match

The Gargoyle Gets His Girl

The Professor Woos The Witch

The Witch's Halloween Hero – short story

The Werewolf's Christmas Wish – short story

The Vampire's Fake Fiancée

The Vampire's Valentine Surprise – short story

The Shifter Romances The Writer

The Vampire's True Love Trials – short story

The Dragon Finds Forever

The Vampire's Accidental Wife

The Reaper Rescues The Genie

The Detective Wins The Witch

The Vampire's Priceless Treasure

The Werewolf Dates The Deputy

The Siren Saves The Billionaire

The Vampire's Sunny Sweetheart

Death Dates The Oracle

Shadowvale Series:

The Trouble With Witches

The Vampire's Cursed Kiss

The Forgettable Miss French

Moody And The Beast

Her First Taste Of Fire

Monster In The Mirror

A Sky Full Of Stars

Sin City Collectors Series

Queen Of Hearts

Dead Man's Hand

Double or Nothing

Standalone Paranormal Romance:

Dark Kiss of the Reaper

Heart of Fire

Recipe for Magic

Miss Bramble and the Leviathan

All Fired Up

URBAN FANTASY

The House of Comarré series:

Forbidden Blood

Blood Rights

Flesh and Blood

Bad Blood

Out For Blood

Last Blood

The Crescent City series:

House of the Rising Sun

City of Eternal Night

Garden of Dreams and Desires

Want to be up to date on all books & release dates by Kristen Painter? Sign-up for my newsletter on my website, www.kristenpainter.com. No spam, just news (sales, freebies, and releases.)

∽

If you loved the book and want to help the series grow, tell a friend about the book and take time to leave a review!

Nothing is completed without an amazing team.

Many thanks to:

Cover design: Cover design and composite cover art by Janet Holmes using images from Shutterstock.com & Depositphotos.com.
Interior formatting: Gem Promotions
Editor/Copyedits: Chris Kridler
Proofs: Nancy Brunori

Made in the USA
Middletown, DE
11 August 2024